Praise for
APRIL HENRY and
HEART-SHAPED BOX

"April Henry delineates character with dazzle, insight, and grace. In *Heart-Shaped Box*, Henry probes past and present with power and perception. This is a compelling entry in a deservedly acclaimed series."
Carolyn Hart

"Henry hits all the right notes as she deliciously skewers those former classmates most of us can't forget—old boyfriends gone to seed, high school hussies and those who peaked during their teen years. And no reunion mystery is complete without the nerd turned computer millionaire."
Ft. Lauderdale Sun-Sentinel

"Definitely a new series with staying power."
Margaret Maron

"Excellent. One of Northwest mystery fiction's best new stylists."
Portland Oregonian

Also by April Henry

SQUARE IN THE FACE
CIRCLES OF CONFUSION

HEART-SHAPED BOX

A Claire Montrose Mystery

APRIL HENRY

AVON BOOKS
An Imprint of HarperCollins*Publishers*

This is a work of fiction. Names, characters, places, and incidents are products of the author's imagination or are used fictitiously and are not to be construed as real. Any resemblance to actual events, locales, organizations, or persons, living or dead, is entirely coincidental.

AVON BOOKS
An Imprint of HarperCollins*Publishers*
10 East 53rd Street
New York, New York 10022-5299

First Avon Books paperback printing: February 2002
First HarperCollins hardcover printing: February 2001

Avon Trademark Reg. U.S. Pat. Off. and in Other Countries, Marca Registrada, Hecho en U.S.A.
HarperCollins ® is a trademark of HarperCollins Publishers Inc.

Printed in the U.S.A.

10 9 8 7 6 5 4 3 2 1

Acknowledgments

Bringing a book into the world requires the assistance of many others. I'd like to thank Kevin Beckstrom of Oregon's DMV for sharing so many excellent vanity license plates with me. When I needed help getting the details right, firefighter Mike Bell and his wife, Pat; Manhattan prosecutor (and excellent author in her own right) Linda Fairstein; author Jonnie Jacobs, and coroner Brenda McCreight stepped forward to help. And Los Angeles coroner Mike Bower proved invaluable. Any errors are my own.

Author Gregg Main has served as my one-person writer's support group. Carrie Patten is hereby promoted from junior to senior brainstormer. Kelley Rothenberger and Shannon Davis righted the wrongs and found the lost.

On the publishing side of things, thanks go to Carolyn Marino, Erica Johanson, Deb Evans, Diane Jackson, and Leslie Cohen. My former publicist, Lindsay Lifrieri, is destined to go far. Wendy Schmalz continues to be the best friend, mentor, and cheerleader a girl ever had.

   Staff at Kaiser Permanente (most especially Jan Bellis-Squires) have been my best boosters. My husband offers support in so many ways (including not saying one word when I toasted his car's head gasket on my way to my first book signing). And my daughter is always proud to point out her mommy's books at a bookstore.

HEART-
SHAPED
BOX

One

Friday, July 2, 11:43 P.M.
South parking lot of
Ye Olde Pioneer Village Theme Park

Like the long stem of a flower, her neck curved away from him. He hesitated, then softly kissed Cindy's nape, just where the tousled blond curls began. How many times had he kissed her there, at just that very spot? She was finally quiet in his embrace. As if in a dream, he gave her shoulders a squeeze, feeling the press of her open lips against the palm of his other hand.

But his body remembered what had happened, even as his mind shied away from the terrible weight of the truth. His heart hammered like a fist in his chest, reminding him of where he was, of what had happened.

When he said her name again, it came out a whisper. "Cindy?"

No answer. He had to let go, to face what he already knew. His arms loosened. Cindy (what was her last name now? Perez or something like that?) sprawled on the blacktop, her body half-turning as she fell. Her denim miniskirt—Cindy's interpretation of tonight's

Western theme—hiked up, exposing slim, tanned thighs.

He was afraid to look at her face, but when he finally did he found that in the faint, filtered light she didn't look too bad. Her eyes were half-open, and the tip of her tongue protruded between her teeth, but otherwise her expression was oddly calm.

He stared down at her, surprised by the speed of death. Unbidden, memories swamped him. The naughty smile Cindy used to give him, grinning up from the shelter of his arm, her lids at a knowing half-mast. The magpie way she collected things—shiny jewelry, dozens of shoes, pretty clothes, pretty boys. Now a single sob escaped him. He clamped his hand over his own mouth, silencing himself the way he had so recently silenced Cindy.

His mind was racing now, faster and faster, as he calculated what he must do. Leaning down, he grabbed the lapels of her yoked red satin Western shirt and pulled. To his ears, the sound of the pearl snaps popping open was as loud as gunfire. Underneath, Cindy wore a bronze-colored satin push-up bra. He remembered how she used to go braless. Avoiding contact with her skin, he tugged her skirt up farther. He lifted his head and listened. Nothing more than the thrum of distant traffic. Her purse was within arm's reach. Grabbing her wallet, he stumbled off.

Cindy Sanchez had never been comfortable with silence, but now she lay quietly on her back in the overflow parking lot of Ye Olde Pioneer Village. Her blue eyes were still open, but filmed with dullness. The bright blood from her bitten tongue was already beginning to brown as it dried.

Forgotten in her uncurling fingers, manicured to sharp crimson points, was a little wooden box. A heart-shaped box.

Two

Three months earlier

YOU
ARE INVITED
TO THE MINOR HIGH SCHOOL
CLASS OF 1979
REUNION
JULY 2–5
YE OLDE PIONEER VILLAGE
NEAR MINOR, OREGON
WITH SPECIAL GUEST OF HONOR:
SAWYER FAIRCHILD
BE THERE OR BE SQUARE!

Claire Montrose grimaced as she read the last line on the first page of the invitation. That was one of the problems with having come of age in the seventies. It seemed like such a nondecade, forced to borrow its slang from previous times. What had come out of it that was worth remembering? Polyester sweater vests, disco dancing, the Waltons, eight-track tapes? Men's pinkie rings, streaking, smiley faces, Bachman Turner Overdrive? Even the big events, such as the end of the Vietnam War or the resignation of Richard Nixon, seemed like leftovers from the sixties.

Inside the invitation was the schedule of events, encompassing everything from a barbecue to a dress-up dance. While Claire had never been to Ye Olde Pioneer Village, she had read about it in the *Oregonian*. It was a popular spot for Portlanders who wanted a little low-stakes casino gambling coupled with some amusements for the kids. In addition to slot machines and black jack, Pioneer Village offered "family-friendly" entertainment, which included everything from carnival rides to miniature golf to hourly reenactments of a stagecoach robbery. In the evening you could send the kids off to the supervised video arcade while you danced to the music of a washed-up singer still eking out a living performing his one twenty-year-old hit.

Claire sorted the invitation into the pile of other junk mail— unsolicited credit card offers, a plea from Oregon Public Broadcasting (which seemed to regularly forget that her membership was paid up through December), the heap of slick magazines that had been pouring into her mailbox ever since she made the mistake of ordering a vase from Pottery Barn—and carried them to the recycling center Charlie had built under the sink. The invitation slid back out of the bin and landed with a plop on the blue-tiled floor. Claire picked it up again.

Maybe she should go. She was no longer the girl she had been in high school, the girl who was too smart, too tall, too skinny, and who looked much younger than she was. Now maybe all her old handicaps were actually to her advantage. At thirty-seven, it was good to be smart, tall, thin, and look younger than you actually were. And then there was Dante to consider. Claire could bet that no one from her high school would show up with a Metropolitan Museum of Art curator who looked more like a pirate. The part of her that still thought in terms of license plates, a legacy of ten years of working for Oregon's Specialty Plate Department, thought maybe she should BYTDAPL—bite the apple, in license-plate speak. (Until she had quit a few months ago, Claire had spent eight hours a day approving or denying applications for vanity plates, deciding if the abbreviated or encoded messages were obscene or otherwise objectionable.)

But did it really matter if she would hold up well under scrutiny? Would she really have anything in common with people she hadn't seen in twenty years? The first step, Claire decided, was to sit down with her high school annual, look at the faces and think about whether she wanted to see them again.

Claire picked up the phone. Only a few months ago she wouldn't have bothered to call her mother before coming over. Jean had always been at home, sitting in her darkened apartment for hours on end watching— and all too frequently phoning—the QualProd shopping network. Indirectly, it was Jean's addiction to QualProd that had cut the cord binding Jean to the TV. She still watched, of course, but now it was as little as five or six hours a day instead of sixteen. Jean had met her new boyfriend, Zed, at a Shoppers Anonymous meeting. A good fifty pounds lighter than Jean, Zed was a Teamster, a wiry guy who favored half-unbuttoned shirts worn with two gold chains. When he was in town, he took pains to keep Jean and himself occupied and away from temptation, squiring her to stocked trout ponds, line dancing, and monster truck pulls.

But evidently Zed was on the road, because Jean answered the phone on the first ring. She sounded disappointed when she realized it was only her daughter. Claire arranged to come look through the box of school souvenirs still buried in the closet of what was now the guest bedroom in her mother's apartment. Then she changed into a pair of black running shorts and wrestled a running bra down into place. Hoping to catch a little sun, she put on a tank top instead of a T-shirt. After all, it wouldn't do to go to the reunion looking as pale as skim milk. She realized she was already thinking about it as if she would go.

Two hours later, Claire was back in her own living room and staring at what was supposed to be her own picture when her roommate Charlie bustled through the front door, her arms full of shopping bags. Charlie—short for Charlotte, not that anyone ever called her that—said, "What's that, Clairele?"

Claire turned the cover of her high school annual toward her friend. It was embossed with a badly drawn cartoon miner wearing overalls, a plaid flannel shirt, work boots, and an outsize head lantern. Minor had been founded by a miner who had been both unable to spell or to find the gold he was convinced must lie just under the ground. As a mascot, the miner hadn't had the guts-and-glory image of the symbols for rival schools. Secretly, the Minors always envied their opponents with more appropriate names like the Warriors or the Bobcats.

"Pictures from your high school?"

"I got an invitation to the twenty-year reunion today." Claire felt strange saying it—twenty years!—but knew that any complaints to Charlie would fall on deaf ears. At seventy-nine, pretty much anyone seemed like a baby to Charlie. "I'm trying to decide whether to go or not."

Charlie put her Nature's grocery bag on the coffee table and settled down next to Claire on the couch. "Let me see your picture."

Claire found the M's again. Her picture, with its blank background, was easy enough to pick out. It had all the charm of a mug shot. At Minor High, it had been traditional for seniors to spurn the photographer who came to the high school. The plain photographs taken in the cafeteria were for the babies—the juniors, sophomores, and freshmen. Instead, the seniors scheduled sittings at Waltham's Studio Portraits. As a result, all the photos around Claire's were of students leaning against artificial trees or posing in front of a muraled sunset.

But studio portraits had been an extravagance the Montroses couldn't afford. Jean (who hadn't married either of the men who had fathered her two children) barely scraped by on a monthly disability check from a local grocery store chain where she had once slipped on a squashed Thompson grape. The money hadn't really been enough to support a single woman and two growing girls. Claire had started working as soon as she turned sixteen, and her earnings from Pietro's Pizza had been carefully apportioned among the gas, electric, and phone companies, each getting just enough to alleviate the threats to cease services.

Tangled in emotions she couldn't sort out, Claire looked at her old self. Her younger self offered back a tentative smile, half-hidden by flyaway curls. The black-and-white photograph had leached the color from her red-gold hair, leaving it pale gray. Maybe it was just as well. Just before her senior picture was taken, she had overdone it with a bottle of Sun-In, resulting in a halo of bright orange hair. She flushed now, remembering how she had told everyone it was her natural color.

Charlie pulled the annual from Claire's lap and began to page back through it. It was a catalog of styles that had come and gone and in some cases come back again. Cowl-necked sweaters, flared pants, blouses with floppy self-bows, men's shirts with collars as big as elephant ears.

Seen from the perspective of a twenty-year absence, it all looked a little silly. The boys wore ties as wide as six-lane freeways, and their hair was long and shapeless. Most girls had ridiculous-looking feathered bangs that bore the marks of a curling iron (a styling necessity, Claire remembered, as otherwise the wearer was unable to see). Everyone looked both young and hopelessly dated. Claire knew, though, that in two hundred years it would all run together in people's minds, with no clear demarcation between the first and second times polyester was popular, between shrink-to-fit Levi's and jeans worn so big they bagged around the wearer's hips, among clunky wedge sandals from the forties, seventies, and nineties.

Claire thought about the painting she had inherited the year before, a small painting of a woman holding a letter. It had turned out to be a Vermeer, painted around 1665. She had learned a lot about Vermeer as the painting's authenticity was debated. On one of her visits to New York, Dante had shown her a near-perfect copy of another Vermeer painting. For some time, it had even been attributed to the great painter, although it had actually been made twenty years after his death. The only giveaway was the woman's missing sidecurls. The real Vermeer had them, and the fake did not, because the forger had found the style hopelessly dated. Three hundred and fifty years later, the modern viewer couldn't tell the difference. Both women had costumes and hairstyles that the mind simply classified as "old."

Charlie had reached the first page of the annual, which bore the inscription, "Dedicated to our teacher of the year: Sawyer Fairchild." The page was filled with a close-up photo of a young man with an oval face, long dark hair, and sideburns that tickled the corners of his full mouth.

"Isn't that our candidate for governor? The man for whom you wish to vote?" Charlie asked. She was probably the last living American to use "whom" correctly, but then again, her native tongue was German. In Dachau, nearly sixty years before, she had lost a husband, a small son, and all affection for her homeland. Sometimes when people heard her accent, they would insist on knowing what she was. Charlie would always lift her chin and reply that she was, of course, an American.

Claire nodded. "Yes, that's Sawyer. He was so much a part of our class that they've invited him back to the reunion. He was a student teacher for a year before he went into politics. Supposedly, he was teaching us biology, but it was clear he didn't care if we never learned anything about cell division. He wanted to teach us about life. I remember how he used to have us push our desks back and then sit in a circle in the middle of the room. And Sawyer would pull down all the blinds, turn off the lights, and light a candle in the center of the circle. He would have us all hold hands, and we would take turns talking about what we wanted to be when we grew up. Not do, but be." Claire remembered how Sawyer had said that was an important distinction. And how in the dark, kids would talk about things they never had before to anyone. And how everyone else listened and didn't laugh, not at anyone, not even after the lights were turned back on.

"And what did you say you wanted to be, Clairele?" Charlie said in a soft voice, as if they were sitting side by side on the cool linoleum in that darkened classroom, twenty years earlier.

Claire's smile was rueful. "Oh, a teacher. Like about 90 percent of the other kids. We all looked up to Sawyer. He was so different from the rest of the teachers. I think he was the first adult I knew who wanted me to call him by his first name. He wasn't that much older than us, but we knew he had been through a lot. He only started to talk about Vietnam a couple of times, and both times he stopped and stared off into the distance. All the girls were in love with him, and all the boys wanted to be him. Any guy who had the ability to grow facial hair started trying to coax sideburns, hoping Sawyer would notice. But Sawyer treated everyone the same. He paid attention to everyone."

"It sounds as if he had charisma even then."

"He was the first adult I knew who admitted there were things about the world that he didn't understand, and who said that stupid things were stupid. When I think back on it, he couldn't have been more than twenty-five, but he turned that school upside down. The teachers hated his long hair, and he didn't make much of a secret of the fact that he had smoked a lot of pot in the past. But at the same time, they had to treat him as a sort of hero. A year as a POW, a year in the hospital getting skin grafts on his legs, but he still had that terrible limp. All of us kids loved him because we felt he understood us, that he wasn't one of 'them,'" Claire hooked her fingers to make quote marks, "you know, the adults. When we voted him teacher of the year, his name wasn't even on the ballot. I remember there was a big fuss because you weren't supposed to be able to get the award if all you were was a student teacher."

"But he didn't teach after that, did he?" Charlie asked.

Claire shrugged. "He must have figured out that he could influence a heck of a lot more people if he were a politician than if he were a teacher. Twenty-five kids or 2.5 million people—it's a pretty easy choice if what you're hoping to do is make a big difference."

Through the years, Claire had loosely followed Sawyer's career. He had moved to Portland, lost his first campaign for state senate and won the next. While in the senate, he had gained a reputation as a consensus builder who got things done—expanding mass transit and recycling, working for antidiscrimination laws. Then he had been tapped by the White House for secretary of transportation. Despite his high-level job, Sawyer had never given up the spark of iconoclasm that had marked his days as a student teacher. He still refused to wear a tie, and was famous among the White House press corps for showing up at highway ribbon cuttings wearing boot-cut Levi's, snakeskin cowboy boots, and beautiful old Pendleton shirts.

Now Sawyer was back in Oregon, running hard for governor against a one-note antitax activist whose campaign literature lumped Democrats with devil worshippers. Even Republicans said privately that Sawyer would probably win. And most people speculated that a governorship might just be a stepping stone back to Washington, D.C.—only the next time Sawyer would be the one choosing the secretary of transportation.

"Will you vote for him?" Charlie asked, turning the page.

Claire didn't have to think twice. "Of course. Even if
the choice wasn't so limited, I still would." She reached
out and turned the page of the annual open on Charlie's lap.

It began with the highlights of the school year—the
sporting events. As a feeder school for several sparsely
populated surrounding counties, Minor had been able
to pick and choose only the best for its teams. So what if
a third of each class failed to graduate—the football
team always went to state!

The section began with a full-page photo of a football
player forever frozen in midleap, a football tucked under
his arm. The opposing team milled in his wake. Claire
didn't need to look at the caption to know who it was.

"That's Wade Merz. Even I knew he was the best football player Minor ever had." Off the field, Wade had
worn his sunglasses constantly, indoors or out, rain or
shine, and only answered to the nickname Suede. His
hair was blond, but Claire now realized that because of
the sunglasses she had no idea what color his eyes were.

"Did he make a career out of it?"

Claire shook her head. "Three hours before the
homecoming game, he got arrested for drunk driving. I
heard that there was a scout in town that day, but when
the game started, Wade was still sitting in jail. His
grades were terrible, so that would have been the only
way he went to college. The scout left at halftime. Now
Wade owns Wade's Auto Haus. Maybe you've seen it—
it's kind of by Susie and J.B.'s on Eighty-second."

Wade's Auto Haus was sandwiched between a pawn-
shop and an off-brand fried chicken franchise. Although
she hadn't spoken to him since high school, Claire
sometimes saw Wade in the parking lot when she drove
past on the way to her sister's house. It gave her a secret

thrill to see him, to know what he was doing when he knew nothing about her. A big man now running to fat, Wade seemed to spend most of his time polishing cars with his butt. He still wore his trademark sunglasses, but unlike the typical used car salesman, he favored well-tailored suits and crisp white shirts stiff with starch.

Charlie flipped through the pages devoted to the basketball players, lanky and awkward-looking, then the baseball and track teams. Girls were represented only on the track and tennis pages.

"Activities" followed the sports section. The title page was decorated with a few candid snapshots of popular students. "There's Cindy Weaver." Claire touched a photograph. "She's Cindy Sanchez now. She used to date Wade." In the picture, Cindy was surrounded by a half-dozen boys, her face turned up in a laugh.

"That woman who adopted the girl you thought was Lori's?"

Claire nodded. A few months before she had done a favor for an old friend and tried to track down the child Lori had surrendered years before to a secretive adoption agency. At one point, it had looked as though Cindy might have been the one who had adopted the child. Claire tapped a finger on the bottom of the photograph, on the lace-edged white anklets Cindy was wearing with her black spike-heeled pumps. "I'd forgotten about Cindy's jailbait look."

"She did look mature for her age," Charlie said tactfully.

Claire had a hundred memories of Cindy, who had been Minor High's head cheerleader, party girl, and general bitch. Cindy leading a routine, her large breasts seemingly without benefit of a bra. Cindy pulling

Claire's hair while she sat behind her in social studies, for no reason that Claire had ever figured out. Cindy showing up late for graduation rehearsal, her face pale and her eyes red. Later, Claire had heard a rumor that Cindy had spent the morning aborting Wade's baby.

"Oh, look, there's Belinda Brophy." Claire pointed to a girl who she had overlooked in the picture of Cindy. In the photo, Belinda stood literally in Cindy's shadow, looking up at her with the same rapt attention the boys did. "I kind of liked her even if she did hang around Cindy. She was one of those girls who always wanted to be popular, but wasn't ever going to make it." Belinda had been too plump, too plain, too shy. "So she did the next best thing and turned herself into Cindy's closest friend. Of course, Cindy used Belinda just as much as Belinda used Cindy. I don't think Cindy ever did any of her own homework."

The next page showed the cheerleaders with their perfect thighs, their pert little asses barely covered by black skirts with yellow box pleats. Claire remembered how the yellow had flashed as the cheerleaders jumped and kicked through their routines. In every photograph, Cindy was front and center.

Charlie turned the page to a series of photos from the school plays. Their only constant was a girl with Irish good looks: dark hair, blue eyes, and flawless white skin. "That's Jessica McFarland. We were pretty good friends in grade school, but we grew apart when we got older. She was more outgoing than me." Jessica had been cast as the lead in every school production, from *My Fair Lady* to *The Wizard of Oz*. In the largest photo, Jessica stood in the middle of a line of actors taking their bows. The others grinned at the audience, but Jessica looked out with a studied expression, her eyes big and her mouth serious. She drew the viewers' eyes past the half-dozen smiling faces on either side of her.

"Does she still act?"

"I'm not sure. She did for a while. She moved to New York City after graduation. I remember my mom was really excited when she got a part on that soap, *Until Tomorrow*. She used to tape the episodes Jessica was in so that I could watch them after I got home from work. But then her character was killed in a plane crash."

Charlie continued to leaf through the annual until Claire put out her hand. The caption across the two-page photo spread read, SOMEWHERE OVER THE RAINBOW—PROM MEMORIES. The largest photo showed the prom court posed in a half-circle under a crooked crepe-paper rainbow. The girls wore pale Gunne Sax dresses, the boys pastel-colored or all-white tuxes with wide lapels.

Cindy Weaver, who had naturally been chosen Minor's prom queen, was on the top riser, wearing a black halter dress that stood out among the pale froth. A red cape, lined in white satin, was thrown over her shoulders. On her perfectly French-braided blond hair sat a rhinestone-studded tiara. Beside her, Wade wore a matching black tux, and was for once without his sunglasses. His blond hair—grown out from football season—was tucked behind his ears, and he had a thick mustache that had been the envy of the other boys since tenth grade.

A collage of photos surrounded the larger photo of the prom court. A girl smiled shyly as her date leaned over her, trying to pin an orchid to the slick satin of her dress. Clearly no one had told him about the bra strap trick—or he didn't feel comfortable attempting it. Another couple sat side by side, slumped in folding chairs. Even at seventeen they looked tired of each other. In a blurred sea of swaying couples, Cindy danced with her head tipped back, her body pressed close to her partner. The photo's focus was narrowed to Cindy's face, her parted lips, her closed eyes. Even her hands were reduced to white blurs against her partner's shoulders, his head a dark smudge.

Charlie flipped through pages with photographs of club members, the choir, the band, the orchestra. Claire recognized herself in one of the group photos, her curls all but obscuring her eyes.

Before the alphabetized photos began was a single page set in plain type and headlined ACADEMIC HONORS. Claire reached out to turn the page, but Charlie had already found her name. "Look at this! National Merit Scholar. Oregon Scholar. Presidential Scholar Nominee. Your family must have been so proud!" Claire gave her a look and Charlie remembered whose family she was talking about. The older woman's face grew serious. "With your scores, why did you never go to college?"

"We didn't have any money." Claire kept her answer short, knowing that was only part of it. Part of the reason was that she had been scared.

"But all the good schools are what I believe is called 'need-blind.' You should have qualified for many scholarships."

Claire shrugged. "No one told me that at the time. At Minor, we had one guidance counselor, but I'm not sure what he was there for. It wasn't much of a secret that he believed girls should grow up to be wives and mothers."

Wanting to change the subject, Claire took the annual from Charlie and began to turn the rest of the pages, rows and rows of faces. She pointed at a thin boy with straight dark hair parted on the side. With his long, narrow pointed nose he looked something like a drawing of Pinocchio come to life, made the "real boy" he had always wanted to be. "Now this is the funniest story of all. Who would have thought that Dick Crane would turn out to be somebody important?"

"Why is that name so familiar?" Charlie wrinkled her forehead.

"He goes by Richard now."

"Richard Crane—he is that computer millionaire?"

Claire nodded. Dick—or Richard—had invented the Simplex high-speed modem. Now anyone who spent time on the Internet wanted to do it via a Simplex, which was superfast and allowed its owner to use a phone without needing an additional line. Who could have foreseen that a member of Minor High's Bi-Phy-Chem Club—which now sounded like a support group for drug addicts with sexual identity issues—would someday be well on his way to being one of the richest men in America?

"He sat in front of me in calculus, but I don't remember talking to him more than once or twice. He was kind of your typical smart, quiet kid. He worked on the yearbook and was a founding member of the Knights of the Log Table math club. Everyone knew he was a genius, but at Minor High that wasn't anything to be proud of."

"I wonder how the people will treat him now?"

"I kind of hope he comes, just to see," Claire said, turning the page. "Oh, look, there's Kyle Kraushaar."

"Kyle Curlyhair? It fits, doesn't it?" Charlie tapped on Kyle's hat-defying blond Afro.

"I didn't realize that was German. When we were six, I told him there wasn't any Santa Claus. When he was little, he had this terrible stutter, and he couldn't even get any words out, he was so shocked. So instead he ran away, crying. His mom called me up on the phone after we both got home from school, screaming that I was a liar to have told her son that."

"He must not have liked you."

"Are you kidding? He always had a huge crush on me. He even asked me out on my first boy-girl date." Claire smiled at the memory, the awkwardness faded by the intervening years. "I don't know why I said yes. Ever since third grade he had been trying to prove that he liked me by pushing me down on the playground or stealing my lunch. Once when we were playing dodge ball he beaned me so hard that he gave me a bloody nose and I had to go home."

Charlie gave her a sympathetic smile. "What was your date like?"

"Well, we were both fifteen, which meant he couldn't drive. He had his mother pick me up and then we went over to his house and listened to records in the den. Every few minutes his mom came in with another tray of snacks. I still remember the look on her face, like she thought she was going to catch us having sex. The next week Kyle told everyone at school I was his girlfriend, and I had to go around taking it back."

"Was he angry?"

"That was the sad thing. He wasn't." Claire riffled through the pages until she found the photo she wanted. "This was my first real boyfriend. Jim Prentiss." She pointed to a boy with wavy light brown hair who was intently potting a plant in a greenhouse. He wore a puka shell necklace, flared jeans so tight you could see the space between his thighs, a belt with a buckle in the shape of a leaf of pot, and what looked like a hand-crocheted shirt. Her memory supplied the color for his eyes: the green of cat's-eye marbles. "We worked together at Pietro's Pizza. I was head cashier and he was head cook. Sixteen years old and proud I was making twenty cents more than minimum wage. We used to stay in the restaurant after we finished closing it up."

Charlie raised an eyebrow but said nothing, having guessed what two teenagers would do in a building late at night with no adults present. Jean had never talked to Claire about birth control, but Claire had only to look at herself or her sister to know the consequences of unprotected sex. The same week Jim kissed her in the cooler Claire had gone to Planned Parenthood for the pill. She remembered the way Jim used to touch her, his clear experience tempered with a genuine affection. Afterward, they would pass a cigarette back and forth. Claire had felt sophisticated, conversing naked with a boy. When he decided he wanted to see someone else, Jim told Claire straightforwardly and then held her while she cried. It wasn't in Jim to lie, or to be with one girl for more than a few months. Whenever he had free time, he practiced guitar with his older brother in their garage. They had played for a few school assemblies, sweaty and happy, their hair hanging in their eyes, while the girls screamed out their names.

"I heard he got some girl pregnant right before we graduated, and their parents made them get married just before she had the baby. I can't imagine he stayed married long, though." She realized what was unusual about the picture of Jim in a greenhouse. He had basically been a hood. Claire flipped back through the pages. No one had taken pictures of the hoods, of the nerds, of the shy people. Or maybe they did, but their pictures certainly didn't make it into the annual.

Claire was about to close the yearbook when her gaze lit on the photo of Logan West. He had a shock of bright red hair, pale skin, and square-framed glasses that had not yet moved from geekiness to Elvis Costello cool. "There's another kid I've known since kindergarten. His family lived down the block. The last time I saw him was about a week after we graduated. He was wild, shouting that the walls were listening to his thoughts, that people's mouths were turning into volcanoes. He was wearing a kind of helmet he'd made out of tinfoil. Everyone thought it was because he smoked a lot of pot, but later that summer he ended up in Dammasch, the old state mental hospital, diagnosed with schizophrenia." Claire had visited him a couple of times. Now she felt guilty that she had let him slip out of her life.

Instead of answering, Claire turned back to the photos of the prom. "Looking at all these people, I feel like I have double vision. It's been so long since I've thought about them I can almost see them as if they were strangers. At the same time, I remember the weight some of them carried, the weight of popularity. It was as if the rest of us were insubstantial."

RD4MOR

Three

With a snap, Susie shook out a silver plastic cape and draped it over Claire's shoulders. Already Claire was beginning to have second thoughts. Her gaze met her sister's in the mirror. Their eyes were the same—the same almond shape, and the same shade of blue, like the flame on a gas stove. They had the same high cheek-bones, the same narrow straight noses. Even their hands were the same—long with squared-off fingertips—only Susie's were stained yellow with nicotine.

Susie lifted one of Claire's strawberry blond curls and then let it spring back into place. "You won't look stupid," she said, answering an objection Claire hadn't raised. Yet. "This is going to be very subtle. Take a look at your hair real close. You already have blond, brown, and auburn highlights. I'm just going to accent them a little. And I'll guarantee it will take five years off your face and make your eyes look bluer."

"But will it freshen my breath and get rid of my ring-around-the-collar?" Claire asked.

Instead of answering, Susie tugged a close-fitting rubber cap over Claire's head and tied the ends of the white elastic bands under her chin. The cap was pock-marked with dozens of holes. Picking up a tool that looked like a crochet hook, Susie began to pull small sections of hair through the cap.

A thought occurred to Claire. "You don't use this stuff on dead people, do you?" Susie had started working at Moyter's Funeral Home a few months earlier. At her previous job at Curl Up and Dye, she had grown tired of all the clients who seemed to want her to be a therapist instead of a hairdresser. As Susie had pointed out, dead people usually weren't interested in telling her about their ungrateful kids or philandering husbands.

"Relax." Her sister patted Claire's shoulder. "I keep all that stuff separate."

Despite the tugging sensation of having bits of her hair pulled through the cap, Claire closed her eyes and tried to follow her sister's instruction to relax. It was impossible to clear her mind. She just hoped she was doing the right thing by letting Susie talk her into getting highlights.

When she had first returned the card to the Minor High reunion committee, Claire had decided that she was comfortable enough with herself to go as herself. She wasn't going to get caught up in trying to make herself over, the way she heard some people did before attending their reunions. No face lift. No breast implants. No Jenny Craig. No caps on her teeth.

But then an idea began to nag at her the way her mother never had—would it hurt to try to look her best? In the last two months, Claire had worked her way up to eighty-pound pec flys and now benchpressed one hundred and twenty-five pounds. She was determined to draw attention away from her knobby knees and to her shapely shoulders. She loved junk food too much to diet for more than two hours, but now she was restricting herself to potato chips and crackers that said "less fat" on the label.

What to wear was the one problem Claire still hadn't solved. The reunion offered a million different forms of humiliation for people who were on the verge of forty—and who also happened to be stuck in the throes of remembering their youth. Things kicked off Friday night with a Western-themed social. Claire figured she could get by with a denim skirt, a T-shirt, and a bandanna tied around her neck. But what was she supposed to wear to the next day's pool party? Or the dress-up dance Saturday night? Or Sunday's barbecue and salmon bake? Fourth of July in Minor meant the weather would likely be ninety-plus degrees. No hiding less than perfect thighs under pants, or concealing "chicken wing" upper arms with long sleeves.

At Meier and Frank, Claire had bought a swimsuit that, according to its hang tag, could correct six different figure flaws. It promised to nip in her waist, give her cleavage, elongate her torso and legs, minimize her butt, and flatten her abdomen. The only problem was that it took twenty minutes to wrestle herself into it. And once she took it off, the red marks it left behind lasted for hours.

On the same shopping trip she had come close to buying an evening dress that was cut in such a way that no underwear could be worn under it. She'd finally borrowed a dress from her old friend Lori. Lori had insisted Claire try on the high-heeled pumps that matched the dress. At the sight of Claire's awkward, mincing stride, her friend had doubled over with laughter. "You look like a transvestite!" she had managed to gasp out. "You'll have to wear flats, like you always do." Since Claire had planned to do so anyway, she didn't bother pointing out that her strange gait had been mostly due to the fact that Lori's shoes were two sizes too small for Claire's own size ten feet.

Something cold seeped onto her scalp. Claire opened her eyes. Susie was dipping a paintbrush into one of three pots of liquid color. Then she picked up another of the pulled-through sections of hair and began to paint it. "I'll put more of the blond next to your face. It should make you look younger."

"Susie, at a reunion, everybody knows exactly how old you are."

"I know that," Susie gave Claire's shoulder a shove that was a little less than playful. "But you don't have to look it, do you?"

Could Susie be jealous? The only thing she had ever graduated from was beauty school. Their mother, Jean, had left high school at sixteen when Claire's imminent arrival had made itself known. Both of Jean's parents had grown up on farms, quitting school by tenth grade because their help was needed in the fields. Before that, the family history was a little hazy, but Claire wouldn't have been surprised to learn she was the first Montrose to graduate from high school.

Susie picked up a box of tinfoil and began to tear off inch-wide strips. When she had a couple dozen, she started to wrap some of the sections of hair in twists of foil. "This will intensify the color a little bit. That way you'll have two levels of three shades, for a total of six variations of color—in addition to the color of your own natural hair." She caught Claire's gaze in the mirror again. "Don't worry. You'll look great, and no one will have any idea that it didn't grow that way. Plus, you won't have to worry about roots." She picked up the last piece of tinfoil, twisted it into place, and looked at her watch. "Okay, this is going to have to set for forty-five minutes, and then I'll rinse it out. I've got to run down to the store and get some pull-ups for Eric. I've tried everything to potty train him, but it's not working. I even got him this special potty chair that plays a song when you pee in it."

"That would definitely inspire me."

Susie shook her head. "He's learned to get water from the sink and just pour it in instead. Then this other mother at the park told me I should make it into a game by floating Cheerios in the toilet and trying to get him to 'drown' them. I tried it, he wasn't buying. And then I forgot to flush and J.B. found all these floating Cheerios and thought I'd gone crazy. The only thing that sort of works is to give him an M&M each time he pees, but now he's figured out how to make one pee stretch into eight trips to the potty."

"All this talk of peeing is giving me ideas," Claire said, and went down the hall. Confronted by her own image in the bathroom mirror, she let out a little shriek. She looked like a demented superhero or perhaps the bride of Frankenstein on an acid trip. It wasn't just the silver plastic cape. The dye had stiffened her hair, so that it bristled out of the rubber cap at all angles. Light glinted off the sections wrapped in foil.

When Claire came back, Susie had the car keys in her hand. "Why don't you go lie out in the back and get a little color? You don't want to show up at your reunion looking like a ghost."

Claire made a mental note to buy some self-tanner so that her legs wouldn't bear more than a passing resemblance to something that crawled up from the cellar. "I think I'll just stay inside."

"On a nice day like this? You've got to take advantage of the sunshine when you find it."

"I look like a nut case, Susie. I don't want to take the chance of anybody seeing me like this."

"Come on, we've got a six-foot privacy fence back there. And I'll loan you my latest issue of *People* and a pair of sunglasses."

It was beginning to sound tempting. Warm weather always made Claire lazy. "Maybe I'll just go to sleep. But you'll wake me up, won't you?"

"Don't worry. If I let that stuff stay on for more than an hour, it might make your hair fall out."

"Fall out?" Claire froze.

"Don't worry. I'll be back long before that."

Claire peeked out into the backyard before she opened the door all the way. Susie was right, no one would be able to see her here. Stretching out on the lawn chair's white rubber tubes she closed her eyes. Claire put one forearm over her face and let herself relax. She thought of Dante, his dark curls, his smoothly muscled shoulders, the way his breath would catch when she kissed him in the cup of his left ear, just above the gold earring he wore. Even smiling, he looked slightly dangerous, since one of his front teeth had been broken and then mended with a flash of white. None of her old classmates was ever going to believe that he was a Met curator specializing in sixteenth-century art.

Claire was dreaming of Dante, of his slow smile and his gold-flecked eyes. They lay together in his bed, the noises of New York City muffled by the thick walls of the old apartment, built before the First World War. Enjoying the contrast between her paleness and his swarthiness, Claire pressed her body against him. He groaned in pleasure. Then the street sounds swelled in her ears, louder and louder, shouts, a woman screaming in fear.

Claire opened her eyes. The sounds continued.

"You bastard!" A grunt. The stinging sound of a palm against flesh.

She rolled off the lawn chair and crept toward the fence. Peering out between the slats, Claire realized that a woman was being raped in the alley just outside Susie's fence. The woman's blond hair hung wild in her face, and her long breasts were exposed to the world. The man already had his pants loosened around his hips. Bravely, the woman balled her fists and swung at the man, who had his broad back to Claire. The street was otherwise empty, although Claire wondered if a dozen other pairs of eyes were also watching, evaluating, waiting to see if the man had a gun, or telling themselves to mind their own business. This was the kind of neighborhood where people thought the best way to stay out of trouble was not to notice things.

Claire had seen enough. But the phone was inside the house. By the time she reached it, called the police, and they arrived, this poor woman would probably be lying on the ground with her teeth kicked in and the man rutting away on top of her. She made a split-second decision to intervene. Even if the other neighbors wouldn't get involved, surely there must still be some elderly busybody who lived on the street and could be counted on to call 911.

Charlie had passed on a few tips from her Self-

defense for Seniors class. One of them was that screaming or shouting gave you power. The other was that
when you acted, you did so with all decisiveness. There
was no turning back. Shrieking like a banshee, Claire
opened the gate and ran toward the struggling pair.

"Stop it! Stop it!" she yelled. Running up behind the
man, she grabbed his right hand before he could strike
again. She twisted it behind him and then jerked it up
between his shoulder blades. He was a big guy, but most
of his bulk was concentrated in the roll around his
waist. As he twisted in her two-handed grasp, she was
glad that she had begun lifting heavier weights.

"You bastard! Leave her alone!" Claire screamed in
his ear while the man groped behind him with his free
hand, trying to force her to let him go. "Somebody call
the police!" she yelled at the empty neighborhood. The
only thing that answered her was a dog that began to
bark farther down the block. She remembered reading
in a magazine that people were more cooperative about
calling the fire department than the cops, so she decided
to hedge her bets. "Fire! Fire! Call the fire department!
There's a fire!"

The woman gave Claire a strange look, then made a
fist and shook it in the man's face. "Give me my money,
asshole."

Before Claire could decipher the meaning of this, the
woman punched the guy in the stomach. Accompanied
by a hollow explosion of breath, the woman's fist sank
in up to the wrist. Claire was reminded absurdly of
Charlie punching down bread dough.

The man doubled over and threw up on the woman's
scuffed white pumps. Fearful that she would break his
arm, Claire released it. He fell to his hands and knees.

The woman reached down to her waist and tugged

up the yellow tube top over her slack breasts. A tube top. Claire hadn't seen one of those since she was in high school. Looking more closely at the young woman's plump, sullen face, Claire saw that she probably hadn't even been born yet the last time Claire had worn a tube top. The other woman ran her hands down her blue shorts with bright green polka dots, then pushed her frayed, dead-looking hair out of her eyes.

"Thanks," she said, then bent over and tugged the man's wallet from his back pants pocket. She thumbed it open, but the money compartment gaped empty. The wallet bounced off the man's hanging head. "That's the last time you get anything before you pay for it, ass-hole!" She aimed a kick at his ample backside. His face skidded in the dirt. Then she turned to look at Claire again.

"What in the fuck are you supposed to be? Some kind of superpimp or—." A medley of sirens interrupted her question. Without wasting any more time on conversation, she began to cut across the neighbor's lawn, heading in the direction of another alley that ran behind the houses.

A firetruck and a police car pulled up beside Claire and the man, one right after another, sirens blaring, lights whirling. The noise was deafening. The man lifted his head from the dirt, a string of vomit still hanging from his mouth. His soft, blurred features looked familiar. Refreshed by her recent trip with Charlie down memory lane, Claire finally placed him. Good old Suede. Wade aka "Suede" Merz, Minor High class of 1979. Head football player turned overweight used car salesman.

The sirens were turned off, but the lights continued to strobe. The cop and two firemen reached them at the

same time. Claire could see one of the firemen trying
unsuccessfully not to laugh as he took in her silver plastic cape, rubber helmet, and bristling spikes of color-
streaked and foil-wrapped hair.

The cop had a narrow, pale face, and he didn't look
any older than twenty-five. "What's the problem here,
folks?" he asked. He made a point of resting his hand on
the butt of his gun. His gaze was fastened on Claire, not
Wade. In the last few years, a number of mentally ill
people in Portland had committed "suicide by cop."

Claire wasn't sure what to answer. Was it her business
to tell the cop that Wade had tricked a hooker into giving him something for free?

While she hesitated, the cop leaned over Wade, who
was sitting back on his heels. He'd even managed to zip
up his pants. The red imprint of a hand was rising up on
his cheek, and there was a smear of dirt on his chin.

"Did this woman assault you, buddy?"

When Wade looked at Claire, it was clear he was focused on her outfit, not her face. A slow smile spread
across his face. "Just a little argument, officers. Nothing
to be concerned about."

Everything seemed to be calming down until Susie's
old Chevette came tearing up. She was yelling before
she even got the car door open. "Where's the fire? Is the
house okay?"

"Everything's fine, Susie. Just a little misunderstand-
ing."

Susie's confused glance went from the cop to the two
firemen (who were now openly laughing) to Wade. He
sat on the curb, the front of his starched white shirt
stained yellow with vomit. Susie was still confused, but
then she happened to catch sight of Claire's wrist. She
grabbed it to look at her watch. "It's that late? We've got

to rinse your hair out right now." She began to pull Claire behind her.

The cop put a hand on her shoulder. "Not so fast, ma'am. You're interrupting an ongoing investigation. I'm going to have to ask you to allow me to continue without interference."

"If I don't rinse her hair out now, it's going to start falling out. In big clumps."

He stiffened. "All in good time, ma'am."

Great. Now the cop had stopped paying attention to Wade and Claire and was getting angry at Susie. Was it Claire's imagination, or did her scalp suddenly feel tight, as if the follicles were reaching a critical breaking point? She couldn't take that chance.

"Wait a second. There's no problem here, Officer. Right, Wade?"

Wade started at the sound of his name. He gave Claire a puzzled look, but didn't miss his cue. "Right. No problem," he echoed.

"So can I go?"

"There's still the little matter of disturbing the peace," the cop said stubbornly.

"Oh, leave it go, Riley," one of the firemen said over his shoulder as the two men walked back to their truck. They climbed in, turned off the lights, and drove away.

The cop gave the three of them a long look. "I don't know what the hell's been happening here. You should be glad I don't have the time to haul your butts in the way you deserve." Then he turned on his heel and marched smartly back to his patrol car. Claire noticed the back of his neck was an ugly red.

Wade stood up and gave Susie and Claire a half bow. Claire noticed that the palm of his right hand hovered over his shirt without touching it. "Ladies," he said with a nod, then walked off, as dignified as if nothing had happened.

-CSHFLW

Four

Claire tilted the rearview mirror so that she could look at her hair one more time. Despite the heat, and her car's lack of air-conditioning, she had driven to Minor with her window resolutely rolled up. Dante had felt no such compunction, however, so the right side of her hair was tousled. In a corner of the mirror, she caught a glimpse of a crumpled Tootsie Roll wrapper in the seat behind her, caught in a crack between the narrow bench seat and the seat back. She reached back and quickly pocketed it. Normally, her car was cluttered with junk-food wrappers, but when Dante was in town she took pains to keep that side of herself hidden from him. Despite her best efforts, her car was like a real-life example of entropy or perhaps spontaneous generation, as candy and chip wrappers magically appeared even after she vacuumed it.

Claire knew that people sometimes wondered why she still drove an eleven-year-old Mazda 323 with a trunk that no longer locked, why she still shopped at the bag-your-own Winco, why her quitting Specialty Plates was the only visible sign of the fact that she had inherited a multimillion-dollar Vermeer. The answer was that Claire had given nearly all the proceeds from the painting's sale to the World Jewish Restitution Organization. No one knew who had owned the Vermeer before it made its way into Claire's great-aunt's possession in postwar Germany. Still, it wasn't hard to figure out the reason no heirs had come forward, since the Nazis had stripped so many Jews of their art collections before disposing of their owners altogether.

They had even done the same thing to Charlie, taken a little Rembrandt that had been in her family for generations. It was because of Charlie that Claire had initially decided to keep none of the money, but then Charlie had finally insisted that Claire keep a tiny fraction. A lawyer Charlie knew had set up a trust that provided Claire with just about the same amount of money she used to make when she vetted vanity license plates. And that wasn't really enough to afford a better car.

Her hair, at least, still looked good. Despite the best efforts of the police, the firemen, Wade, and the hooker Claire had privately christened "Earlene," Claire's hair had turned out just as Susie had promised. Now as she looked in the rearview mirror, Claire ran her fingers through soft ringlets the colors of paprika and cinnamon, mustard seed and curry. Here and there a strand glinted with the spicy brightness of hot red pepper.

"You look great," Dante said. "You should stop worrying about it."

"I spent twelve years of my life with these people."

She pushed the mirror back in place. "I don't know why, but it still matters what they think about me."

For an answer, Dante leaned over the parking brake and gave her a kiss. Claire began it with one eye half-open, but by the end she had surrendered to the feeling of his lips, surprisingly soft, on hers. It was Dante who finally broke apart. He gave her a cat's slit-eyed smile of pleasure. "We'd better go and get a room before somebody yells, 'Get a room!' at us."

Claire's car was parked in the acres of parking lot that surrounded Ye Olde Pioneer Village Inn. Despite the name, the complex wasn't run by the descendants of pioneers, though, but by the last living remnants of the Tequamish tribe. One hundred and fifty years ago, the white man had decimated the Tequamish through broken treaties and the simultaneous introduction of smallpox, measles, and firewater. The Tequamish had fought back valiantly, but to no avail. Now, through Indian casino gambling, their sons and daughters had found a belated revenge. It was easier, less messy, and a lot more profitable to separate the white man from his wallet than his scalp.

Dante nodded at the hotel. "Should we go check in?"

"Sure," Claire said, giving him a smile that felt forced. She had just caught sight of someone she was sure was Jim Prentiss sauntering into the lobby, his hands in his pockets. Alone, she couldn't help noticing. How would it feel to face her long-ago lover with her new one at her side? Would Jim even care when he saw her? Would she? She felt as nervous and awkward as the day the bus had first dropped her off before the doors of Minor High.

"You haven't moved," Dante pointed out.

"I'm just wondering if people will still be divided into the same groups." Actually, she had decided to give Jim a head start. She didn't feel quite up to staring into those yellow-green eyes of his.

"So what groups were those?"

"The jocks," Claire said, ticking them off on her fingers. "The nerds—those were the smart people who weren't embarrassed to carry an HP calculator on their belt in a zippered case. The hoods—you know, the people who smoked pot and cigarettes and had zero plans to go to college." She felt a flash of disloyalty as she thought of Jim Prentiss, who had more or less fallen into this category. "We called the farm kids goat-ropers. Oh, and then there were the theater people, like my friend Jessica. We thought it was really funny to call them thespians, because it nearly rhymed with lesbians. And of course there were the popular people—the socs." She pronounced it *so-shs*. "They were mostly the ones whose parents had money because they were doctors or lawyers or architects."

Claire shifted in her seat as she remembered longing to be just like them. With money, she could have dressed just like they did, in clogs and a pair of wide-legged San Francisco Riding Gear jeans (with the bottom edges rolled up, unhemmed). Old white tennis shoes and stiff dark jeans from Sears hadn't exactly cut it. With envy, she had watched the socs laugh at jokes she didn't get or talk about vacations spent surfing in Hawaii or seeing *A Chorus Line* on Broadway. Dante, on the other hand, had grown up in New York City, and fit in easily with friends whose families owned megacorporations. She hoped he wouldn't find Minorites, with their pretensions to sophistication, too laughable.

"Which group were you in?" Dante prompted, and Claire realized she had been silent for a long moment.

"Not any group, really. I was smart enough to be a nerd, but I worked after school instead of attending meetings of the math club." It hadn't really been a choice, although Claire didn't tell Dante how much they had needed the money from her job.

They got their bags from the car, with Dante carrying the bulk of them. He hadn't said a word about how much she had brought, even though she knew three suitcases for a three-day weekend were too many.

Behind the hotel was a ten-foot-tall wooden stockade fence. Above the pointed stakes she could see the Ferris wheel lifting people up into the air in rocking suspended cars, as well as a half-dozen other rides that looked a lot less gentle. Faint screams trailed behind the roller-coaster riders as they did a corkscrew loop. Claire swallowed as she looked at the Tilt-O-Whirl, remembering an unfortunate picnic at Oak's Amusement Park that had begun with four beers and ended with her riding the Tilt-O-Whirl and praying to God to let her die.

They passed three or four other couples in the parking lot as they walked toward the hotel, but Claire didn't recognize anyone. Either they had come for the casino gambling and not the reunion, or they had all changed a lot since high school. When she wasn't looking at the other people, Claire automatically scanned the parking lot for vanity plates. She found a RKNROL and a TOUCHE, which someone had illegally defaced by adding a painted accent mark.

Dante nudged her shoulder, and when she looked up at him, he gave her a reassuring smile. Even if Claire was uncertain about herself, she could relax a little when she looked at Dante. His white T-shirt contrasted nicely with his dusky skin and his curly hair as black as a crow's back. How could she feel insecure when she had Dante on her arm?

"Hey, Warty! Warty!" Heads turned as the cry cut through the parking lot. Claire froze. What was worse— to acknowledge this greeting or ignore it? Finally she turned and saw Jessica galloping toward her. How could Jessica have done this to her? Hadn't she seen that Claire was with a man who wouldn't understand this once humorous reference to their youth?

"I had a little skin condition in second grade," Claire murmured quickly to Dante. She couldn't look him in the eye.

As soon as Jessica caught sight of Dante, she skidded to a stop. Claire could practically watch her childhood friend grow up before her eyes, going from a giggly eight-year-old to a sophisticated thirty-eight in an instant. She wore silver-colored silk shantung capris and a matching boat-necked top with three-quarter-length sleeves. Dressed in jeans and a T-shirt, Claire felt instantly dowdy.

"Well, well—who's this?" Jessica smiled up at Dante with eyes as blue as a summer sky. Her thick black hair was cut close to her face.

Dante put the bags down and shook Jessica's hand while Claire made introductions. "Jessica McFarland, this is Dante Bonner. Dante, Jessica. Jessica used to be on *Until Tomorrow*."

"Until I was in a plane crash. Or at least my character was," she explained, directing her attention to Dante. "They had the whole cast involved in a midair collision. Some of the characters were killed off, some were severely burned. My character was one of the ones who died. Even if my character had lived, they probably wouldn't have kept me playing the part. When the bandages came off, voilà, you had a whole new cast of young actors willing to work for scale."

"But didn't the new actors look a lot different than the old actors?" Dante asked.

Jessica shrugged her small shoulders. She was only five feet two—a full eight inches shorter than Claire. The longer Claire stood next to her, the more she was beginning to feel wider, taller, and sturdier. "They just explained that the plastic surgeons did the best they could. Some of the new cast even had different color hair than the people they were replacing. I don't know how they expect the audience to believe that it all happened because of plastic surgery!" She shook her head, then smiled. "But the whole thing has really turned out to be a blessing, because it's freed me up to do theater." She gave the word an English spin. *Thee-uh-tuh.* "I was just saying to Meryl the other day that dying has proved to be the best career move I ever made."

Claire's mind filled in the blank. Could Jessica mean Meryl Streep? "So you're acting in plays now?" The longer she stood next to Jessica, the more she felt hulking. Monstrous. When she was in high school, she had longed to be the same size as Jessica. To be diminutive. To shop in the petite department. To wear size five shoes. She had wanted to have boys be able to pick her up and twirl her like a baton.

Jessica's answer was a snatch of song, "Give my regards to Broadway." After a bit of soft shoe, she dipped low for the bow. As usual, Jessica had drawn an audience. When she raised her head, five or six people broke into a patter of applause. A radiant smile lit her face. She bowed her head again before turning to pull open the door.

In the circular lobby, they were greeted by a huge wooden bear that appeared to have been hastily carved with a chain saw from a single length of pine. Jessica had fallen into an animated conversation with two of the women who had watched her mini-act, so Claire and Dante went up to the check-in desk. It was fashioned of plastic logs, and the young woman behind it wore a poke bonnet and a long calico-print dress.

"Montrose, Montrose, Montrose," the woman said, tapping her teeth with the butt end of a white ballpoint pen. "Where have I heard that name before? Oh, yeah— I have a package for you."

"A package?"

For an answer, the woman slipped a small padded manila envelope into Claire's hands. It bulged in the middle, filled with something hard that was a little smaller than a closed fist. The outside of the envelope was bare, except for a printed label reading, CLAIRE MONTROSE, MINOR HIGH REUNION, JULY 1. There was no return address—but then there wasn't any stamp, either.

"Who left it for me?" Claire asked, but the only answer she got was an uninterested shrug, the woman's mind already turning to the growing line behind them. After handing back Claire's credit card, she stepped from behind the counter to summon a bellhop. Claire saw that the feet peeking from underneath her pioneer dress were shod in aqua-colored Nikes.

Dante and the bellman loaded their bags on top of his cart, and then followed the cart to the elevator. Claire still carried the little package. The bellman's breeches and shirt were fashioned of Ultrasuede, and a matted synthetic coonskin cap sat on top of his head.

The hotel had been fashioned in the shape of a wagon wheel. The hub corresponded to the circular shape of the hotel's lobby. The spokes were long blocks of rooms, three stories tall. Once the bellman opened the door to their room, Claire saw the covered wagon theme had been carried over to the interior decoration. The room was lit by a sort of chandelier fashioned from an ersatz wagon wheel. The canopy on the bed was designed to mimic a covered wagon. But the decorator's ingenuity only went so far. The TV still looked like a TV, the phone looked like a phone, and when Claire poked her head in the bathroom, she was relieved to find a toilet instead of a two-hole privy.

The bellman palmed Dante's tip and left. Claire slipped her thumb under the envelope's flap. "Maybe it's our name badges," she guessed. She shook the contents into her hand.

Out tumbled a heart-shaped wooden box a little smaller than Claire's palm, handcarved from dark-red wood that glowed under the light. The top was decorated with three freeform curlicues and a simple flower. On the left side was a silver hinge. Claire thumbed it open. Inside, glued to the bottom, was a picture she recognized right away, because it had only been a few weeks since she looked at it with Charlie. Aside from her alphabetized photo, it was the only other picture of her that had run in the annual. Whoever had put the photo in the box had scissored Claire from the group of forty or so members of the National Honor Society who had surrounded her. The photo showed only Claire, sitting cross-legged on the ground.

Dante looked over her shoulder. "Why did someone send you that picture? What does it mean?"

"I don't know. It's from my annual." She pointed at the edge of a coat behind her, the slice of another arm on her left. "These are other people from the honor society." She looked inside the envelope. "There's nothing else. No note or anything."

Dante said in a singsong voice, "Someone's got a crush on you."

"I don't know. Do you really think so?" Claire felt a secret thrill. "I wonder who it could be?"

"Did you have many boyfriends in high school?"

"Only a couple. And I can't see any of them doing this."

"So it's a secret admirer then?"

"I guess so. So I'll have to wait until someone 'fesses up." Claire put the heart-shaped box back in the envelope and set it on the nightstand.

"So what's first on the agenda?" Dante sat on the edge of the bed and bounced experimentally.

Claire ignored the hint. "Tonight there's what they are calling a mixer in the Hoe-Down Room. The dress is supposed to be Western casual, whatever that means. I'm sure the guys will all just wear jeans, but I don't know what the women are supposed to wear. Do you think I could get away with a denim skirt and a white T-shirt?"

"I'm sure anything will be fine. People are going to want to see you, not what you're wearing."

Claire thought to herself that Dante, who usually understood women, for once was completely wrong. She was sure that all the other women there would be checking out everything from body fat to marital status to income levels. But instead of arguing with him, she said, "I'm too nervous to think about eating. If you're hungry, why don't you go ahead and order from room service? I'm going to take a shower before I change."

In the bathroom, she regarded herself critically in the mirror. Her confidence in her appearance fizzled. She was a mature woman now—so why did she feel as if the person looking back at her was still an insecure girl?

Since her birthday fell five days before the cutoff for enrollment, she had been the youngest in every class. How Claire had longed to be older—or to at least look older—when she was in high school! It had been embarrassing, being the last to be able to get a learner's permit and then a driver's license. Senior year, some of her friends were getting into bars with fake ID, but Claire didn't even bother exploring the option, not when she was seventeen and looked several years younger. Once when she was eighteen, she had gone with a date to a movie. The old dragon lady taking tickets had asked her how old she was. Confused, Claire had inquired if the movie was R-rated. It turned out that the movie was PG—and that the ticket taker thought Claire qualified for the under-twelve discounted children's ticket. That had been her first and last date with that particular guy.

But now she was finally all grown up, a woman with actual curves instead of an awkward stork wearing men's shrink-to-fit Levi's, sized 26–36. Maybe now she could even pass for sexy. She tried out a "come-hither look," but in the mirror she appeared simply to be a woman in search of her bifocals. Had she moved from being too young to being too old, skipping over the vital middle part of being just right?

And then she saw it. The beginnings of a huge pimple threatening to erupt just below her mouth. How could she show up at her class' twentieth high school reunion with a zit the size of a slice of pepperoni decorating her chin? She turned on the shower. Maybe she could steam it out.

Under the warmth of the shower's spray, Claire closed her eyes and began softly singing as much as she could remember from "My Sharona." Which wasn't much. She remembered lying sprawled on a blanket in the park with Logan the spring of their junior year. They had listened to a giant boombox, and she had nodded in agreement when he told her that the Knack was destined to be as big as the Beatles. That was back when the radio still played music for Logan, although a few months later all he seemed to hear from it were voices that told him he was stupid and deserved to die. Once she had ripped the batteries from the back and held them out to him in her shaking hand, but he had screamed that the radio was still broadcasting, that the voices were still talking about him.

Lost in memories, she didn't hear the bathroom door opening. She only lifted her head from the spray when two strong hands gripped her shoulders. Claire gasped. Dante kissed her nape just below the shower cap. She tried to turn to kiss him, but he held her fast as he nuzzled her. Forgetting all about how she looked, Claire closed her eyes and gave herself up to his attentions.

Afterward, they sprawled on the bed. Claire propped herself on her elbows to look at Dante. He was half asleep, his eyes closed, a faint smile curving below his strong nose. It wasn't easy, maintaining a relationship while living in cities three thousand miles apart. They had developed their own rituals to stay in touch. They E-mailed, they sent each other bizarre postcards, they called. When they had phone fights, they worked to resolve them as quickly as possible—and they never hung up on each other. Living apart, the phone was their lifeline.

Once or twice a week, they planned "dinner dates." They set up a time, each cooked a nice dinner, and then they got on the phone and ate together. (It helped that Claire didn't mind eating at 5:00 P.M., while Dante, a native New Yorker, thought 8:00 P.M. was just the right time to sit down to dinner.)

Whenever they finally did reunite, they eased back into it. They had learned not to book surprise romantic weekend getaways or shower each other with dozens of long-stemmed roses. Instead, they were more likely to go out for lunch at a neighborhood restaurant or to take a walk—anything where they could just talk. It was way too much pressure to be "on" all of a sudden when they hadn't seen each other for a month or more.

Even though Claire had really wanted Dante to be by her side for this reunion, she hoped he wouldn't be too bored. For anyone who hadn't gone to Minor High twenty years ago, it was sure to be a dull weekend.

AWAWEGO

Five

Just outside the Hoe-Down Room was a folding table covered with a line of shoe boxes. Sitting behind the table was Belinda Brophy. She looked basically the same as she had in high school, just a little more tired and a little more plump. The name badge applied to her black leather jacket read BELINDA BROPHY-MULLER and showed a picture of the younger Belinda, her hair crimped by a curling iron. Today's Belinda had a fuss-free perm. "Well, hello, Claire Montrose," Belinda said, her hands poised above the shoe boxes, which were labeled with different stretches of the alphabet. "So what's your married name now?"

Dante leaned forward before Claire could answer. "She decided to keep the Montrose."

"How—modern!" Belinda simpered, distracted by Dante's proximity. She handed over Claire's name tag and they moved away.

Claire pasted on her name tag, all the while complaining to Dante. "Maybe I shouldn't have come. I'm afraid people are going to spend all night asking me about my occupation, my marital status, and how many kids I have."

"Just let me know if it makes you change your mind," Dante answered. He had talked about marriage, and even about kids, but Claire was undecided. She had long ago determined that if and when she ever did marry it would be forever—and part of her still doubted that Dante would always want her.

She put her hand on one of the double doors to the Hoe-Down Room, but didn't push it open. It seemed to faintly vibrate from the noise inside. "Go on," Dante urged into her ear. "I'm right here with you." He reached out and swung open one of the doors.

The noise of conversation and laughter, mingled with the sound of Rod Stewart's "Do Ya Think I'm Sexy?" spilled out into the hall. At first, it was overwhelming. Claire guessed there were more than a hundred people in the room, gathered in knots, or sitting at small glass-topped tables underneath the glassy-eyed stare of stuffed animal heads. The largest group was congregated in front of the bar, where a harried bartender was pouring drinks with both hands. A crumpled straw cowboy hat was tilted back on his head and he wore fringed chaps over his jeans.

Dante and Claire found an empty table at the edge of the room. At first, Claire didn't recognize anyone. But then in a process similar to entering a darkened room, her eyes began to adjust to the changes twenty years had wrought. In general, the women seemed to have held up better than the men. The women all had their hair, for one thing, while a good portion of the men had receding hairlines, or had gone completely bald or turned gray. A lot of the guys had gained weight, too, ballooning past the point of recognition, including one guy in an orange tank top that made his stomach look like a pumpkin. He was staggering from group to group, shouting, "Party!" and pumping his fist in the air.

"Let me guess." Dante pointed at a blond, slender woman who was flitting from table to table, blowing air kisses, tossing her newly gilded locks, and smiling so hard it looked as if her teeth were in danger of bursting through her cheeks. "A cheerleader?"

"Bingo. Cindy Weaver. Or I guess she's Cindy Sanchez now. Head cheerleader and prom queen. She never much cared for us little people. I was a weird kid in high school. I literally walked around school with my nose in a book. One time I was going down the hall and someone stuck out their foot and tripped me. I don't know for sure that it was Cindy, but I'll never forget looking up and seeing her standing there laughing at me."

"Did you know her in grade school, too?"

"She moved into the district in third grade. Everybody thought she was glamorous. Her mom used to set her hair every night on sponge rollers. I thought she looked like a fairy princess. By fifth grade she was wearing pantyhose and a bra, when the rest of us were still in white knee-highs and undershirts."

They watched as Cindy squealed and lunged for another woman, who managed to hold her at arm's length. "That's Maria Markgraf that Cindy is hugging. She was a cheerleader, too, but she wasn't nearly as mean as Cindy." Judging by the way she was dressed, Maria had become a well-paid executive. One of the few women in the room not clad in denim, she wore an open-necked cream-colored silk blouse under a camel-colored gabardine pantsuit. It wasn't exactly "Western wear" but it was elegant. Her thick auburn hair was pulled back into a French twist. She settled back in her chair and exchanged a smile with the woman next to her. Claire said, "That woman with all the freckles, the one sitting next to Maria, is Jill Proctor. Jill was part of the horsey set, which meant her family had a lot more money than we did, but she was always pretty nice to me."

A waitress wearing a tan Ultrasuede dress cut past them. A black feather dangled from the headband that held back her straight light brown hair. Balanced on the palm of her hand was a round tray filled edge-to-edge with glasses. Dante raised two fingers, but the waitress was too harried to notice him.

Dante turned the gesture into a point and indicated a thin man wearing a fringed leather jacket so elaborate that a single cow must have died for the fringe alone. "Wait a minute—that guy over there looks like Richard Crane. The computer guy." A dozen people were crowded around Richard's table, shaking the man's hand and slapping him on the back as he awkwardly held court. Even sitting down, he looked storklike and gawky.

"Yeah. That's Dick. I guess I should say Richard now. Minor's one real claim to fame." Richard glanced up for a minute, and his gaze caught Claire's. He gave her a little wave, and Claire was surprised to feel her face flush. Was she no better than the rest of them, willing to fawn over him now that he was rich and famous?

"Wow! I didn't know you knew the guy who owned Simplex!"

"I didn't really know him. No one really knew Dick—I mean, Richard. He always hid behind his camera. He was on the yearbook staff. Everyone used to make fun of him because he walked around with a pocket protector stuck in his shirt and a calculator hooked on his belt. You always read that he's got such a reputation as a loner —but I just think he never had a chance in high school to develop any social skills."

Dante scanned the room. "So which of these people *were* you friends with in high school? Besides that woman who called you Warty, I mean."

Claire managed to keep a neutral expression on her face while she reminded herself to kill Jessica. "Since I had to work after school, I didn't have a lot of close friends." She spent a few minutes locating the current versions of people from the group she used to eat lunch with. Claire nodded in the direction of a dark-haired woman wearing a sleeveless black turtleneck. "That's Becca Brody. She's really slimmed down since high school." Next, Claire pointed at a tall, plain-faced woman who wore her hair carelessly pinned back. "And that's Rachel Munroe. Even though her father was a doctor, they didn't have any money. He mostly treated migrant workers' children in a free clinic."

She scanned the crowd for a few more seconds. "That woman over in the corner, the blonde passing around the pictures—that's Nina Lisac. She was Becca's best friend. She got pregnant when we were still in high school and got married before we even graduated. It was kind of a Minor thing to do."

Dante again endeavored to catch the waitress's eye, but failed. "I think I'll have to go to the bar if I want something to drink. What would you like?"

"Could you get me a glass of red wine, please?" She watched him go, smiling to herself as more than one woman turned her head to follow his path.

"Claire." She started as a man's voice murmured in her ear. A hand cupped her shoulder. "You look good."

She turned in her chair, her heart already beating a bit faster because of the surprise of his touch and his voice.

At first, her old boyfriend Jim looked the same, just a little more weathered. His wavy light brown hair had thinned a bit, but the heart-shaped face was the same, as were the heart-stopping pair of green eyes. Why was it, Claire wondered, that crinkles around men's eyes were sexy, but that crinkles around women's eyes only fed a billion-dollar-a-year face-cream industry? Unlike a lot of Claire's other male classmates, at least Jim hadn't picked up a paunch along the way. His weathered Levi's fit him like a dream, and his green short-sleeved polo shirt showed off well-muscled, tanned arms.

There was a moment where she could have gotten up and hugged him, but it passed. Instead she offered him her hand, and he shook it, a little awkwardly.

"So what have you been doing with yourself, Jim?"

He looked away from her as he pulled out one of the free chairs. Straddling it, he set his long-necked beer bottle on the table. "I'm working for the local beer distributor."

"In sales?" She imagined him talking store owners into stocking new varieties of beer, enticing them with free posters of scantily clad women dancing around giant beer bottles.

"Actually, I make deliveries. I like to say it combines the two things I like most. Beer and travel. Plus, there's always the employee discount."

Jim laughed, but she thought he seemed embarrassed. He used to talk about doing something exotic after he graduated, but really, what had life ever offered him? Even graduating from high school had been exotic for his family. His dad had never been in the picture. His mom had been a waitress, with no aspirations beyond making it to her next cigarette break. Claire flashed on a memory of Jim's mother's white Famolare shoes, worn with heavy-duty support hose that had made her legs look like plastic.

Jim was now looking down at his open hands. "Did my hands feel rough to you?" He stretched out his arms and spread his fingers. "I've been trying to remember to put cream on them every night. I figured I'd be shaking hands a lot this weekend, and I didn't want to scare anyone. After heaving boxes all day and pushing around a handtruck—well, my hands are always pretty banged up. And don't get me started on the broken bottles." His hands were bundles of tendons and muscles, laced with the ridges of scars. Claire couldn't help noticing the lack of a wedding ring.

He seemed to follow her thoughts. "So was that your husband? Do you guys have the two-point-two kids?" The soft voice was the same. Listening to it, Claire had to suppress the urge to scoot closer to him, as if he were drawing her into the same magic circle they had shared more than twenty years ago.

Claire shook her head. "I'm afraid I haven't gotten around to all that yet. How about you? I remember hearing you got married." She refrained from using the phrase "had to."

Jim shrugged and looked away. "That didn't last long. For the moment, I'm single."

She changed the subject. "Do you still play music?"

"I'm in a band." He tilted his beer to his lips and took a long swallow. "If you can call it that. We mostly do weddings. I spend a lot of my time singing "Louie, Louie." I'm one of only thirty-seven people in the United States who actually knows all the words." He looked past Claire. "Here comes your boyfriend or whoever he is."

Claire turned. Dante was walking toward them, his eyes on the two glasses he was trying to keep safe from jostling elbows. "My boyfriend. Here, let me introduce you."

"That's okay. I need to go out and get a smoke." Jim gave her a nod, and was gone before Claire could urge him to stay.

Dante put a glass into her hand. "Who was that?"

"Jim Prentiss. We used to be pretty close, a long time ago. Talking to him made me realize how lucky I am not to be a waitress at the Apple Tree Truck Stop, wearing the thickest support hose they make." Claire couldn't help thinking that Jim made quite a contrast to Dante's old conquests. Dante's former girlfriends tended to have trust funds, degrees from Harvard, and to wear ugly, abbreviated clothes from designers so hip that Claire had never heard of them. "I'm afraid Minor is going to seem a long way from New York City."

In answer, Dante put his arm around her shoulder and gave a squeeze. "Hey, I wanted to come, remember?" He changed the subject. "So do you think he's the one who gave you that heart-shaped box? After all, he came right over to the table as soon as I was gone."

For a moment, Claire had forgotten about the box. "Jim? I don't think so. He asked me about his hands, whether they felt rough. I think he was worried about impressing some other woman. Or women. Not me."

They sat quietly for a few minutes, sipping their drinks

and watching the crowd swirl and eddy about them. There were glad cries of reunion as people rediscovered each other, exchanged photos of their children, teased each other about lost hair and gained weight. A few conversations seemed more serious. Claire saw Sawyer Fairchild, the gubernatorial candidate, talking to Richard Crane, their heads close together. Nearby, a woman waited patiently. She had the kind of prettiness particular to Miss America contestants, with teeth like Chiclets and straight brown hair worn shoulder-length with the ends curled under. Sawyer and Richard's conversation ended with the two men nodding and shaking hands.

Cindy was still going from table to table, acting more the politician than Sawyer ever would. But Claire noticed that Cindy stayed away from her area of the room, as if Claire were emitting some kind of invisible force field. A few months before, they had met unexpectedly. Cindy had bragged about the wonders of her new maid, an illegal immigrant who, according to Cindy, was happy to work for two dollars an hour. Claire had done her one better, though. When Cindy had paused long enough to ask what Claire was doing these days, Claire couldn't resist saying that she now worked for the IRS.

Claire spotted Wade Merz standing just a few feet from them, scanning the room. His eyes glossed right over Claire and then came back again, his expression puzzled and a little wary. Claire realized that without her rubber highlighting cap and silver cape, Wade wasn't too sure who she was. She hazarded a guess that he was probably under the impression he had sold her a car (and judging by his wary expression, a lemon) at some point. While Claire watched, the waitress walked between them with her now empty tray. Wade stopped her by laying a hand on her upper arm.

"Excuse me, but I'd sure like a heapum big vodka tonic." He gave her a smile that made his crooked nose more prominent. "Say, you don't look like an Indian. Or should I say squaw?"

"Squaw is an old white word for pussy," the waitress said. "So don't use it. And, for your information, I *am* half Tequamish *and* was raised on the reservation." Her utterly mirthless smile lent credence to the tale that the Tequamish used to celebrate victories over their enemies by eating their hearts—pulled, still beating, from their chests. Although anything, Claire supposed, sounded better than ground acorn pancakes, which had been the staple item in the Tequamish diet.

Wade ducked his head so he wouldn't have to meet the waitress's gaze. "I'll be sure to remember that, miss."

Claire had been so busy eavesdropping that she didn't notice a man approaching from the other side of the room.

"Hello, Claire. Long time no see."

She turned, but didn't recognize the speaker. She and Dante both stood up. He was a tall man, two or three inches over six feet, but pudgy, his hair a faded gingery gray. In a room filled with denim, he wore a snug gray suit and a wrinkled red tie. Behind thick glasses, his eyes regarded her, blinking slowly. Claire tried to be subtle, but finally she had to glance at the high school picture on his name tag. The bony pale face, shock of hair, and square-framed glasses were instantly familiar in ways this plump stranger wasn't. Could this really be her old friend, the skinny redheaded boy who had always been in motion, going faster and faster even as he went crazy?

"Logan?"

"I know. You're surprised." His voice was flat, but she thought she detected the hidden trace of a smile. Logan smacked his lips. "You probably didn't think we'd ever run into each other again, did you?"

"I didn't think that," Claire lied. Although that was exactly what she had thought, that surely Logan must be dead or permanently disappeared by now, crushed in the endless cycle between the streets and hospital stays. Her joy at seeing him was tempered by the thought that he looked as if he had barely made it out alive.

Finally, she remembered her manners. "This is my friend Dante. Dante Bonner, Logan West. Logan and I go way back. We've known each other since we were five."

"And we went way forward, too," Logan added. "Claire was the only person from high school who visited me at Dammasch. The state loony bin," he added for Dante's benefit. Claire started as Logan grimaced, throwing his head back, his jaw thrusting upward. He continued talking as if nothing had happened. "Dammasch was the model for the hospital in Ken Kesey's *One Flew Over the Cuckoo's Nest*."

Dammasch was closed now, for good reason. There had been stories of attendants who preyed on the people they were supposed to care for, of inmates left tied to their own beds for days. With a twinge of guilt that it had only been a few times, Claire remembered her visits to Logan. They had talked—or rather she had talked—while Logan had shuffled down the hall beside her, restless with no release. Occasionally he turned to look at her, his glazed eyes without recognition. Even though he wasn't talking, he chewed the air, smacking his lips. The corridors of the hospital stank sharply of urine and vomit and bleach, and Claire tried to breathe through her mouth. The other inmates had been no better off than Logan, shouting, screaming, staring silently at the TV bolted on the wall or at the dust motes flickering in the air. Each of the three times she visited, Claire had thought how could Logan not be crazy, in a place like this? Each visit there had come a moment when words failed her, and she had simply walked beside him, holding his trembling hand. Later she had learned that the restlessness and the terrible repetitive movements were all side effects of the drugs meant to keep the visions at bay. No wonder that Logan's mother had told her that every time he was discharged, he threw his meds away.

Now Claire found that all the things that one normally said to an old friend seemed too much like prying. *So what are you doing these days? What have you been up to? Did you finally settle down?* And yet, Claire really wanted to know. She tried a neutral tack.

"How are things going for you, Logan?" She found herself taking his hand between her palms.

His mind was still in the past. "You know, you coming to visit is about the only thing I remember about Dammasch. At least, I think it is. I've been hospitalized all up and down the West Coast. After a while, it all runs together. Gurneys. Being pinned down by restraints like a bug. One-on-one suicide watches. Being so zoned out you drool on yourself. If you don't like the Haldol, try the Mellaril or the Stelazine or the Prolixin. Do you know what kind of memories I have? I remember what hospital I was in when Ronald Reagan got shot. The hospital I was in when Princess Di got married. I remember what hospital I was in when the Challenger exploded." His voice was bitter.

"But things are different now?" Claire prompted.

"About a year ago I got a doctor who put me on this new drug. Risperdal. I didn't think it would work, but five months later, the voices stopped." He spoke gingerly, as if talking about the voices in too much detail might somehow bring them back.

"That must have been a relief, after all those years."

"Are you kidding? When I realized they had stopped, I curled up in the bathtub. I stayed there for four days. It's like you drive a car for years and it's got a rock caught in the wheel well. Then one day you take the rock out and something's missing. It doesn't feel like your car anymore. It's the same way about the voices. Sometimes I think, 'This isn't my head. My head has voices in it.' Now I just tell myself that if it gets too bad I can always stop taking the medicine." He ran his hand across his mouth, hard, as if he were wiping off his expression, then attempted a smile. "Now I live on my own in a real apartment. Not even any roommates. Do you know—I've never lived alone this long before. I've got a job. I even have a cat."

"Where do you work?" Dante asked. Claire wondered if he was glad to be able to ask a normal question.

"Arby's. The same place I worked in high school. I think they even have some of the same meat in the back of the cooler." Logan said it with a sardonic smile, the corner of his mouth lifted as if he were laughing at his own joke. It was Logan's old smile, pasted on a stranger's overweight face. Then even the smile was gone, and he smacked his lips again.

"Why don't you sit with us?" Claire asked, gesturing to the two empty chairs at their table.

Logan shook his head. "No, that's okay. I see somebody over there I want to catch." He took off through the crowd before Claire could stop him.

Dante took a long sip of his drink, his expression thoughtful. "Sometimes you get reminded how lucky you are."

"You should have seen him back then, Dante. He was smart and skinny and funny and shy. And really good at basketball, which is kind of hard to believe, looking at him now. I think we were about sixteen when everything started. I remember we were in his living room, watching TV and talking, when all of a sudden he said, 'I'm not stupid. I'm not.' And I said, 'Of course you're not.' Because nobody would even think to call him that. But then I realized he wasn't talking to me." Claire sighed. She felt like crying for what had been and what was never to be.

"Claire! Claire Montrose!" Rachel Munroe, the doctor's daughter, waved at them, then came over to where they were standing.

"This is Rachel." Claire turned to Rachel. " I guess I don't know your last name. Is it still Munroe?"

"Yes." She extended her hand to Dante. "Rachel Munroe. I'm married, but I kept my name. Seemed easier all the way around."

"Dante Bonner."

Claire said, "I heard you're a doctor now, like your dad."

"Yep." Claire noticed that Rachel already had a lot of lines on her face, but they were all from smiling. "A pediatrician."

"I'm doing some volunteer work. And Dante works at the Metropolitan Museum of Art."

"The Met?" Rachel looked interested. "What do you do there?"

"I'm a curator, primarily specializing in Old Masters." Rachel tilted her head to one side. "That must be fascinating," she began, but then another woman ran up to Rachel, screaming her name in excitement. With a wave in their direction, Rachel let herself be led off.

Next, Jessica came up to their table. She wore a denim skirt and a white cotton shirt topped with a fringed and beaded buckskin vest. "Is this chair free?" She didn't wait for an answer before sitting down. She leaned close to Claire. "What did you do to your chin?" Flushing, Claire put her hand to her face. Here she was, thirty-seven years old—old enough to know better than to pick at her face in an effort to improve it. She imagined the pimple blinking redly, a beacon on her chin, emerging from the seven layers of foundation she had put on it.

Jessica raised her voice to a normal level. "Did you hear what Kyle is doing these days? He's Minor's chief of police!" She turned the full wattage of her smile on Dante, blinking her heavily made-up eyes. "That guy over there"—she pointed to a man with faded blond curls and a potbelly perched above stick-thin legs—"is Kyle Kraushaar. He used to be Claire's boyfriend."

"No, he didn't!" Claire interjected, stung. Back when they were friends—before Jessica climbed the social ladder of Minor without so much as a wave goodbye—had she let the other woman bruise her ego so easily? "I listened to records in his living room one time. One time!" She refrained from mentioning that Jessica had done a hell of a lot more than listen to records with half the men in the room. "And that was twenty-three years ago."

"Twenty-three years, Claire? Can you believe it? We're old now, Claire. Old!" Suddenly dejected, Jessica slumped in her chair.

Claire said, "What about that actress I see on TV sometimes? You know, the one who says life begins at forty?"

Jessica waved a disparaging hand. "Well, for her, plastic surgery began at twenty-eight, so what does she know?"

"You guys aren't old," Dante said. He was eighteen months younger than Claire, so it was easy to be magnanimous.

"Huh!" Jessica snorted. "Men don't have to worry about turning forty. They have to worry about turning ninety, and even then they can father children. They just can't recognize them or pick them up."

Dante realized it was better to change the subject. "So when we met out in the parking lot, you were saying that you're acting on Broadway."

"I finally feel that I have found my calling. There's something about playing a part in front of a thousand people that gives you so much more energy than trying to emote in front of a bored cameraman and a director who would much rather be doing music videos."

Dante leaned toward Jessica. "What shows have you been in?"

Envy pinched Claire's heart. Couldn't he see how shallow Jessica was?

The wattage of Jessica's smile increased. "*Les Miz*, of course, and—"

A woman's shout stilled all conversations.

"Two, four, six, eight! Who do we appreciate! Yeah Richard! Yeah Richard! Yeah Richard!"

It was Cindy, who seemed to be reliving her days as Minor's head cheerleader. She had kicked her high heels under a chair. In lieu of pompoms, she shook a crumpled napkin in each fist. At each repetition of Richard's name she leaped higher in the air, the muscles in her tanned legs flexing. Richard—Claire had to keep reminding herself not to think of him as Dick—watched her, goggle-eyed.

Jessica leaned over to Claire. "Cindy's husband doesn't look very happy, does he?"

Claire followed Jessica's gaze. About a dozen feet away, Kevin Sanchez sat alone at a table. A tall, darkly handsome man, graying at the temples, he wore a white dress shirt with the sleeves rolled up. His right elbow rested on the table, so that the gin and tonic in his hand covered the set of his mouth. He couldn't hide the narrowing of his coal-black eyes, though, as he watched his wife shimmy her hips in front of a computer multimillionaire.

A few of the women in the crowded room were whispering to each other, shaking their heads, but Richard still only had eyes for Cindy as she shouted his name while she twisted and danced. Her hips swung, her hands clapped, and even her head bounced from side to side, so that she looked like a nodding toy puppy dog in the back window of a car. She landed in a full side-to-side split that made all the men smile, and then bowed from the waist.

Richard, flushed to his hairline, began applauding. He got to his feet, still clapping, calling out, "Bravo! Bravo!"

Jessica leaned over to Claire. "Are you thinking what I'm thinking?" she stage-whispered.

"What's that?"

"That I still hate Cindy just as much as ever."

A man's voice cut through the din, his tone high and girlish and mocking. "Cindy, oh Cindy, can I kiss you?"

Heads turned. It was the drunk guy in the orange tank top. Claire vaguely remembered him from high school as one of the people who used to stand across the street from the school, smoking. He stood in the back of the room, one arm looped around a pillar as if for balance, his face twisted and ugly.

A woman nearby tried to shush him, but his call came again. "Cindy, can I kiss you?"

In a flash, Kyle was upon him. "All right, buddy, I think you've had enough." Kyle grabbed the guy's wrist, doing something to it that allowed him to lead the drunk man out of the room like an overly tired child.

All eyes went to Richard and Cindy. He was looking down at the table, his face scarlet. His right thumbnail slipped into his mouth and he began to nibble it industriously.

Cindy leaped to her feet. Into the shocked silence she said, "Of course, Richard can kiss me." She leaned over and theatrically presented her cheek—and a wide expanse of cleavage—to him. Richard's head bobbed forward and he gave her a quick peck. Then he leaned back and called out in a raised voice that trembled slightly, "A round for all my old friends from Minor. On me." The bartender rolled his eyes while the rest of his body sprang into action. With one hand he began squirting drinks from a plastic hose, while setting beer bottles on a tray with the other. With one hip he closed the cooler door, while simultaneously kicking the dishwasher door closed with his other foot.

"What did that bit about kissing Cindy mean?" Dante asked.

Jessica said, "I think Richard went on exactly one date in high school. He took Cindy to the movies. She was about seven steps above him on the social ladder, so

God knows why she said yes. Anyway, at one point during the movie, he asked if he could kiss her. Unfortunately, it coincided with a time when there wasn't much on the soundtrack, and a lot of people in the theater heard him. And the next Monday at school, Cindy kindly filled in the details for anyone who wasn't there. For months he couldn't walk down the hall without guys yelling 'Cindy, can I kiss you?' after him."

"So did Cindy say yes the first time?"

Jessica snorted. "You clearly don't know Cindy very well. I wouldn't be surprised if the whole reason she went out with Richard in the first place was to humiliate him. She had a way of finding your weak spot and working on it."

Watching the other woman's mouth crimp, Claire wondered what weak spot of hers Cindy had exploited. Then Jessica's lips broadened into a smile.

"Just think how stupid Cindy feels now. She could be living in a thirty-thousand-square-foot lakeside mansion in Seattle instead of still being stuck in Minor, Oregon." Jessica opened her mouth to say something more, when an expression of delight blossomed on her face. Claire followed her gaze. Wade Merz was beckoning to Jessica, holding a glass out to her in invitation.

"Excuse me," Jessica murmured, and was off like a shot. Claire turned to apologize for her, and was surprised to find Dante watching Jessica, an unreadable expression on his face. Instead of saying anything about Jessica, Claire excused herself to go to the restroom.

As she cut past Richard's table, he looked up from the woman he was talking to and gave her a smile. Claire was still mad at herself for being pleased that he remembered her. Would she have felt the same way if he worked in a factory instead of being responsible for employing thousands of people who worked in factories?

"Hi, Claire—long time no see. Say, do you know Martha?" Claire vaguely remembered Martha Masterson, a quiet woman who had sat behind her in advanced English. She had always worn a white plastic headband that pulled her hair back from her high forehead. Now her thick dark blond hair was cut in a flattering pageboy and her large gray eyes were no longer hidden by glasses. "She and I are both refugees from the Bi-Phy-Chem Club, only neither of us got too far away. She does"—he turned back to her, a theatrically quizzical expression on his face—"what is it—organic chemistry research? Anyway, something I barely understand."

Martha gave him a playful push on the upper arm. "Don't tell me you don't understand it. If you hadn't tutored me, I wouldn't have done so well on my chemistry advanced placement exam. Thanks to your help, I got enough credits to enter college as a sophomore."

"That's the thing, though. I only understand chemistry up through the college freshman level. Not the postdoc work you're doing." He turned back to Claire. "What about you, Claire? What are you doing?"

Her answer felt inadequate. "I volunteer with the SMART program. It's a program to teach at-risk kids to read."

"Hmm. Very noble. Do you have any children yourself?" She saw him glance at her left hand.

"No, at least not yet." Her bladder sent up another distress signal. "Say, would you excuse me for a second?"

As she continued to pass through the crowd, Claire heard scraps of conversation from combinations of people she would never have imagined together. Cindy was telling a table full of people Claire recognized as former hoods about her career "in the spirit industry." Wade seemed to be putting the moves on Jessica, and her face was alight as if the whole thing wasn't fueled by a half-dozen vodka tonics. And Kyle was talking to a restless-looking Becca. Claire caught a snatch of his monologue. "So I drew my gun and I said, 'Do you want to bet who is gonna fire first? Because I shoot to kill, buddy!'"

"Hey, Clairice! It's been a long time."

She turned. Sawyer Fairchild. He was clean-shaven now, his dark hair gone silver at the temples in the way that seemed only to happen to men.

"I guess since I've been following your career, it doesn't seem as long to me." She had forgotten how he used to call her Clairice. Like the other kids, she had preened at any sign that Sawyer had singled her out.

"I'm flattered. I hope I've made the kind of decisions you can support."

"I'm a dyed-in-the-wool liberal. The worst kind. So I'm all for the Portland urban-growth boundary, better schools, and gay rights."

Making a face, Sawyer slapped himself on the cheek. "I'm doing it again, aren't I? Running for office. And tonight's supposed to be about seeing old friends. Have the last twenty years been good to you?"

She nodded. "The last few years, especially. I'm definitely having more fun than when I was seventeen."

Sawyer opened his mouth to reply, but just then a half-dozen women waving cocktail napkins descended on them, asking "the future governor" for his autograph.

Claire mouthed a goodbye in his direction, then again made her way toward the bathrooms, which were behind a partition that held a pay phone. The women's restroom door was labeled the She-Pee Room and featured a cartoony illustration of an Indian (or should she say Native American?) woman sneaking behind a tepee. She took her place in the long line for one of the four stalls. Nina, one of her old circle of friends, fell in behind her. Nina's once long blond hair was cut short now, a feathery cap that suited her small features. They hugged each other stiffly, each unsure of how much pressure to exert.

Nina broke their awkward clinch. "So what are you doing with yourself these days, Claire? And when did you get married?"

"Mostly volunteer work," Claire said, thinking of Rainy, the seven-year-old girl she was slowly and painfully trying to teach to read this summer, despite the distractions of television and a never-ending series of new "dads." "And Dante and I aren't married."

"Dante? That's a fancy name. Is he foreign?"

"Born and bred in New York City." She could tell by Nina's expression that this was tantamount to being foreign-born. "What about you? What are you doing now?"

"I sell real estate part time, but mostly I watch after my grandkids. They're the only good thing that came out of my marriage to Gene, even if it was indirectly."

"Grandkids?" Claire echoed with a rising sense of horror. She hadn't given much thought to having children, yet here was someone she knew for a fact was two months younger than she was who already had multiple grandchildren.

Finally it was Claire's turn for a stall. She sat down just as something rattled in the stall next to her. There was the sound of a loud exhale followed by the hiss of something being sprayed, and then a quick, sucking inhalation. Drugs? Claire wondered, sniffing the air experimentally. But when she and the woman next to her pushed open their stall doors at the same time, Claire saw it was Cindy—slipping a blue asthma inhaler into her purse. The other woman did not even acknowledge Claire's presence, and quickly washed her hands.

Six

The tables of the Hoe-Down Room were littered with crumpled napkins and empty beer bottles and glasses, some marked with lipstick. Reuniongoers who had little kids—or those who could simply no longer stay up late—had already gone back to their hotel rooms. About three dozen people remained in the bar, talking quietly while drinking Full Sail Ale under the gaze of glassy-eyed elk, deer, and one moth-eaten buffalo.

When the scream ripped through the air it froze everyone in place. A woman's scream, high-pitched, wordless. Then Claire began to realize there were words within the scream, run together into nonsense.

Belinda Brophy-Muller scrambled through the double doors. Her staring eyes did not see any of the old classmates who gaped at her. And now Claire could make out the two words that ran together in harsh cadence.

"She's dead! She's dead! She's dead!"

Belinda sank to her hands and knees. She was past thinking, past caring what other people thought. As she rocked back and forth, her denim skirt rode up until it was almost as high as her black leather jacket, exposing the uncertain flesh of her thighs and the bottom edge of her flowered cotton panties.

Some of the people in the room jumped to their feet and ran toward her. Others shrank back in their chairs. Claire noted that she and Dante were the kind of people who got to their feet. Kyle had gone home an hour ago, so they had no one to turn to but themselves.

Jim Prentiss asked the question everyone was afraid to. "Who's dead, Belinda? Where?"

"She!" The words were a bark. Belinda sat back on her heels. She put her hands to her throat and began to stutter. "She, she, she, she . . . "

Dante cut through the knot of people around Belinda and knelt in front of her. He put his finger under her plump chin and lifted her head so that she was forced to look him in the eye. The sight of a stranger's face seemed to calm her.

"I saw you leaving here a few minutes ago, right?" Dante's voice was calm, unhurried.

Belinda nodded. Her breath came in jerks.

"And then . . . you went out in the parking lot?"

She nodded again, more slowly.

Step by step, he continued to lead. "And then did something happen when you were walking to your car?"

A final nod, her eyes wide and frightened. Her breathing began to speed up again.

"What happened, Belinda?" His voice was a priest's or a counselor's, inviting confidences.

Her shrill voice was in the present tense, as if Dante

had hypnotized her and she was seeing it all play out again before her eyes. "I see something lying on the ground. At first, I think it's a doll, a big, big doll. I go over to look, and, and, and—it's Cindy. Her clothes are all messed up. And her eyes, her eyes are open. But she's not moving!"

The room was as silent as if it were empty, while three dozen people held their breath. Claire looked over at the table where Cindy's husband had been sitting, but it was empty except for one line of various types of glasses marked with lipstick and another of squat unmarked glasses, each holding a wedge of lime. Kevin's jacket was gone.

"Did you touch her, Belinda? Can you be certain that she was dead?"

Shaking her head, she began to stutter again. "N-n-n-no."

"Call 911 and get an ambulance," Dante snapped over his shoulder to the bartender, who immediately picked up the phone. "And the police." He stood up and gently lifted Belinda to her feet. "Show me where she is."

Her head whipped violently back and forth.

"Just point me in the right direction then." His tone was coaxing. "I need to see if I can help your friend."

Belinda let him lead her. A few feet behind, about a dozen people followed, Claire among them. There was still absolute silence. Wade came out of the He-Pee room and joined them. His eyes were alight as if he suspected a prank or hoped for an outing. They went past the gaming rooms, where cigarette smoke hovered above the heads of the gamblers hunched over slot machines, clutching white plastic buckets full of quarters. They hadn't looked up for the woman screaming, and they didn't watch as the silent, wary group walked past them now. When Dante pushed open the outside doors, the hot and heavy air pressed on them, in contrast to the air-conditioned cave of the Hoe-Down Room.

Belinda weakly waved her hand in the direction of the far reaches of the parking lot, then sank to the side-walk and began wailing again. A couple of the women gathered around her, while the rest of the group more slowly followed Dante's loping run through the half-empty parking lot. Sawyer, hindered by his limp, brought up the rear.

There was a second's pause at the sight of Cindy's body, half-naked, awkward, and terribly still. As soon as Claire saw it, she knew that was what it was. A body, emptied of life.

Cindy lay on her back, one leg twisted underneath her. One of her red high heels had come off and it lay a few feet behind her. A few yards farther away sat her purse. Her blouse had been ripped open to display her full breasts, spilling out of a gold-colored satin bra. Her denim skirt was around her waist, exposing a tiny pair of matching gold-colored bikini panties. Claire was able to note all these details without feeling any emo-tion, but she found she couldn't look at Cindy's face, at the pale-blue eyes, half-open and dull, and the way the swollen tip of her tongue poked between her lips.

Claire could see why Belinda had wrapped her own hands around her throat while she stuttered the news about her best friend. Angry red marks were clearly vis-ible on Cindy's long neck. Careful to touch nothing else, Dante knelt and pressed two fingers just below them, at the side of her throat.

Claire already knew the answer before he shook his head and announced, "No pulse."

"Should we do CPR?" Richard Crane ventured. His narrow face was drained of all color. Martha stood behind him, and now she patted him on the shoulder, comforting him even before Dante spoke.

Dante shook his head again and stood up. "Her skin is cool. I think she's been dead for a little while."

Moaning, Wade Merz stumbled away and threw up at the base of a lightpost. Even after he was done being sick, his shoulders continued to heave. Claire guessed he was crying. She had a sudden memory of Cindy and Wade at the prom together, both young and beautiful and proud of it. Back in the days when everyone was young and no one could imagine Wade stiffing a twenty-dollar hooker or Cindy's half-naked broken body stretched out under the yellow vapor lights.

Claire felt sick and strange, as if she were hallucinating. Everything was beginning to look two-dimensional, as unreal as a stage set. Pretty soon Cindy would get up and wash the makeup off her throat and go home.

She heard a soft mumbling, words she couldn't make out. She looked around. Logan stood twenty feet away from their little group, moving his lips as he looked at Cindy's body. Claire couldn't tell if he were talking to himself, to Cindy, or to someone he only imagined was there. He shifted from foot to foot, his hands twisting against each other as if he were washing them clean. His face had altered, and he somehow looked more like the old Logan. Was Logan's new drug strong enough, Claire wondered, to keep him anchored even in this reality as terrible as any nightmare?

"At least we should make her decent," Sawyer Fairchild said. Claire hadn't realized he was standing behind her, but now he moved past her and leaned down to tug together the edges of Cindy's shirt.

"No," Claire said, and grabbed his hands. They jerked and trembled in her own. She wondered if he was remembering all the bodies he had seen in Vietnam. "That's evidence. You have to leave her the way she is until they take photographs."

"What difference does it make if I cover her up?" His voice was low and unsteady. "Do you think Cindy really wants the whole police force staring at her breasts?"

"There could be fingerprints on the buttons, maybe even the cloth," Dante said quietly to Sawyer. He put his hand under the other man's arm and moved him back a few feet. "You don't want to mess that up."

"Hey, what's this?" Moving too fast for Claire to stop her, Jessica snatched something small and dark from Cindy's hand.

"Let me see," Sawyer said.

"No," Claire said, running over to them. Sometimes she wished she didn't have the hall monitor-type personality. If only she wasn't always aware of the rules and acutely uncomfortable when they were broken. If only something inside of her didn't squirm in protest when people talked during the movies or took eleven items into the nine-items-or-less express line. "It's important not to get anyone else's fingerprints on—."

Claire stopped, staring at the object Jessica held in her hand. It was a box. A heart-shaped box. And as far as Claire could see, it was identical to the one in the package she had received at the hotel earlier in the day. She was too stunned to protest when Jessica thumbed it open. Inside was the picture of Cindy dancing at the prom, her head thrown back and her eyes closed.

Claire barely heard the angry bull-like roar as someone came shoving through the crowd. At the sight of his wife's body, Kevin Sanchez staggered backward. "Cindy, what have they done to you? My God, what have they done?"

Claire's gaze was drawn back to the box Jessica still held in her outstretched palm. The box Claire had gotten a few hours earlier was twin to the one Cindy had been holding in her dead hand.

TAGURIT

Seven

Kevin was still screaming his wife's name, but to Claire it was as if the sound were being swallowed up, absorbed by the empty darkness that surrounded them. She felt as if she were high above their little group, observing with great detachment as they shouted and cried and ran around. Was this how God felt when he looked down at the earth? she wondered. Indifferent and far away?

Then Dante wrapped his arms around her and Claire felt herself come back into her body. "You look like you're about ready to faint," he said into her ear, and she realized that he was right. As she pressed her face against his shoulder, the tight strings of her body began to loosen.

The feeling of isolation was further shattered when everything arrived at once in a whirl of strobing lights and ululating sounds—first an ambulance, then a police car, and finally Kyle, hurrying toward their little group from the direction of the hotel. As he got closer, Claire could see fear and self-importance chasing themselves across his face. The patrol car and the ambulance skidded to a stop.

Kyle had to shout to be heard over the sirens. "Step back, people, step back!" Everyone obeyed but Kevin, who still knelt in the gravel, pressing his wife's body to his chest. Cindy's head lolled back at a sickeningly boneless angle. Claire saw the Adam's apple in Kyle's throat bob as he swallowed hard. He tugged his belt upward. Mercifully, the sirens ceased wailing, leaving a welcome well of silence.

Two cops spilled out of the police car and a pair of paramedics jumped from the ambulance. They all converged on Cindy, then slowed when it was clear she was beyond help. Paying no attention to the new arrivals, Kevin kept his face pressed into the hollow of his wife's bare shoulder.

One of the paramedics leaned down and picked up Cindy's wrist. Kevin lifted his head and roared, "Let go of her!" The startled man complied. Kevin shrugged Cindy closer and buried his head in her hair. "What have they done to you? What have they done?" he moaned again, a question with an answer he didn't want to believe.

Kyle appealed to the small crowd. "Can someone tell me what happened here?"

There was a pause, then Dante's voice cut through the beginning babble. "Belinda came out in the parking lot and found Cindy here. Then she went back to the bar to get help. Some of us came out to see if we could do anything, but . . ." Dante's words trailed off.

"How long ago was this?"

"About five minutes."

Claire checked her watch. She was surprised to realize Dante was right. Everything seemed to be moving too slowly. Noises were louder, colors brighter. Shock, she thought. Fight or flight, and she could do neither.

Kyle leaned over and spoke to Kevin. "Buddy, you're gonna have to let go of her. You need to let the paramedics do their job." Head down, Kevin continued to rock his wife's body. Kyle laid a gentle hand on his shoulder. "Come on, man, you can't help her now. Let us do our jobs, so we can find out who did this to her." Kevin seemed to shake his head, or he could have been dropping kisses on his dead wife's hair.

Kyle walked over to Claire and whispered in her ear. "What's his name? I can't remember."

"Kevin."

Kyle turned back and leaned down again. "Kevin, you gotta let go of her. Do you hear me, Kevin? Do you understand what I'm saying? There's gonna come a point where you can't hold on to her forever. I promise we'll take good care of her."

After what seemed an interminable pause, Kevin slowly eased Cindy back to the ground. He did not raise his eyes from her face. One of the paramedics knelt beside her and picked up her wrist again, but clearly it was only a formality.

Kyle turned to the taller of the two cops. "Marc, why don't you take Kevin here back to the hotel, find someplace quiet, and get him a drink. Tell the manager I'm gonna need a room that I can use for the duration. I'll come in in a few minutes to take his statement."

The small group was silent as they watched Kevin, slump-shouldered and stumbling, being led away by the policeman.

"Oh, I almost forgot. When we found her, Cindy was

holding this." Sawyer took the heart-shaped box from Jessica's hand and offered it to Kyle. "I guess we should put it back where it was."

"No! Damn it!" Kyle's voice rapped out. "So you mopes have been touching things?" His glance, full of contempt, swept over them. Claire followed his gaze. Richard looked as if he were about to collapse. Wade was as serious as Claire had ever seen him. All the color had drained from Jim's face. Even Jessica seemed drained by the all-too-real drama. "Once you've disturbed the crime scene, you can't just put things back the way they were." He turned to the remaining cop. "Greg, get an evidence bag and take this from Mr. Fairchild."

Kyle turned back and regarded them as if they were all equally guilty. "Now let me get this straight. You all came out here together. Was there anyone who saw Cindy out here, in the parking lot, dead or alive, prior to that?"

Kyle's gaze examined each of them in turn, but he was answered by silence. A few people shook their heads.

"And if Belinda was the one who found the body, then where is she?"

Claire answered. "She stayed back at the casino, I guess. She was really starting to lose it."

As they were talking, the cop named Greg—who looked to be no more than twenty—bagged the heart-shaped box and put it in his trunk. Then he took out a roll of yellow crime scene tape. He began to mark out a rough square, about two hundred feet on each side, with Cindy's body in the center. He wrapped the tape around light poles and, in one case, around the antenna of a car, a gray Dodge Dart spotted with rust patches.

"Hey, that's my car," said Jim. "And I have to go home tonight."

"Not in that car, buddy," Kyle said. "That car is now officially part of the crime scene, at least until I say otherwise. Tell the hotel that I asked them to comp you a room." He raised his voice. "Greg, take these people back to the Hoe-Down Room. Tell Marc to get their names, addresses, and phone numbers, as well as room numbers if they are staying here. Then I need all of you to not leave until I can talk to each of you. I hafta ask you about what happened tonight. And don't go talking about this case with each other while you're waiting. We need you to tell us only what you saw, not what others think they saw."

Greg lifted up the crime scene tape, and they dipped under it, one by one. As they left, Kyle was methodically walking from corner to corner of the crime scene, taking photos of the body from every angle. Claire flinched at every burst of light from the flash.

Kyle's idea that they would be sequestered from the other reuniongoers evaporated the minute they approached the hotel. Greg was no match for the two dozen people who surrounded them as soon as they entered the lobby, asking if it was true that Cindy Weaver was really dead. The people who had found her body were the center of attention. Questions buzzed past them.

"What happened to her?"

"Was she shot?"

"What did she look like?"

"How long had she been dead?"

Jessica took center stage, her low voice pitched to cut through the din. "It's true. Cindy Weaver Sanchez is dead." There was a pause between each word. Jessica could have been announcing the passing of a queen. "When we found her, Cindy was lying on her back like this." She dropped to her knees in the entryway. Twisting one leg behind her in imitation of Cindy's awkward sprawl, she lay back on the carpet, which was patterned to look like a Pendleton blanket. Her denim skirt crept up her legs until it reached her crotch, but Jessica didn't seem to mind. "She had been savaged. Her blouse had been ripped open, her skirt was up around her waist." Jessica sat up on her elbows, her hands at her throat. "And there were these terrible marks on her throat."

"That's enough, lady." Greg barked, finally realizing he had to take control of the scene. "You heard what my boss said—no talking to each other about the scene. Get up off the floor." Jessica didn't move until he extended a hand.

"Greg, what is happening here?" The other cop appeared on the scene, shaking his head. "This way, people, this way." He led them back to the Hoe-Down Room that Claire had been planning on leaving thirty minutes before. Now it looked as if she was in for a long night.

They sat back in their same places. Dante handed her her gin and tonic. Slivers of ice were still floating in the glass.

When she reached out for it, Claire realized she was shivering, a fine quaking shiver that ran up her back, down her arms, and out through her trembling fingers.

Dante scooted his chair next to Claire's and put his arm around her. "You're still shaking."

"You are, too." It was true. Dante looked as if he wanted to forget what he had seen. Now that there was nothing to occupy him—no one to direct, no one to soothe, no pulse to check—Dante seemed to have lost his bearings. He picked up his half-full glass and put it down again without taking a sip.

"The only other time I've seen a dead body that wasn't lying in a coffin was when that guy fell out the window." Claire knew what he was talking about, a man who had fallen sixteen stories while they both watched, horrified. "You didn't have to get too close to know that guy was dead. But tonight—I was hoping when I touched her throat that I would feel something. Just a faint, thready pulse." He closed his eyes, but she could still see his eyes moving underneath the lids, as if he were replaying what had just happened, only making everything right. "But the minute I touched her, I knew she was dead."

Marc, the older cop, had to shout to be heard over the babble of voices. "Okay, people, now listen up. Me and Greg here are gonna take your names and addresses. We will also ask you your whereabouts during the last two hours. And if you are one of those people that found Cindy's body, then our chief of police is going to want to debrief you. Tonight." There were scattered groans and a comment about how late it was getting. "Settle down, people. We'll get you out of here as quick as we can. In the meantime, we don't want any of you who were out in the parking lot to compare notes about what you might have seen or heard."

The room seemed more crowded than it had been before Cindy's body was found. But Claire noticed that one table remained empty, a silent island in the middle of several dozen chattering people. The table where

Cindy had sat—empty now, except for the glasses marked with her lipstick.

GON4EVR

Eight

FROM THE INTERVIEW WITH KEVIN SANCHEZ

The night manager had vacated his own office for Kyle. It was a narrow, windowless space. Three sides were lined with wire shelving stacked with cardboard boxes. There was scant room for the scarred metal desk. On a bare section of shelving sat the things that had once been on the desk: a Rolodex, a handmade ashtray, a lumpy ceramic pot holding pens and pencils, and a framed picture of a woman and a young girl. When Kevin saw this last he pressed his lips together so hard they turned white. His eyes were red from weeping, his voice hoarse from screaming his wife's name.

"First of all, Mr. Sanchez, I want to thank you for your cooperation at such a difficult time. Your wife," Kyle sighed noisily, "your wife was a beautiful woman. I want you to know that we're gonna catch this guy."

Kevin nodded, his face drawn. "Thanks."

"There's a couple of things I need to get out of the

way. I'm gonna need to take your picture so that I can show it to the hotel staff. That way, if they tell me they saw Cindy with a man, and then they point at your photograph, I'll be able to rule that out, okay? You being her husband and all."

A curt nod. "All right. If that's what you need to do."

Kyle looked through the viewfinder of the Polaroid camera, then put it down again. "What's that mark on your shirt?" It was dark brown, a roughly oval blotch about the size of a half-dollar.

Kevin looked down, but his view was blocked by the open collar of his white dress shirt.

"There. Just below your left shoulder."

"What are you—oh, God. It looks like blood. I guess that's what it must be. Cindy's blood." He touched it gingerly, tenderly, almost stroking it. "When I went out there and saw her lying on that hard ground with everyone gawking at her, I just wanted to hold her. To protect her. I guess part of me knew she was dead, but I just couldn't believe it."

"It's a hard thing." Kyle nodded in agreement. He picked up the camera and snapped the picture, leaving Kevin blinking from the flash. "I'm also gonna need your fingerprints. Same story. It makes it easier to find the perp if we have everyone else's fingerprints on file."

Kevin turned his hands over and looked at them. His fingers were long and narrow, unmarked by anything but the plain gold band on his left hand. While Kyle rolled his fingers on the ink pad, Kevin held his upper body rigid. From one of the restaurant's cardboard boxes, Kyle handed him a little package of moist towelettes (the restaurant handed them out after barbecue meals), and Kevin wiped his fingers clean.

Picking up his narrow tan notebook, Kyle flipped it open. "Okay, could you please state your name, address, and occupation for the record?"

"I'm trying to be cooperative, officer, but I don't see how this is going to help anything. Shouldn't you be out there finding out who killed my wife instead of going through all this rigmarole?" Kevin ran his hands through his hair. There was so much gel that his fingers left furrows.

"That's what we are doing. I've got one of my men talking to the hotel staff, trying to find anyone who might have seen what happened out there. The other one's working the crime scene, getting fingerprints and looking for any other evidence."

"That's just two people. Two! You need more than that!"

"Look, I've got exactly eight cops working for me. That's to cover seven days a week, twenty-four hours a day. The best I can do at any one time is two, and that's stretching it. Right now, I'm working off the clock, but here I am, questioning anyone who was at the reunion. And don't forget about the medical examiner. He will be looking for the time of death, et cetera. He's already sent swabs to the lab."

"Swabs?"

Kyle's words were a mumble. "From the . . . the body." He began to tap his pencil rapidly on the edge of the desk.

"But why—you don't mean Cindy was raped, do you?" Kevin's face paled. "Oh, God. Some son of a bitch raped and strangled my wife?" He gripped the arms of his chair until his fingers turned white.

Too late, Kyle began shaking his head. "I'm not saying that at all. We just hafta look at all the possibilities.

Then we can rule them out." Thankful for the chance to change the subject, he asked again, "So, what is your name, address, and occupation?"

"But I still don't see why you need to ask me these stupid questions. I already gave that other cop some of the same information."

Kyle nodded. "I understand why you feel the way that you do. But for us to catch the perp who did this, we're gonna need information. Lots of it. If you make me give you a reason for every question I ask, it's gonna take a lot longer."

"All right, then. Kevin Sanchez. 3434 Pine Terrace, Minor, Oregon. I'm a senior partner with Denight, Sanchez, and Torch. That's a law firm in Portland."

"And Cindy? What was her occupation?"

Kevin's voice became high-pitched, strangled. "My God, she's really dead, isn't she? I keep forgetting that. Just—just a minute." His ragged breathing filled the small space. Pressing hard, he passed his hands over his face, leaving his expression blank. "Okay. Cindy is a sales rep for Nelsons, the biggest cheerleading outfitter in the country. And she also does some consulting with local cheerleading teams."

"Like the Blazer Dancers." Kyle nodded. "She told me that."

"Yeah. Like the . . . the Blazer Dancers. Like them."

"And how long were you two married?"

"I still don't see why you have to ask these questions. You should be out there," he waved his arm behind him, "finding the guy who did this to her."

Kyle's voice was flat. "I know this is hard, but please humor me."

"We've been married for sixteen years. Together for twenty. We met in college. I was a senior and she was a freshman." A soft smile transformed Kevin's face. "She was the most beautiful thing I ever saw. They used to call us day and night, because she was so blond and I was so dark. While she finished up school, I went to law school at Lewis and Clark. We got married the same year I joined my dad's firm. That was hard on her. Cindy never understood about those ninety-billable-hour weeks. And then my dad died when he was only fifty-two. Those were big shoes to fill."

"What kind of law does your firm practice?"

"Estates, mostly. It's not a particularly dramatic area." The police chief looked up as a tension entered Kevin's voice. "They won't ever make a TV show about the kind of cases I handle."

"Why do you live in Minor instead of Portland? Isn't that a long commute?"

"Cindy grew up here. Even if it's changed a lot, she still feels like this is her home turf."

"And how would you rate your relationship with your wife?" Kyle strove for a jovial, "you can tell me anything because I've heard it all before" tone, but it fell flat. "Any troubles in that arena?"

There was a long silence. Kevin finally broke it, his expression now impassive, haughty. "Are you saying you are looking at me as a suspect in my own wife's death? I think I may need to make a phone call to my attorney."

"Look, I gotta ask the question. You know that. It's part of the procedure."

"You may think that this is an area you need to examine, but let me assure you that you're wrong. Cindy and I got along very well. She's a beautiful woman. We've been—we were—married for sixteen years. We have a daughter—Alexa. Oh, God. Alexa." He half got up from his chair, then sat back down heavily. "How can I tell her that her mother is dead?" Then Kevin interrupted himself, his voice taut with anguish, "Tell me, do you think she suffered? Do you think she was in much pain?"

"No," Kyle said. Perhaps too quickly. "I don't think she suffered. It would have been over in a minute or two."

"Do you know how long a minute or two is when you can't breathe?" He buried his face in his hands and spoke from behind their shelter. "I know another attorney who got a death penalty conviction just by having the jurors sit still for two minutes and think about how long that would be to die. When they deliberated, it took them less than fifteen minutes to decide that the guy who did it didn't deserve to live either."

Kyle didn't disagree. Instead he changed the subject. "I need you to think carefully. Has there been anything out of the ordinary lately that upset your wife? Any arguments with people she knew? Or even people she didn't know? Has she said anything about someone, say, stalking her?"

There was a long pause, then Kevin shook his head. "No. Cindy gets along well with everyone. She's a real people person."

"Was there anything she was uptight about in regard to the reunion? Anyone she didn't want to see tonight—anything like that?"

"Not at all. On the contrary, she told me she was looking forward to it. Sure, maybe she was a little bit nervous. She didn't want anyone to think that she was over the hill. I tried to tell her that all the people here were going to be the same age as she was." Kevin's next words were in the same tone he must have used with his wife. "People you went to high school with are definitely going to know how old you are, so there's no need to worry about it."

"Did you notice her talking to anyone for a long time tonight? Or having a particularly intense conversation with anyone?"

Kevin shrugged. "I'm afraid I don't know most of the people she went to high school with. I guess I met some of them at the ten-year reunion, but that was, well, ten years ago. I mean, I knew Belinda, of course. She's been Cindy's best friend forever. But all I really know about tonight is that it seemed to me that Cindy talked to everyone. Even you, officer."

Kyle ignored this remark. "So you didn't see her having any kind of an argument?"

"No. Not that I saw. I did see her looking kind of annoyed after talking to this guy she called Suede. You know, the car dealer guy. His real name is Wade Smarts, or something like that. She told me they dated a long time ago." Kevin straightened in his chair. "Maybe you should have him in here for questioning."

"Don't worry. We will be interviewing him shortly. Did she ever talk about him to you?"

His answer was slow, reluctant. "Not that I can recall."

"What about this box that was found with Cindy's body?"

"What box?"

"When her body was first found, there was a little wooden heart-shaped box in her hand. So you didn't see it? You never held it?"

"No. I didn't even know she owned anything like that."

"We also recovered her purse from the scene, but there's no wallet in it. Does she normally carry a wallet?"

Kevin nodded. "It's black eelskin, with a checkbook inside and all her credit cards."

"If you could come up with a list of all her accounts, that might be helpful." Kyle tore a blank page from the notebook and pushed it toward him. "Just list everything you can remember. If you have cards you both carry, then maybe you can get the number off what you already have in your wallet. I'm going to take a hard look at the people who were in here tonight, gambling. See if any of them ran out of funds and then came back with more." He looked down and made another note. "We're almost done, and then I can let you go. Could you just sketch out for me the last time you saw your wife alive? And what you did from that time until the time the body was discovered?"

"Cindy had a headache, but she didn't want to leave. There was some Advil in her suitcase, and she said she was going back to our room to take it and then come back. I said, 'Why don't we both go and not come back?' It was getting late. But she wasn't ready to leave. You'll probably find that there are a dozen people who can tell you I spent all night at that table, watching Cindy do her thing. My role was to be the spouse and to look interested when people I had never met before talked about something that happened twenty years ago. Then she left, only she didn't come back. I was wondering if she had lain down on the bed for a few minutes and fallen asleep, although that didn't seem very likely. I mean, Cindy had been talking about this event for weeks. I didn't know what to do. I knew she would be mad if I went to look for her and lost our table. Then after a while, well, I had had a couple of drinks and I really had to go to the bathroom. So finally I spread my jacket over the table so no one would take it. So I missed

Belinda coming in, and then everyone was running outside to see what had happened. When I came out of the
men's room, the whole bar was in an uproar, talking
about how Belinda had found Cindy's . . . Cindy's—oh
God, you know. And then I ran outside and . . . and—
and found her."

Kyle looked up from his notebook. "You said she was
going back to your hotel room?"

Kevin nodded.

"Then why do you think she was found in the corner
of the parking lot farthest away from the hotel?"

"I don't have any idea. Someone must have tricked
her or lured her out there. Maybe this guy pulled a gun
and marched her out there. I still—I still can't believe it.
How can she be dead? How could she die without my
feeling it? You'd think I'd feel it in here when it happened," Kevin thumped his closed fist against his chest,
"or that I would think I heard her voice calling me.
Something. After nearly twenty years you'd think we'd
be that connected. But I had no idea. I was just sitting
there drinking a gin and tonic and wondering when she
would hurry up and come back."

"You said you don't know of any arguments she had
tonight, or of anyone stalking her. Did your wife have
any enemies?"

Kevin's laugh was unexpected. "Who are you kidding? Cindy was the most popular girl at Minor High.
She was beautiful. She was head cheerleader, for god's
sake. She dated any boy she wanted. You don't think that
was reason enough for someone to hate her, even after
twenty years?"

Nine

Belinda's frayed blond hair had half-fallen down from its pins. She swiped it from her raccooned eyes. The room was warm, but still she wrapped her black leather jacket tight around her. "I feel awful, Kyle. Do you really have to talk to me? You've got my photograph and my fingerprints—isn't that enough? I didn't see anything except the—the body. And that was just for a second. Now my head hurts so bad. I feel like I'm going to be sick." Her voice was like that of a little girl's, pitched high and breathy.

"Belinda, I gotta talk to you tonight, before you start forgetting things. If you need to, use this." He leaned down under the desk, reappearing with a round metal wastebasket. There was a clang when he set it down.

His tough-love approach just resulted in a fresh burst of weeping. Kyle sighed noisily. "You still pal around with Cindy, right? I've seen you guys around town."

"I, I, I . . ."

"Take your time." His tone was impatient. He rummaged around on the wire shelves until he found an open carton half-filled with white boxes of generic tissue. Ripping one open, he pushed it in her direction.

Finally, Belinda managed a nod. Her face was puffy and blotched from weeping. "She is my best friend."

"Was she looking forward to this reunion? What kinda mood had she been in lately?"

"What kind of mood? A good mood, of course. You know how everyone liked her at school, how popular she was, so of course she was looking forward to seeing everyone again. I was over at her house last week and she must have tried on everything in her closet, trying to figure out what to wear. Cindy was really revved up about this. She was very excited—and a little bit nervous."

"Nervous," Kyle echoed, and wrote that down. "So Cindy was nervous—did she say anything about receiving any threats, or—."

"No," Belinda interrupted. "Excited nervous, not scared nervous. She was looking forward to seeing all her old friends."

"What about her old enemies?"

"I don't know what you're talking about." The silence hung between them until finally she was forced to break it. "All right, maybe there were a couple of people in high school that didn't like her that much. But, Kyle, that was twenty years ago. If someone from our high school hated Cindy enough to kill her, they could have done it a long time ago. And, besides, I can't think of anyone who would have really wanted to kill her. You saw what she looked like, the same as I did! How could anybody do that to another human being?"

"You'd be surprised what people are capable of." He

tapped the end of his pen on the open notebook. "Who were her enemies in high school? I can think of a few people, but I don't want to put words in your mouth."

"That's just it, Kyle. What I'm trying to tell you is that maybe there were a couple of people she wasn't in sync with, but there wasn't anyone you would call an enemy."

"Give me a for instance of someone she wasn't 'in sync' with."

"Come on, Kyle, you know. The people who weren't—popular. Like Dick—I guess I mean Richard. Or Jim Prentiss. Or that Claire Montrose. Or even you. The way I remember it, you didn't get along that good with her either." She hesitated, wiping a balled-up tissue under her nose. "Didn't you ask her out on a date once?"

"I don't remember that." He switched subjects so fast that it left Belinda flustered. "You were Cindy's best friend. How would you describe Cindy's relationship with her husband? Have there been any tensions between them? Any fights? Have either of them had affairs?"

"Of course not!" The tissue thudded into the wastebasket. "Their relationship was—excellent." Belinda lifted her empty hands, palm up, to her shoulders, then let them drop back to her lap. "This is going to be so hard on Kevin. They were very close."

"Did anything unusual happen tonight? Did Cindy have any arguments or confrontations?"

She hesitated. "I'm not sure it was really anything."

"What?"

"Well, that Logan West. Did you see him? He's all big and, and—hulking now. He was watching her all this evening. Did you notice that? Cindy . . . Cindy," Belinda's voice sputtered to a stop, but then she recovered.

"Cindy told me Logan was giving her the creeps tonight. Everyone knows that he went crazy after high school and had to go to the nuthouse. I don't know why he would want to come back here and make everyone else uncomfortable."

Kyle shrugged. "Maybe he had old friends he wanted to see, same as everyone else."

Belinda's tone was dubious. "Maybe."

"Did you leave the Hoe-Down Room tonight any time between, say, nine P.M. and midnight? Before you found her?"

"Why are you asking me that for, Kyle? Do you think I killed her?"

"You saw her. You think a woman did that? I'm wondering if you were outside and might of seen something."

"No. I didn't leave."

"Do you remember anyone being gone for a long period of time?"

Belinda shrugged. "People were in and out all the time. You know that." She straightened up. "Wait a minute—I remember at one point I was looking for Wade. I want to buy a used car, and I thought he might cut me a deal. But I couldn't find him anyplace. I even went out and looked at the slots, but he wasn't there." She looked up at him, her blue eyes wide. "You don't think he could have done it, do you? He really loved her in high school. It just about killed him when she broke up with him."

Kyle didn't answer her question. "Did you see Cindy leaving with Wade?"

"I told you, I didn't know she had left. So I don't know who she left with—or if she left with anyone."

"Then who was the last person you saw her talking to?"

"I've been trying to remember, but I'm not sure. She wasn't staying in one place for very long. I remember looking around for her when I left, but I couldn't find her. I just figured she was in the bathroom."

"But you didn't check?"

She shrugged. "Why should I? I knew she had to be around somewhere, since Kevin was still there. I said goodbye to him and told him to tell Cindy I'd see her in the morning. Then—" she hesitated, her words coming slower, "then I left."

"I want you to walk me step by step through what happened. What time was it when you left?"

"I don't know, exactly. Sometime around midnight. I just remember thinking how much I wanted to go to bed."

"Then why did you go out to the parking lot instead of your hotel room?"

"Because I still had two bags left in the car. I'd brought two in with me when I checked in, but I couldn't carry the other two."

"So you came alone to the reunion?" He eyed her wedding ring.

Unconsciously, Belinda began to twist it. "My daughter came with me."

"Okay. So you decided to go back to your car. You left the hotel. Did you go out the main doors?"

"Yes." Her voice trailed off.

"Did anyone come in those doors as you were walking toward them?"

"I don't think so." She closed her eyes, shutting out all distractions. "No. No one came in while I was leaving."

"All right. When you left, did you see anyone outside?"

"Yeah. There were a couple of people out there smoking. Jim Prentiss. And that Logan West. And I think maybe there was one other person who was leaving just as I was walking by." She hesitated. "But I don't remember right now who it was. I didn't look in Logan's direction very long. You know what they say about crazy people and animals—you don't want to look into their eyes for too long, 'cause it makes them mad. So we just kind of nodded at each other."

"Were they talking to each other?"

"Logan and Jim? No, I don't think so."

Kyle made a note. "And how did they seem to you?"

"What do you mean?" Belinda seemed puzzled.

"Did they seem upset to you? Or out of breath? Did you maybe notice scratch marks on their faces or hands, for example?"

She was shaking her head before he even finished. "I didn't see anything like that. They just looked—normal. I'm sure I would have noticed if they didn't. I just said hello and kept on walking. I was tired and wanted to be back in my room."

"And then you began to walk through the parking lot. Did you hear anything or see anything out of the ordinary before you saw the body? See anybody running or hear any shouts or . . . ?"

"No." Her voice stretched the word out until it trailed off. "No."

"Are you sure? You sound like you remembered something."

"It seemed like I thought of something for a moment, but now it's gone. It's probably nothing. I was so tired when I went out there. I was mostly just wishing I was already in bed." She grabbed another tissue, her voice arcing higher. "But now I don't see how I can sleep! If I close my eyes I just see her the way she was when I found her. Her eyes half-open and looking at me but also looking *through* me. Like she didn't care what she saw."

"And where was her purse when you found her? Was she holding it?"

Belinda shook her head. "No. It was lying a few feet away. I think there was some stuff spilling out of it."

"Do you remember seeing anything in Cindy's hands?"

"What do you mean? Like she grabbed a hunk of the guy's hair or something? No, I didn't see anything. But I hope she did. I hope she hurt this guy something good."

"I do, too." Kyle tapped the pen against his teeth. "You know what I might do? I think I'm gonna call in a hypnotist from Portland. See if they can walk you through what happened tonight. Get you to remember in more detail."

"I don't know if I can do this all over again, Kyle. I don't want to keep thinking about it and thinking about it. I want to remember Cindy the way she was. She was so beautiful. So, so beautiful. I know. People were always saying that to her when we were together."

Ten

A strange, nervous energy infected the Hoe-Down Room. The harried bartender couldn't keep up with the fresh onslaught of demands as people crowded four deep around the bar, offering to buy each other rounds. All around them conversations grew louder, as some people cried at the thought of Cindy's being gone and others shuddered at the horrible manner of her death. Fueling everything was their giddy relief at simply being alive. Even though the police had only asked those who had found the body in the parking lot to stay, no one wanted to miss out on the excitement.

It wasn't real to most of them, Claire realized as she looked around the room. Only the dozen or so people who had found Cindy's body looked truly shaken. Richard was chewing his nails, pausing every few seconds to search for another sliver he could nibble away. He looked like some sort of industrious animal, like a squirrel or a woodpecker or a beaver. Martha sat slumped next to him, but the two of them weren't talking. At another table, Sawyer rested his head in his hands, his palms hiding his eyes, while his wife rubbed his shoulders. Even Jessica was unusually somber as she dug through her sleek Coach purse.

The two people who had been closest to Cindy in high school seemed the most affected. Until one of the cops had escorted her out to be interviewed by Kyle, Belinda had wept brokenly in the back of the room. And Wade was leaning against a wall, his arms crossed, his face shadowed by the moose head mounted above him. On the way back to the casino, he had wiped his shirt sleeve across his face, erasing all traces of vomit and tears.

But, Claire noticed, two of the little group who had found Cindy's body in the parking lot were missing. Logan West and Jim Prentiss. She was particularly worried about Logan. Had the sight of Cindy's violated body sent him back over the edge of insanity? And what about Jim? Just as she was wondering where he could be, he slipped into the room and joined the crowd around the bar.

At the next table, Becca was talking to Nina. Her next words fell into an unexpected pool of silence. "Poor Belinda." The silence rippled out, like a stone thrown into a pool. "Poor Belinda," Becca repeated. People turned to her, and she flushed to her hairline, but continued on. "I can't imagine what it would be like to find the body of your best friend. How horrible." Around the room, people shook their heads, murmuring in agreement.

"Who could have done it?" a woman asked.

Jim shrugged. "Some sad sack probably saw Cindy walking along, not paying any attention to where she was going, and holding this big purse. Maybe he'd lost everything at the tables, and he was just looking to score a little cash. And then one thing led to another."

"Or maybe it was a Tequamish," Nina ventured. "Everyone knows Indians can't hold their liquor." She shrieked as the waitress stumbled and spilled the remains of a bottle of beer down the back of her neck. With a false smile that didn't reach her flat dark eyes, the waitress apologized.

"Why are you talking about whoever did it as if they were a stranger?" Martha asked. "Occam's razor would say that the most likely person to have a motive to kill her would be one of us."

Someone in the back of the room started to laugh, but then stopped abruptly when people turned their heads.

"Occa-what?" Jessica asked.

"Occam's razor. It says the simplest explanation that accounts for all the facts is probably the right one. Why would a stranger want to kill Cindy? If they wanted her money, all they had to do was take it. It's more likely that it was someone who had known her for a long time."

Wade stepped forward, his face hardening. "Just what are you saying?"

It was Maria Markgraf who answered him. "Oh, just look around the room, Wade. Martha is right."

"What do you mean?"

"You can start with me, if you want. Who was head cheerleader senior year? It should have been me, but instead it was Cindy. She sweet-talked that faculty adviser into recounting the votes, and somehow it ended up that Cindy won by three. Now, wasn't that convenient." Maria drew the last word out sarcastically. "And she didn't care if that meant the end of our friendship."

As Maria spoke, a hush fell over the room. Even the

bartender had stopped to listen, a half-filled glass forgotten in his hand. Claire didn't know if everyone was stunned by Maria's venom, or by the fact that someone was finally speaking the truth about Cindy.

Maria continued. "Take you, Wade. She knew you were interested in me right at the beginning of the school year, so it was like a challenge to her to get you. And after she got tired of you, she broke it off." Wade shook his head and turned away, his back rigid. "She thought that being beautiful and rich and head cheerleader gave her a license to look down on everyone. Even Kyle—do you think he really feels that bad about her being dead? Remember how he used to stutter when he was a kid and she would make fun of him?"

There was a long silence, then other voices began to chime in.

"She slept with my boyfriend and then as soon as he broke up with me she dropped him."

"She had all the male teachers snowed."

"I heard she gave Mr. Berkman a blow job to get an A in social studies."

A voice cut through the babble. A trained voice, used to projecting itself even to the two-for-one seats in the nose-bleed section. Jessica.

"I think you're looking at this all wrong. You're all talking about Cindy's death as if whoever did this was just out to get Cindy. But remember what Martha said— it's the simplest explanation that fits the facts. All the facts. And you're leaving out the most important one. I think that the person who killed Cindy may be after me as well."

Jim's skeptical voice cut through the babble that began to return. "What makes you think that, Jessica?"

"Because when we found Cindy out on that cold

ground,"—well, it hadn't been cold, Claire thought, but she guessed an actor was allowed a bit of poetic license—"you saw what she had *clutched*" —Jessica gave the word "clutched" dramatic emphasis—"in her hand." She had everyone's attention now. "A heart-shaped box. Hand-carved out of wood. And inside, there was a photo of Cindy cut out from the annual." With a flourish, she pulled something from her purse and held it up so everyone could see. There was a murmur as people craned their necks. "Well, look at what I got when I checked in to the hotel. An identical box! Only this one has my picture in it! Which means that somewhere—perhaps in this very room—a killer is watching me. Waiting for his chance to—."

Claire only had a second for startled recognition before another woman's voice cut Jessica off.

"You mean Cindy got one of these, too?" Jill asked. She reached into her own purse and then held up what looked like an identical box. "The desk clerk gave me this when I checked in. No note or anything else. Just this box in a little manila envelope. And inside there was a picture of me when I was in riding club. I thought it was from my old boyfriend until I saw that Maria got one, too." Maria nodded.

The center of attention had slipped away from Jessica and now swung from woman to woman as one after another confessed to having received a box identical to the ones Jessica, Claire—and poor dead Cindy—had received.

"Becca got one too," Becca said, instantly transporting Claire back to her high school days, when she had found Becca's habit of talking about herself in the third person incredibly annoying.

Nina reached into her pocket and then waved a box

over her head. "I didn't know what it meant—just that someone picked the worst picture to remember me by."

"I got one," Claire added, although she didn't know if anyone but Richard heard her in the hubbub. For a few seconds his frightened gaze met hers.

"All of you got boxes?" Jessica asked, looking deflated. Claire watched as she slipped her box back in her purse, no longer the center of hushed attention.

While Jessica sat slumped and silent, the four other women who had received boxes began to compare them. The rest of the room crowded around. Claire thought about going back to her hotel room to get hers, but then realized the cop had told them they couldn't leave until Kyle had finished his questioning. She joined the crowd clustered around Jill, Becca, Maria, and Nina.

The boxes were roughly similar. Each was slightly smaller than a woman's palm, hand-carved out of some dark reddish wood, with a single silver hinge. The top of each box was decorated with curlicues and flowers. As far as Claire could tell, they were close duplicates of the box she had received.

In the commotion, Jim pulled her aside. They stood beside an empty coat rack made out of upturned deer hooves. The hooves looked plastic. She hoped they were.

"So you got one of the boxes, huh?" He shifted from one foot to another. "What do you think it means?"

"I honestly don't know."

"Say, I need you to do me a favor, Claire."

"What's that?"

His smile was private and somehow sad. "You're not the old Claire anymore, are you? The old Claire would have just said yes."

The old Claire never found someone strangled in a parking lot, either, Claire thought. "Why don't you tell me what it is?"

"I need you to say we walked back here together, okay? If anyone asks, say we walked back to the Hoe-Down Room together, that you stayed outside with me for a second while I had a quick smoke. There was so much going on that nobody will remember exactly what happened. But I don't need anyone asking questions about where I was for five minutes."

"Since we both know that didn't really happen, what were you doing instead?"

He looked away from her, running his index finger around the cup of a hoof. "Don't ask me that, okay? Because I can't tell you."

Claire looked at him without speaking. Had she really opened her body to him all those years ago? Now Jim was a stranger to her, with his tanned, lined, tired face. He reached out and caught one of her hands in his. They were rough as sandpaper. Had he squeezed these same hands around Cindy's neck?

Claire felt as if the world were falling away beneath her feet. She didn't know what was true and what wasn't. With an effort, she drew a deep breath and steadied herself, Jim's fingers still gripping hers tightly. He had always been honest with her. He had been gentle and sensitive and kept their lovemaking private, when so many boys would have boasted to each other.

They looked at each other without speaking. The color of Jim's eyes seemed darker, no longer the yellow green of a cat's, but almost a blue green, the color of the sea before a storm.

He gave her hand one more squeeze, then dropped it, turned on his heel, and was gone before she could either promise to lie for him or to press him to tell her where he had been.

When Dante came up behind her and touched her shoulder, Claire started. "Should I be jealous? You seemed to be having a very intense conversation there."

Now was the perfect time for Claire to tell Dante what Jim had asked. Instead she said lightly, "Jim's pretty shook up about Cindy's death. Maybe they were closer than I knew in high school." As she said the words, she wondered if her lie contained a kernel of truth. A few times while she and Jim had been dating, Claire had burned with jealousy when she caught him greeting Cindy with an almost imperceptible nod in the school hallway. Now it wasn't so hard to imagine that Cindy, who had always loved a beautiful man, might have gone slumming once or twice.

But could Jim have killed Cindy? No. She couldn't imagine a world where Jim would tear at a woman's clothes and then put his hands around her neck. She decided that she wouldn't volunteer anything about Jim's being missing in action right after Cindy's body was found. If someone asked—well, then she would have to tell the truth.

The young cop named Marc came into the room. "You. He wants to talk to you." Paying no attention to the people clustered around the boxes, he pointed at Claire.

OPNYDE

Eleven

FROM THE INTERVIEW WITH CLAIRE MONTROSE

The younger policeman escorted Claire down a narrow hallway to a small office that Kyle already had made his own. When she walked in, he was tapping his pen on the metal desk, looking up at the pipes that ran along the oppressively low ceiling. He stood up to shake her hand with his own damp one, then gestured at a chipped wooden chair that sat opposite the desk. Claire sat down, smoothing her denim skirt. Was it good—or bad—that she, after all her agonizing, had ended up dressed exactly the same as everyone else?

Kyle wore a short-sleeve golf shirt. His hair was beginning to recede to the crown, leaving a little island in the middle, just above his forehead. He had let this part grow longer than the rest, resulting in a puff of hair three inches long. Maybe he had had hopes of swirling it across the bare spots, but tonight it just hung there, bobbing whenever he nodded his head. Claire thought to herself that women might have to bear a thousand indignities, from push-up bras to brow tweezing, but at least they didn't have to decide what to do when their hair was only half gone.

Although she remembered when Kyle had been as thin as a pencil, now his belt sagged under the weight of both his gun and his belly. His face had the weathered look of someone who spent a lot of time in the sun with a cigarette clenched between his teeth.

"So when did you decide to go into law enforcement, Kyle?"

"I've been on the job since eighty-one." She could hear the capital on "the Job" in his voice. "Of course, there are a few perks to this line of work. Like you meet a lot of women when you're wearing a badge. Cop groupies, for one thing. A lot of ladies out there have a thing for a man in uniform. All my wives have always been jealous of that. You get pretty girls rubbing against you, swearing that they will do anything, absolutely anything so they don't get a speeding ticket. Or so the Dee-Wee won't show up on their record and bump up their insurance."

"A 'dee-wee'?" Claire echoed. Was Kyle bragging about his prowess with women in an attempt to hit on her?

"To you civilians, it's called driving under the influence. A DWI." He cleared his throat. "So—you single? Notice you're still a Montrose. And no ring." He waggled his own left hand at her, which still bore a faint white stripe around the ring finger. "My third wife, well, it turned out we didn't exactly see eye to eye. But I haven't soured on you gals yet."

Great. Kyle seemed to be viewing Cindy's murder as some sort of cop version of *The Dating Game.* "That's very flattering, Kyle, but I'm in a long-term relationship."

"With that Danny guy?"

"Dante." She had wondered who would be the first to mangle his name. "His name is Dante."

"Oops! Got me there." Pointing his index finger at her, he made a "p-choo" noise with his mouth, like a kid pretending to be a cowboy, turning his finger into a gun. Given his current profession, Claire found the gesture a bit disconcerting. Then he looked away and drummed his pen on the desk. "Remember when you used to come over to my house and listen to records?"

She had been to his house a grand total of one time, but felt it wasn't politic to say so. "Sure, Kyle. I remember." How could she forget those three long hours with Kyle sweating and silent beside her on the couch as he studied the liner notes of a Hot Tuna album as if he had never seen them before?

Kyle's mind returned to the business at hand, and he picked up the camera. "I'm gonna need to take your photo, Claire. It's a formality. Strictly for identification purposes. I think we can already rule out any of you gals, right?"

"What do you mean?" Claire was still asking the question when he lifted the camera to his face. Afterward she pressed the flat of her hands over her dazzled eyes. She heard the camera whir as it spat out the photo, and then a click as Kyle put it down on the desk to develop.

"You saw how he left her. Clothes half ripped off. I'm thinking what we're looking at here is a botched robbery slash attempted rape. You get a load of some of those skels who hang out in front of the slots? A bunch of lowlifes who gamble until the ATM machine won't give them any more money. And Cindy looks rich. She was hammering those drinks back pretty regularly, so my guess is she didn't notice when the perp followed her out hoping to score some easy cash. Then he took her purse, and got a little too turned on when she put up a fight."

Skels, dee-wees, perps—Kyle seemed to be using as much cop shoptalk as possible. Something nagged at Claire. "You think someone raped her?"

"Well, I won't know until we get the lab reports back. But you saw how he left her, naked to the world. And how she was acting earlier tonight. Half-sloshed, doing a cheerleading routine for God's sake, like she was still in high school." He lowered his voice, as if his words were more for his own ears than Claire's. "It's kind of funny, isn't it? Who would ever have guessed that twenty years later it would be Cindy Weaver trying to impress Dick— I mean Richard—Crane?" He shook his head. "Cindy always was a hot little number. Maybe with all that she had to drink, she could of sent someone the wrong signals."

"What are you talking about?" Outrage surged through Claire. She straightened up in her chair. "If someone thinks a woman is sexy does that give him the right to rip her clothes off and kill her?"

"Simmer down, Claire. That's not what I was saying."

That *had* been what Kyle was saying, but she decided it wasn't worthwhile to argue the point. Instead, Claire thought about how they had found Cindy. Kyle was right, Cindy's purse had sagged open, hollow-looking, as if someone had taken something from it. And again, she saw Cindy's breasts, nearly spilling out of the gold satin bra, and how her skirt had been tugged up around her waist.

The Polaroid had finished developing. Claire picked it up and looked at it. In the photo, she wore an uncertain half-smile that didn't fit the occasion. After years of being ordered to smile for the camera, she guessed it was reflexive. Due to some oddity of the flash, her hair appeared blond instead of red, a cascade of curls falling past her shoulders. Her eyes were wide, her skin washed-out and pale. And glaring like a beacon at the edge of her chin, her zit seemed to have shrugged off its protective covering.

"You're still a damn-fine-looking woman, Claire." Kyle didn't give her a chance to reply, which was just as well as she didn't know what to say that wouldn't sound as if she were begging for more compliments. "Oh, I almost forgot. I need your name, address, phone number, and occupation." When she looked at him questioningly, he said, "It's just for the record. Plus if we need to get a hold of you later." He drummed his pen against the edge of the desk the whole time he spoke, and she wondered if his nervousness was giving him away.

Claire told him her name and address, while another corner of her mind tried to decide whether to make up a phone number or give him her real one. She wouldn't put it past Kyle to call her up and ask her out, Dante or no Dante. But in the end, she gave him the right number. Her occupation gave her pause. She finally settled on, "I do volunteer work."

Kyle tipped her a wink. "I read in the *Oregonian* about how you inherited that painting that everyone made a fuss about. Must be a nice life." Claire kept quiet, figuring it wasn't worthwhile to point out that she had given 99 percent of the painting's proceeds to the World Jewish Restitution Organization. When he realized Claire wasn't going to rise to the bait, Kyle said, "How well did you know Cindy?"

"As you probably remember, we didn't exactly run in the same circles."

"Yeah, Cindy was the top dog at Minor, wasn't she? Or maybe I should say top bitch."

"Kyle! Don't forget she's dead." She remembered what Maria had said about Cindy making fun of Kyle's childhood stutter. Even though Maria had said it had taken place behind Kyle's back, he must have known.

"Did you talk to her tonight?"

Claire shook her head.

"Did you see her having any kind of argument or disagreement?"

"No. The only time I really paid attention to her was when she was doing that cheering thing."

"What about Logan? You were friends with him before, right? Did you notice him following Cindy around, watching her?"

"What are you talking about?"

"There have been some reports that he was acting strangely around her."

"Logan might be a little different, but he's a little different around everybody, not just Cindy."

"Uh-huh." Kyle nodded his head, clearly not convinced. "Did you leave the bar before you found Cindy's body? Did you notice anyone leaving the bar tonight anytime after nine o'clock?"

"Well, I know I didn't leave." Claire tried hard to think about who had been in the Hoe-Down Room and who hadn't. But it had been too chaotic to remember if anyone had been missing for ten or fifteen minutes. People had been in and out of the room all the time—to grab a smoke, to go to the bathroom, try their luck by dropping a quarter in the slots. Finally, she had to shake her head. "No one in particular."

"Before I forget, let me take your fingerprints." He reached for her hand, and she tried not to stiffen. "This is just a formality," he said as he pressed Claire's fingers against the black ink pad, then rolled them on a piece of stiff white paper. "Did you touch anything at the scene?"

Claire tried to remember. "No, I don't think so. Dante was the first one to touch her, and he told us she was cold. Wait a minute—Cindy's box. Jessica picked it up and I told her not to. I knew she shouldn't be touching it."

"Did you touch it yourself?"

Claire thought back. "I don't think so. I was just starting to tell Jessica to put it back when I realized the box was identical to the one I got."

He looked up from his notebook, his expression alert. "The one you got—what are you talking about?"

She realized Kyle didn't yet know that there had been other boxes besides the one found in Cindy's hand. Quickly, she sketched it in for him. As he took notes, his self-inflated posture seemed to sag.

"So you're saying that in addition to Cindy, you, Jessica, Becca, Maria, Jill, and Nina all got these boxes?"

Claire counted on her fingers. "That's right. What do you think it means? Some people said it might be a serial killer. Do you think that's a possibility?"

"A serial killer? They could be right." He gave her a humorless smile. "I guess the only way we'll ever know is if we find another one of you ladies dead."

ANIL8

Twelve

FROM THE INTERVIEW WITH RICHARD CRANE

As he picked up the camera, Kyle said, "Hey, you used to be the one taking the pictures, but now it's me."

Richard held himself stiffly as the picture was taken. The flash from the Polaroid reflected off the shiny fuschia satin cowboy shirt Richard wore under his elaborately fringed jacket. The long nose that jutted from his pale face cast a strange shadow, like the blade of a knife.

"What did you say you were going to use this for again?" Richard asked.

"With the hotel staff or any witnesses we turn up. We can't keep everyone here, and most of you are only in town for the weekend. So I need to get your name, address, and occupation for the record."

"Richard Crane, 320 Cherry Street, Seattle, Washington. I'm the CEO of Simplex Corporation. We manufacture a line of high-speed modems."

"So, Dick, I mean Richard, how well did you know Cindy?"

"I wouldn't say that I really knew her, at least not well. As you know, she was a very popular lady at our high school. But Cindy and I didn't exactly move in the same circles. I would venture to say that I probably knew her better than she knew me. I don't think I was really on her radar screen."

"Is that so?" Kyle made a note, then looked up. "What about you dating her, as was referenced tonight?"

Richard flushed to the top of his high forehead. "That was only once, and a very long time ago. I doubt she remembered me."

"I didn't get that impression. The way I remember it, she was leading a cheer for you."

"She was just showing me a little of one of the new routines she's working on for her business as a cheer-leading consultant. I guess we were the last people to ever see her cheer." He pushed the hair out of his eyes. "God, what a waste. A woman like that, cut down in her prime."

"What did you talk about with her tonight?"

"We exchanged a few words. She seemed very inter-ested in my line of business, wanted to know how things were going, how many units we were selling, things like that."

"Things like that," Kyle echoed, not bothering to hide the sarcastic spin to the words.

Richard set his jaw and looked Kyle straight in the eye. "I found she evinced interest in everyone. We all knew her, didn't we? Or at least we wanted to. I was sur-prised to see her husband with her tonight, but she told me she had only asked him to come along because she was nervous. Nervous! As if she had any reason to be nervous."

Kyle looked up, his face alert. "What do you mean, you were surprised to see her with her husband tonight?"

"I'd heard that they were in the process of getting a divorce."

Kyle started. "A divorce? Where did you hear this from?"

Richard looked down at his narrow white hands. He laced his fingers together, then lowered them to his lap. "I don't really remember. I guess it must have been a rumor."

Kyle made a note. "Did you see her arguing with anyone tonight?"

"There may be one person you ought to be talking to. Sometime in the latter part of the evening, I went to the restroom. And when I came out, Cindy was standing near the door talking to Wade Mertz. You know, the man who was on the football team? She seemed angry. And he was holding his cheek, and I saw a red mark on it. Like she had slapped him."

"Could you hear what either one of them was saying?"

"No. Her tone was too low. But it was intense. Intense and angry."

"And Wade? Was he angry, too?"

Richard's tone couldn't mask his disappointment. "No. No, he wasn't. He appeared to be laughing. And that was just making her angrier."

"Were you aware of anyone leaving the bar after, say, ten P.M.?"

"To be honest, I didn't pay much attention to who was in the bar and who wasn't. There were a lot of people. It was kind of overwhelming. Everyone had a lot of questions about Simplex."

"How about Logan West? Did you talk to him or see him leaving at any point?"

"Is he a suspect?" Kyle let the long silence stretch out. "I suppose you can't answer that. I remember in eighth grade we had a lot of the same advanced classes together, but by our senior year, Logan was . . . broken. Now that you mention it, I might have seen him go in and out a couple of times. But then again, he is a smoker, isn't he? Although maybe he wasn't there during the last part of the evening. I can't be sure, though."

"And did you yourself leave the bar at any time tonight?"

"No. No, I didn't. Not until—" Richard's voice broke for the first time "—not until I saw Cindy lying on the ground."

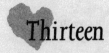 Thirteen

"Take my picture?" Jessica was already pulling a compact and a tube of lipstick from her purse. "Give me just a second."

"This isn't for publication, Jessica." Kyle drummed his pen on the desk. "It's just in case we turn up witnesses. I don't need someone telling me they saw Cindy when it turns out they saw you."

Jessica's words were muffled as she pursed her lips to meet the scarlet wand. "But I'm brunette and Cindy is—I mean was—blond." Slipping the cap back on the lipstick, she gave her reflection a satisfied smile. Then she remembered the occasion for her primping. She looked up at Kyle, her eyes widening as she suddenly began to blink back tears. "I still can't believe this has happened. It is beyond belief. Cindy was just so full of—life! When I saw her lying there, alone, cold, violated . . . I wanted to cry out—where is the justice? Why has someone so alive been taken from us?" A tear spilled down her cheek. "Quick—take the picture before my mascara starts to run."

The camera whirred and spat out a picture. Kyle put it face down on the desk. "You and Cindy ran in different circles in high school, right?"

"There was still this connection between us." She thumped her cleavage with a closed fist. Kyle's gaze lingered on the gentle sway of her breasts.

"A connection?"

"At Minor, we may not have run in the same circles, but we admired each other's work, you know? We both knew excellence when we saw it. Cindy was born to be a cheerleader—and I was born to tread the boards, as we say in the theater world." Seeing Kyle's blank expression, she added, "That means I was meant to be onstage."

"Did you talk to Cindy tonight?"

"A little bit. She wanted to know what it was like to work with people like Nikki Kidman and Kevin Spacey." If she was hoping for a reaction from Kyle, an acknowledgment of these famous names, Jessica didn't get it. "Then she told me a little bit about her experience being on ESPN judging the national cheerleaders' competition."

"What kind of mood would you say she was in?"

Jessica shrugged her shoulders. "Good. Cindy always liked being able to talk about herself. I'm sure you remember that from high school." Kyle scribbled something in the notebook, and she leaned forward. "What are you writing down, anyway?"

He flipped the notebook closed and pulled it back. "Sometimes the smallest clues can catch a perp."

"So you've worked on this kind of case before?"

He gave her a curt nod.

"It must be especially complicated because you know everyone involved."

"I'm a professional. I've learned how to separate my emotions from the facts." He flipped open the notebook again, although now he held it closer to his body. "Did you see Cindy arguing with anyone tonight?"

Jessica was already shaking her head. "No. But I did see something else you might be interested in."

"What's that?"

"Well." She drew the word out as she leaned closer to him. "I could be wrong. I only caught a quick glimpse. I was looking for Sawyer to ask him how his campaign was going. I couldn't find him, so I pushed open the doors to go look at the casino, see if he was maybe out there. And you know who was out there?" She didn't wait for an answer. "Belinda and Kevin. He was leaning over that table. And I don't think they were just talking. I saw the look on her face. I think they might have been kissing."

Kyle raised an eyebrow, his expression alert. "Kissing? You saw them kissing?"

Jessica reluctantly shook her head.

"Touching?"

Another pause, another shake of the head. "It was the way they looked. They looked guilty and out of breath. As an actress, that is just how I would portray someone who had just been kissing."

"But you didn't actually *see* them kissing."

"No." Jessica pushed out her lower lip. "But I know what I saw."

"Uh-huh. One last thing. I need to ask you about this box Cindy was holding. How was she holding it in relation to the rest of her body?"

"Cindy was lying on her back and her arm was stretched out next to her side. At first, I didn't really notice the box because her fingers hid most of it."

"Why did you pick it up? You know it was a very stupid thing to do, disturbing a crime scene like that. There's a chance your fingerprints destroyed the perp's."

She dropped her gaze. "I'm sorry. I was just so startled to see that Cindy was holding a box that looked the same as the one I had gotten."

"Did you get it when you checked in, like the other girls?"

"Yes, in a manila envelope with a printed label with just my name on it."

"If you still have the envelope, I need that, as well as the box. We'll dust everything for prints and see if we get lucky."

Jessica shifted in her seat. "They're both in my hotel room. I'll have to get them for you later."

"Who do you think is behind these boxes?"

"I have no idea. I can't even think of why the six of us all got them. We really don't have anything in common that I can think of. We weren't all friends in high school. We didn't hang out with the same group of people. We don't really look alike. We have different careers, different interests. We don't live in the same towns now. About all we have in common is that we graduated from Minor High twenty years ago. And maybe one other thing."

"What's that?"

She looked up at him, her blue eyes wide. "Maybe someone wants all of us dead."

Fourteen

Wade looked at the photo Kyle had taken of him, then slid it back across the desk. "Not the most flattering photograph I've ever seen."

Kyle looked down at Wade's square, pudgy face, which nearly filled the photo, and then back at the real Wade. His blond hair, streaked with gray, was tamed back into ripples with hair gel. The skin around Wade's blue eyes was swollen, his face ruddy. Refraining from comment, Kyle flipped to a new page in his notebook.

"How well would you say that you knew Cindy?" Kyle paused, pen poised.

"You do know that's kind of a silly question, don't you, Kyle?" Wade sighed and tugged at the front of his tailored lightweight denim shirt, which was pulled taut across the bulk of his abdomen. "We started going out right at the beginning of senior year. I was in hog heaven that fall." He smiled, his voice soft with reminiscence. "There I was, the big man on campus, right? And

I had my arm around Cindy Weaver, the most beautiful lady I had ever seen. If you would have asked me twenty years ago, I would have told you we were going to get married." He made a sound like a laugh. "Just like I thought I'd have a career playing pro ball. But things didn't work out that way, did they?" He shrugged, then looked down at his hands, open and empty in his lap. "I'll have to admit it felt a little strange to see her tonight. Cindy is still a very attractive-looking lady. Twenty years and it's like nothing touched her." There was a pause. When Wade spoke again, there was a catch in his voice. "It was quite a shock, I'll tell you, to see her like that out in the parking lot. It made me literally, physically sick. Just a few minutes before, I'd been thinking about how things used to be between us, and then to see her like—like that."

"Did you leave the Hoe-Down Room at any time before Cindy's body was discovered?"

A shake of the head. "No. I was there the whole time until Belinda ran in screaming."

"How about anyone else? Did you notice anyone who was gone for more than a few minutes?"

"I'm afraid I can't help you there. The only person I really had my eye on was the waitress. I can tell you for sure that she didn't go any place."

Wade's attempt at levity met no response. "Did you see Cindy having any kind of argument or disagreement tonight?"

Wade was already shaking his head before Kyle finished his question. "Nothing like that. Cindy was just having a good time, talking to everyone. Nobody in particular. Well, maybe a little more to people she thought it might benefit her to know. Cindy always had an eye out for that kind of thing. That's just how she was."

"We've had reports that the two of you were seen arguing." Kyle kept his voice neutral, but his hand—which was drumming the pen nervously on the edge of the desk—betrayed him.

Wade began to get out of his chair. "What are you talking about? What are you thinking?" Kyle drew back when Wade raised his balled hands. Just as soon as it had begun, the rage subsided. Wade fell back into his chair, uncurled his fingers, and put his hands over his face. He finally broke the long silence.

"Are you crazy, huh, Kyle, are you crazy?" He dropped his hand and looked at Kyle with an expression of disgust. "Do you think I would be so mad at her for dumping me twenty years ago that I would strangle her now? Do you think I could forget about what she used to mean to me and just stone-cold kill her?"

"Someone said they thought you left the bar with her." Kyle didn't have long to wait for Wade's reaction to this fiction.

"What is this all about? I like women, I've never denied that. Ask any of my ex-wives or girlfriends. Lord knows there are plenty of them around. All of them will tell you that I'm an asshole. That I drink too much. That I like to go to Vegas and lose all my money. And that I played around on them. Every one of them will tell you that. That I slept with ladies I met in bars, in restaurants, in airports. That I have sold cars to ladies and then sealed the deal in the backseat. But I have *never* hit a lady in my life."

"Speaking of hitting, we have reports that Cindy hit you tonight. Would you care to explain that?"

Wade sagged in his chair. "It was just a little slap. I made a little joke to her, that's all. I made a little joke about doing something for old times sake and she didn't see it the same way. But Cindy doesn't have a sense of humor any more. She doesn't want to be reminded that it's been twenty years since anything happened. Jesus! Are you suggesting that that means I killed her?"

"The old Cindy," Kyle echoed, without answering Wade's question. "That reminds me. Why did the two of you break up, anyway?"

"It's none of your business why we broke up."

Kyle continued to look at Wade, until he was forced to expand.

"That was twenty years ago. It didn't have anything to do with what happened tonight. She just said she thought we were too young to be so serious. I hadn't really told her how I felt, but I guess she knew."

"But didn't that make you angry? You'd already lost your football scholarship, and now you're telling me you had no bad feelings toward Cindy for breaking up with you just when you needed her the most?"

"You think I don't know that what's past is past?" Wade snorted. "I've spent twenty years learning that, Kyle, twenty goddamn years."

Fifteen

Sawyer was rubbing his temples when Kyle told him about the need for a photo. "What?"

I said, "I need to take your picture."

Sawyer was enough of a politician to lift his chin at that, although his face was etched with fatigue. He blinked away the flash.

"Did you know Cindy in high school?"

"Not really. I think she might have been in one of the biology classes I taught. And I remember seeing her around the halls, dressed in her cheerleading outfit. Although it would be hard to forget that after seeing her cheer tonight. Some people leave high school and don't ever change. Others—well, look at you, for instance. At first I was surprised to hear you had made a career of law enforcement, but the more I thought about it, the more sense it made. I remember how methodical you were back in high school. And chief of police— congratulations!"

Kyle tried, but couldn't hide his smile. "Thank you." He made a note. "So did you talk to Cindy tonight?"

"Only for a moment. She told me she would vote for me." Sawyer managed a half-smile. "You want to know something? Absolutely everyone I talked to tonight assured me they were going to vote for me. In a way, I was disappointed to hear that. Twenty years ago, I came into Minor High on fire to teach one lesson: that the most important thing in life was to be honest and to hold true to your principles. I guess it didn't stick."

"I remember what you said." Kyle nodded, then looked away and tapped his pen three times on the edge of the metal desk. "So—did you happen to notice anyone having any kind of disagreement tonight with Cindy?"

"That's the thing, Kyle. I might have. I slipped outside for just a minute. I wanted to breathe some air that didn't taste like it had already been in the lungs of a hundred different people. Since the smokers were to the left, I went to the right. And while I was standing there, I heard two people arguing. I'm pretty sure one of the voices belonged to Cindy."

Kyle straightened up. "Who was the other person?"

"That's the problem. I don't honestly know. All I can say for sure is that it was a man. And I got—how can I say this—the impression that it was her husband."

"Did you see either of them?"

"No. They were standing behind one of those huge SUVs. The kind of thing that gets about eight miles to a gallon."

Kyle ignored this side trip to environmentalism. "When was this?"

"Sometime between eleven and midnight. I wish I could be more precise. I still don't like to wear a watch."

"What did you hear them saying?"

Sawyer leaned forward and rested his forehead on his fingertips. "The man said something like, 'How could you do this to me?' And Cindy—at least I think it was Cindy—said, "Everything isn't always about you, you know.' Her tone was quite sarcastic."

"What makes you think this was her husband? Kevin Sanchez?"

Sawyer shrugged. "That's just the thing. I don't know why I thought that. I've never heard him speak. I wasn't even introduced to him tonight. Maybe it was just the way Cindy was talking to him, with this overwhelming disdain. In my experience, the only people you treat like that are people in your immediate family." Through pursed lips, he blew out a puff of air. "It doesn't make sense though, does it? I mean, why would a man rape his own wife?"

"Rape isn't usually about sex." Kyle tapped the butt end of the pen on his teeth, thinking. "And I'm not 100 percent certain that it was rape."

Sawyer looked at the other man with unseeing eyes. "Finding her like that—it brought back some memories. I remember this Viet Cong nurse we found, on her back like that. Her belly was slit open and someone had pulled her entrails out." The words were flat, unaccented.

Sixteen

"I see whoever has this office normally smokes." Jim pointed to the lumpy handmade ashtray sitting next to the Rolodex on one of the wire shelves. "Do you mind if I do?"

"Not at all." The ashtray appeared to have been molded from bright blue Play-Doh that had cracked as it dried. Kyle set it on the desk between them. "I've been dying for a smoke myself. I think you're the first smoker I've talked to tonight."

There was a moment of silence, broken only by the scratch of matches and the deep, grateful inhalations of smokers with a half-century of addiction between them.

Jim blew a stream of smoke out of the side of his mouth. "Yeah, there aren't that many of us left, are there? My girls keep bugging me to give it up, but . . ." He let his words trail off, then tipped his head back and blew a series of perfect smoke rings that floated up to the ceiling.

"I don't think my lungs would know what to do with just plain air." Kyle's laugh ended in a cough. He tried to cover it by asking in a voice that was only slightly twisted, "So, how well did you know Cindy? If I remember, not that well."

A shrug. "She was high priestess to the football team, and I was—what? A stoner? A hood? Anyway, not in the same class, that's for sure."

"Except you were," Kyle said. "So to speak." Tucking his cigarette in the corner of his mouth, he made a note. "Did you talk to her tonight?"

"Nah." Jim took another drag on his cigarette. "I don't think she said one word to me."

"I think I've only heard that from one other person. The way she worked the room, you would have thought she was running for office instead of Sawyer." Kyle's lips curved into a smile, but he dropped it when it went unanswered. "So did you see her having any arguments, anything like that? We've had reports that she was seen arguing with someone in the parking lot."

Jim raised his shoulders and let them fall. "I didn't see anything like that."

"Besides you and me, who else was out there smoking? Seems like they would be the most likely to have seen something."

Jim began to tick off on his fingers. "You, me, Logan. Jessica came out and bummed a cigarette off me once. So did Wade. I hate people who pretend to themselves that they aren't smokers because they don't buy their own cigarettes. Oh, and that guy in the orange tank top—can't remember his name—the one who was drunk off his ass?" Kyle had his pen poised until Jim added, "Except I saw his wife shove him into their car around ten at night. So he probably wasn't around to see whoever took Cindy out into that parking lot."

"So you think she was taken? Like with a gun?" Kyle looked at him with renewed interest.

"Taken, went—how do I know what happened?" Jim ground his cigarette out in the ashtray.

"So while you were out there smoking, did you see anyone wandering off in that direction?" He elaborated. "Toward the place where you guys found Cindy's body? Cindy or anyone else?"

Jim shook his head and lit another cigarette.

"After Belinda came in and you guys were going out there, did you notice anything unusual? Anyone hanging out on the edges, watching? Sometimes perps like to stay someplace where they can watch people find their—handiwork."

A grimace. "No. Once I saw Cindy's body, it was hard to look away. I just couldn't believe it was really happening."

"Did you notice anything unusual about the body?"

"I've never seen anything like that before, so how do I know if it was unusual? All I know is that I never want to see anything like that again. Cindy may have had her faults, but no one deserves to die like that."

 # Seventeen

Claire waited for Kyle to finish interviewing Dante, wanting nothing more than to be asleep. But even as she slowly blinked her burning eyes, she knew there was no way she would sleep for more than a few minutes at a stretch. It would probably be days before she could sleep without meeting Cindy again in her dreams.

The room had grown quieter as the reality of what had happened sank in. More and more of the people who hadn't been there when Cindy's body was found began to leave, as well as those who had finished up their interviews with Kyle. No one seemed sure if Cindy's death had been a random act, a planned attack, or the first strike of a serial killer. Alert for unseen danger, people walked back to their hotel rooms in little groups, like herd animals ready to start at the slightest sound.

"Wait a minute," Maria said, just before she and a group of about a half dozen were getting ready to leave. She scanned the faces in the room. "Where's Logan?"

"Where is Logan?" Jill echoed. She looked at Jim, who was standing next to her. "Didn't you say he was one of the people who was with you when you went out to Cindy's body?"

"He was," Jim agreed slowly. "But I don't think that Logan would ever be——."

"He was watching her tonight," Jessica interrupted. "I saw him watching Cindy. And he had this *intense* look in his eyes."

"Are you sure he was watching her any more than anyone else?" Claire asked. "Everyone was watching Cindy tonight. She made sure of that." But it was as if she hadn't spoken. The people in the room were alert again, eager to find an answer to all their fears.

"I think I remember him taking woodshop," Jill said.

"And when we went out to Cindy's body, he just stood off to one side and shifted from foot to foot. He was talking to himself. Mumbling. It gave me a chill. And then," Jessica spoke slowly, "he didn't come back with us. Maybe he only came out to revisit the scene of the crime."

"Only a small percentage of the mentally ill are violent," Sawyer said. "Just because he's schizophrenic doesn't mean that he would kill."

"Don't you read the papers?" Maria asked rhetorically. "I live in New York City. Just in the last month a man was pushed in front of a subway train and a woman was beaten to death with a brick. Both by schizophrenic men in their midthirties."

"Even so," Sawyer said. "If Logan did kill Cindy—and

I'm not saying that he did—it wasn't him that did it. It was his *disease*."

"Disease, my ass," Wade interjected. "If Logan killed Cindy, then *he's* the one who did it. Not some disease."

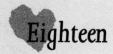

Eighteen

Dante rolled over when Claire slipped out of bed. "Where are you going?" he murmured, his voice still draggy with sleep. It was seven in the morning.

In answer, Claire waved her left Nike at him. Dante groaned and pulled the pillow over his head. He lifted it long enough to ask, "Is it full daylight out?" When Claire nodded, he said, "Don't go anyplace where there aren't any other people." He waited until she nodded again before he let the pillow drop back over his head.

Claire went back to trolling through one of her suitcases for her right running shoe. Originally they had been packed toe to toe, but everything had shifted when she had taken out clothes to wear the night before. The night before. The memory of Cindy's broken body flashed again into Claire's memory, the same vision that had woken her again and again throughout the night, until she had finally gotten out of bed and peeked between the blinds, relieved to find the sky a hot, hard blue. Her dreams had all been nightmares where old faces morphed into new, unfamiliar guises, punctuated by Belinda's half-mad keening. But at the center of every dream had been the slack sprawl of Cindy's body.

Claire's fingers touched something stiff—the missing shoe. She finished getting dressed, then smeared a cool squirt of forty-five SPF sunscreen over her face, neck, shoulders, and arms, giving her face and hands an extra coat for good measure. Lately the freckles on the backs of her hands seemed to have enlarged. A less-than-generous person might even describe them as age spots.

As she stretched her hamstrings, she watched Dante. He had pushed the pillow away from his face and sunk back down into sleep, his fists slowly uncurling. His mouth had fallen open, showing strong white teeth. She admired his hawklike nose, the dark shock of hair, the contrast of his olive skin against the rumpled white sheets. If only she could crawl back in beside him and go to sleep—but she knew that if she did, her dreams would only catch up with her again.

In the elevator, she ran her tongue over dry lips and decided to stop by the breakfast buffet to get something to drink. The dining room—called "the Feed Trough"—was nearly empty. Only a few couples sat at the scattered round tables topped with tablecloths printed to look like burlap feed sacks. The food buffet was self-serve, with Sterno keeping stainless-steel tubs of miniquiches and hash browns warm. Claire was surprised to see Belinda ahead of her, piling a plate high, until she realized the woman she thought was Belinda was really a girl— no more than sixteen. That would be Belinda's daughter, Claire decided, as the girl's hand wavered between a muffin and a cinnamon roll before finally choosing both. They shared the same pudgy body, dishwater blond hair, and nearly lashless eyes. Claire got another shock when she saw who Belinda's daughter was sitting with—a boy with the same broad face and jutting nose as Wade Merz. He was perhaps a year or two older than the girl. While Claire watched, the girl fed the boy a bite of muffin, and he playfully nipped her fingers.

What would it be like, Claire wondered, as she snagged both a cup of Coffee People coffee and a glass of orange juice, to have a child who resembled you so strongly? And what would it be like to have a child who was nearly an adult? She liked to think that she had years left to make the decision about having kids, but most of the people from her class were nearly done with childrearing.

Claire drank both her coffee and her juice while reading a copy of the *Minor Mail-Tribune* someone had left behind at one of the tables. The paper was just sixteen pages, filled with local news (COUNTY FAIR TO OPEN WEDNESDAY), in addition to cartoons and a couple of stories from the wire services. Cindy's murder must have happened too late to make it into print, but judging by the paper's contents, it would be big news when it did. Minor didn't seem to have a lot of crime. The half-page FOR THE RECORD column was mostly taken up with notices of divorce filings and a few drunk-driving arrests. Claire wondered just how much experience Kyle really had in solving murders.

As she was leaving the dining room, Claire ran into a couple she vaguely remembered from high school. The pair had been inseparable from ninth grade on, constantly nagged by the hall monitors to eliminate their PDA—public displays of affection. Claire felt a little prick of surprise (or was it jealousy?) that after twenty-plus years together they still walked with their arms around each other, hips—a little bit more ample now—bumping companionably.

"How are you guys doing?"

"Awful!" said the woman. Her round face was happy and animated. What was her name? Sherry? Cherry? Sharee? "We just heard about what happened to Cindy. We'd already gone to bed when it happened, but imagine—a murder only a couple of hundred yards from where we were sleeping!"

The husband—Tim? Tom? Ted?—squeezed his wife's shoulder. Claire wondered now how she had recognized them. Seen closer to, they looked like fun-house mirror reflections of their old selves—wider, spread out, and even a little shorter. "The wife wants to leave, but I told her it's pretty obvious who did it."

"Who?" Claire asked.

"That husband of hers. Kevin Sanchez. Only he's a soon-to-be-ex-husband. We read about it in the *Mail-Tribune*. They filed for divorce six months ago."

Claire was surprised. "But he was here with her last night." Although maybe *with* wasn't the operative word. Cindy's husband had been seated off to one side, sipping his drink, eyes at half-mast, and face expressionless as he watched his wife work the room.

The woman snorted. "Cindy always had to make sure she had an audience. She must have found some way to talk him into coming. That way she could make a fool of herself doing those cheerleading routines"—she waved imaginary pom-poms in the air—"and still be sure there was at least one person to clap."

"If that was the reason he was here, he didn't look like he was playing along," Claire said.

"That's right," said the man. "Maybe they had an argument out in the parking lot about how she was acting. Or maybe she went out there to have a rendezvous with someone and then Kevin discovered them. I mean, it makes sense if he did it. Just look at all the people who get murdered. Nine times out of ten, it's the spouse." He and his wife exchanged a glance Claire couldn't interpret.

"Maybe you're right," Claire said, filing away the information for future reference. If Cindy's husband were the killer, then there was no need to worry that the heart-shaped box was a killer's calling card. "So what are you guys up to these days?

"We have a shared practice." Doctors? Claire wondered, and then rejected the idea. She couldn't see the two of them submitting to long hours of study about anything except the other. Dentists, then? Her internal musings were interrupted when he slipped a cream-colored card into her hand. "Here's our card. Well, we'll see you around later today, okay?"

Without waiting for an answer, he and his wife turned and walked away, as close as a pair of Siamese twins, steps perfectly matched. They would be a cinch to win the sack race. Claire remembered how self-absorbed they had been in high school. She realized they hadn't asked a single question about her own life. At least now she could find out their names. She looked down at the card in her hand. In flowing script, it read: "Cherie and Todd Walter, pet psychics. What is your beloved pet thinking? Learn what they want and need. Past-life regressions also available. Readings can be done in person, via photographs, or over the phone."

Claire wanted to throw the card away, but she was

afraid that the Walkers might see. Instead, it went in the waist pouch that held her Walkman. What kind of people hired a pet psychic? Claire wondered. Charlie's cat had died about five years before, and the older woman hadn't been able to bring herself to get a new one. But maybe Dante would like to invest in the Walkers' services for the two white kittens he had rescued from a dumpster. For all he knew, in a past life they had been worshipped by Egyptians, pampered by Marie Antoinette, shared tidbits of fried baloney with Elvis Presley. And to think that all of that might be revealed from a photograph.

Claire glanced at her watch before she reached out to open the door. Nearly eight o'clock. Stepping outside, she slipped on her sunglasses. The day was already warm. She started to tuck the buds of her headphones into her ears.

"Hey, Warty!"

Damn. How come everyone remembered a nickname she hadn't thought of for twenty years? She turned around. It was Jim, a mischievous grin splitting his face. His tanned face was definitely lived in, but still Claire felt her breath speed up. How could a man with wrinkles still be sexy? It wasn't fair. "Don't call me that," she said, but her voice came out more sultry than sulky, betraying her.

"How you doing this morning?" He gave her a little nod and a once-over that Claire couldn't help noticing. She hoped it wasn't too obvious that she was holding in her stomach and standing with her shoulders back. "I couldn't sleep last night, thinking about— you know— going out to that parking lot. But in my dreams, I always woke up right before we found her."

Behind him, the yellow-and-black crime-scene tape fluttered at the edge of the hotel's parking lot. Claire shivered. "Yeah. I won't pretend I liked Cindy, but it's hard to believe she's dead. I dreamed about it all night, too."

There was a pause while Jim turned to look over his shoulder at where they had found the body. "So, who do you think did it?"

"At least you're asking, instead of telling me it has to have been Logan. I couldn't believe the way everyone in the bar started acting like he must have done it."

"You and me—we've known Logan since grade school. Most of those other people didn't meet him until high school, so by the time they got to know him, he was already starting to go off the rails. Logan's no crazier than you or me now. Maybe even less." His smile was more a twitch of his lips, as if he was thinking of something that wasn't really funny. "Besides, a whole bunch of people didn't like Cindy. Then there were all the guys who were halfway in love with her, at least back then. Maybe someone followed her out to the parking lot hoping they could get a kiss for old time's sake, and she said no."

"That doesn't seem like much of a reason to kill someone," Claire objected. "Especially in such a—a personal way. It's not as though they stood ten feet away and shot her, just made one little mistake that they couldn't take back. But strangling? Somebody had to put their hands around her neck and squeeze for a long time. They had to have meant it."

"Well, at least we know it was a guy. That eliminates half the potential suspects."

This was Kyle's scenario, too, but Claire realized what

had been bothering her about it. "Why, because someone tried to rape her? Are you sure about that? Do you remember how Cindy looked when we found her? Her panties looked as if no one had touched them."

Jim looked away. "Well, maybe the guy shot his wad too soon or couldn't get it up."

"Or maybe someone just wanted to make it look like a rape. Which means a man or a woman could have done it."

"A girl wouldn't be that strong."

"A *woman*," Claire emphasized the word, correcting him, "a woman still might have done it. Women are stronger than they used to be. Where I work out, half the people lifting weights are women. And Cindy wasn't that big. I'm at least six inches taller than her. And she probably made more women angry at her than men. She didn't suck up to women as much. Cindy wanted attention and beautiful things and to be lusted after— and women weren't really in a position to give those to her."

"What about Belinda? She was Cindy's best friend."

"Yeah, right," Claire said. "She was Cindy's gofer. Cindy's sycophant. Somebody there to tell Cindy how great she looked. Somebody willing to trade being the most popular person in school's best friend in return for being treated like dirt. And for Cindy, Belinda was someone she didn't have to make sure she looked her best around. She knew Belinda would love her, no matter what. I'll bet Belinda saw the real Cindy more than anyone else ever did. But that doesn't mean that Cindy liked Belinda for anything more than what she could get out of her."

"So what are you saying? Do you think Belinda did

it? That she strangled Cindy and then pretended to have been the one to find her? Ran in to us crying crocodile tears and all the while she was the one who killed her?"

It was an interesting idea, and one that Claire hadn't thought of. "I'm not saying she's a natural-born killer. But what if she and Cindy had a fight and she ended up killing her accidentally? Then she would naturally be hysterical and upset."

Jim shook his head. "I can't believe Belinda would do that. Besides, Belinda didn't have any marks on her. I can't see how someone could do that and not have marks."

"Think of the way Cindy's throat looked, though. I think the person who did this stood behind her. Even if Cindy struggled, she might not have been able to reach whoever did this. The finger marks were on the front of her throat, not the back." Claire found it was less upsetting to keep thinking of Cindy this way, in pieces, reducing the memory of her body to a neck or a pair of untouched panties.

"But Belinda's not in the best shape, and Cindy certainly kept her figure." His expression was noncommittal.

"You're probably right," Claire admitted, "that it was a guy. Maybe one of the guys she slept with in high school. From what I hear, that would be half of the guys at Minor High." She watched Jim out of the corner of her eye, but his face betrayed nothing. Claire had always wondered if Jim had slept with Cindy a time or two. Cindy liked to take chances, to walk on the wild side. When the silence became uncomfortable, Claire changed the subject. "Are you going to tell me where you went last night?"

"I went home and checked up on my girls. They were

all sleeping and the house was locked up nice and tight. Sometimes they're not as careful about that as they should be. And what if there's some nut out there killing girls?"

Relief washed over Claire, followed quickly by annoyance. "Why didn't you tell me that in the first place? Why did you ask me to lie for you?"

"Don't you remember? It was just my luck that old Kyle decided my car was part of the crime scene. I had to"—he cleared his throat and looked away—"borrow someone's car. And I didn't exactly have permission."

Some things never changed, Claire thought, shaking her head. Jim slipped easily back and forth across the line between right and wrong, which for him wasn't a line at all, but a gray area a mile wide. "So how old are your kids again?"

"Nineteen, six, and four. The oldest is from my first marriage. The younger two are from my second."

Claire had noticed his bare left ring finger last night. "But you're not married anymore?"

With his eyes on the ground, Jim ran the back of his thumb across his mouth. "Last summer, she just woke up one morning and decided she didn't want to be married anymore. And she didn't want kids, either. She wanted to"—he hooked his fingers in quote marks—"see what she was missing. Live life while she still could."

"That must be hard."

"It's not easy. The oldest is in community college, but she does a lot for her sisters. I don't want to get her all worn out before she's even twenty, though." Jim looked as if he were going to say something more, but instead he patted Claire on the shoulder. "I'd better let you get going before it gets too hot out here. I can tell it's going to get pretty warm today. Driving an un-air-conditioned truck has at least taught me that much."

Claire thought she heard a note of sadness in his voice. A half-forgotten conversation floated through her head. Hadn't he once told her he wanted to be an astronaut? And now here he was, more than twenty years later, piloting a beer truck instead of a rocket ship. Nineteen seventy-nine had probably been about the last year that an unplanned pregnancy had led to a shotgun marriage. Nowadays no one cared. Nearly half the births were to single women, many teenagers, and it was only the girls—and their children—who were made to suffer for bad choices.

"It was good talking to you, Jim," she said, meaning it. "Maybe I'll see you around the amusement park later, okay?"

"Yeah. Catch you then. And be careful out here, okay? Don't go where you will be alone."

Claire wasn't worried. It was broad daylight, she wasn't drunk, and she couldn't think of one enemy—or frustrated would-be lover—she had in the world. "I'll keep safe." Jim surprised her by ducking in and depositing a quick kiss on her cheek. She inhaled in surprise, but he had already pushed open the swinging door and disappeared into the lobby.

ICUNIYQ

# Nineteen

Pressing the button on her Walkman, Claire began to run, accompanied by John Mellencamp singing about lost loves, lost lives, and lost chances. She had been a fan back in the days when the record company had tried dubbing him John Cougar. After only a hundred yards, she knew it was too hot. It was already over seventy degrees, and she didn't like to run when it was much warmer than that. Still, she kept on.

As she put one foot in front of the other, Claire thought about what the Walkers and Jim had told her. Could Kevin Sanchez have killed his wife? His anguish had been genuine, she was sure of that. If he was acting, he must be such a sociopath that even he didn't know the truth. But could it be that the genuine anger and grief he had felt at Cindy's death had really been directed at himself?

Over and over, Claire's thoughts kept returning to Cindy, not as she had been in life, but the parts of her that death had left behind. The loose spill of her breasts. The awkward angle of her tanned legs. The blood layered over her lipstick. Claire saw again the bruises that had encircled Cindy's neck, crosshatched by the raw furrows where she had clawed at her own throat while she slowly starved for air.

Why had someone killed Cindy? She had been casually cruel to so many—but would that cruelty have still hurt enough, twenty years later, to cause someone to put his or her hands around Cindy's throat and not stop squeezing no matter how much she struggled? And what did it mean that both Claire and Cindy—as well as nearly half a dozen other women—had gotten identical heart-shaped boxes with their photos in them? What did they have in common, other than that they had all graduated from Minor High the same year? The group of them hadn't been friends, hadn't even existed on the same social plane.

Were they all marked for death, as Jessica had initially feared? Was the heart shape of the box a private joke of a killer's? Claire tried to remember who had taken wood shop twenty years ago, who might still have the skill to carve two halves of a box so that they neatly matched up. The thought of the sharp tools that such a task must require caused a shiver to dance over her skin, despite the heat of the day. In some ways, the idea of a knife— slicing, stabbing, flesh parting before the silver shine of it—was more frightening than that of a gun.

Another runner crested a hill and ran toward her, a skinny man with long arms and legs. It was easy to see why he was thin, as he wasted so much energy in excess motion. Instead of pumping like efficient pistons, his arms flapped and flailed like broken-winged birds. The aviator sunglasses he wore threw her for a moment, but

Claire finally recognized who it was. Richard Crane, which was kind of a surprise. He hadn't been the athletic type in high school. Then again, neither had she. A second later she realized that was the first time she had thought of him as Richard first, not Dick.

They both paused as they came even with each other, jogging in place. Richard pushed his sunglasses to the top of his head, exposing his pale face and the dark circles under his eyes. He said something that she couldn't make out over John Mellencamp.

Claire pulled off her headphones. "Pardon?" Waves of warmth were radiating from him, and she took what she hoped was a subtle step back.

"You shouldn't be out here alone, Claire. Where's that guy you were with last night—your, um, husband?" His face reddened.

"Boyfriend. And he's still asleep."

"Then let me run with you. You know, just to be safe?"

The street was busy with cars, and Claire wanted to be alone with her thoughts. "That's okay. I'm being careful."

His face coloring even more, he looked away. "I didn't mean to be pushy." Richard was the kind of guy who didn't have a clue about people, Claire thought. He'd rather be tinkering with something mechanical. In high school it had been cameras and now it was computers.

"I don't know if I buy that Cindy's being killed has anything to do with those boxes we all got." While she was talking, Claire wiped the sweat off her forehead and then dried her palm on the bottom of her shirt. "Although I have found myself trying to remember which guys took wood shop in high school. You weren't one of them, were you?" Claire said it in a teasing way. Wood shop had been known as a great place to fashion your own bongs and pipes. The only people who had taken wood shop at Minor High had been the hoods, the goat-ropers, the ones destined to be mill rats. People like Jim, she remembered suddenly. When she looked up, Richard was shaking his head violently.

"What are you saying? I never took wood shop." He looked frightened.

"I was just teasing, Richard." She patted his sweaty forearm. "You seem as if you're still pretty upset about everything. How are you doing?"

He had stopped jogging and now his shoulders curled over, forming a little cave for his heart. "I can't stop thinking about Cindy. She was always so—alive. I mean, one minute she's showing me one of the new cheerleading routines." Claire had her own recollection of Cindy bouncing around in front of Richard, and she saw that his memories were probably more flattering. He hadn't seen the same Cindy that Claire had—drunk, wobbling, a little loud, trying desperately to get his attention now that he was one of the richest men in America. Obviously, she had succeeded. "And she just looked—great! And then less than an hour later to see her like that—." He waved one arm, his words trailing off, then swiped at his eyes. "Damn! Even the sweat-proof sunscreens still get in your eyes." He looked up at the merciless sky, his Adam's apple bobbing as he swallowed some emotion.

Richard had loved Cindy, Claire realized. Or thought he had. Twenty-year-old memories, carefully edited and lovingly hand-colored. "Hey, I've got to go before it gets too hot altogether, but I'll catch you later, okay? And I promise I'll be careful."

She managed to run the rest of the long access road

that led from the parking lot without anyone else wanting to talk to her, and then turned out onto the highway, the half-mile that separated Minor proper from Ye Olde Pioneer Village. The side of the road was made up of palm-sized smooth stones that skittered under her feet, so Claire ran just on the edge of the macadam, facing traffic. The occupants of the few beat-up cars and jacked-up trucks passing her stared openly, as if they had never seen a runner. Maybe they hadn't. After all, Minor wasn't Portland yet, despite the spillover from the city. Claire amused herself by looking for vanity plates. The HE WON plate on a nearly new Chevy Blazer hinted at a story. AMBER fell into the most common, and boring, category that Claire used to have pass across her desk—that of people's first names. Then she saw one that truly made her smile—a white VW Rabbit with a plate reading ML8ML8.

Her body had found its rhythm now, breathing easy, arms loose, legs scissoring past each other. She kept one eye out for groups of men in pickups and the other for the glint of broken beer bottles. Her heart leaped in her chest when a green Geo blew past, barely grudging Claire an inch. The woman driving it gave Claire the finger. After it passed she saw that it sported a bumper sticker reading, PRACTICE RANDOM ACTS OF KINDNESS AND SENSELESS BEAUTY.

Pumping her hot fists, she mouthed along with "What If I Came Knocking?" a song that asked a would-be lover if she would risk everything for a chance at love. It helped keep her mind off the too-stiff heel notch in her new Nikes that was chafing her left Achilles tendon.

She was in Minor proper now, although she didn't recognize anything. Nothing in this section was more than five years old. She tried to find a straight street to run along, but it was all curving cul-de-sacs lined with cookie cutter two-story houses in beiges and tans. "French colonials" no Frenchman would ever recognize, each dominated by a two- or even three-car garage. In Portland, the style was known as a "snout house," and had been recently banned by the city council.

The streets were Sunday morning quiet, even though it was only Saturday. A few people were out working in their gardens. Claire reached behind her and turned the music up a tick. Her legs settled into a fast, easy pace, and she felt the bodywide equivalent of a smile engulf her. Sometimes this happened when she was running. It was a wholly physical feeling that began and ended in her body. It didn't involve thought at all. You couldn't count on it or coax it, although it did help to be running downhill and listening to some favorite music. It was like the nonsexual equivalent of an orgasm. She'd never mentioned it to other runners. She'd read about runners who would get a blast of endorphins at the nineteenth mile of a marathon, but this feeling sometimes happened to her on the second mile of a five-mile run. If the secret ever got out, maybe there would be more runners.

She looped back onto the highway. Up ahead, she saw the neon signs for Ye Olde Pioneer Village. As she reached the end of the access road, Claire glanced right and left, checking for cars before she entered the acres of parking lot around the casino.

A red pickup stood alone on the outskirts of the parking lot. Something about it seemed out of place. She stopped to look closer. Her breath caught. What she saw threw her in a panic. Sprawled on the bench seat was the still form of Jessica McFarland, her head thrown back at an unnatural angle, her dress pushed up around her thighs. A thin edge of white showed at the edge of her eyes.

Claire found herself tiptoeing as she went closer, holding her breath as if someone could hear her, as if it would make a difference. She looked around, but she was all alone. She pulled off her headphones and turned off the music, her gaze never leaving the sight of her old friend's body.

So Jessica hadn't been paranoid after all.

HEBGBZ

Twenty

Claire wasn't aware she had made a sound until it reached her ears. The panic she heard in her own half-strangled sob notched up her fear at the sight of Jessica's broken body, graceless in death. Hearing herself made Claire realize this was real. Her arms prickled as the hair along them rose.

She and Jessica had been so close when they were twelve. Did she owe it to her dead friend to open the pickup door and check for a pulse, see how cold Jessica's body was? Or would she only replace whatever fingerprints the killer might have left at the scene with her own?

While Claire was still debating what to do, Jessica's white hand rose slowly in the air, then dropped to her face and rubbed her still half-open eyes.

Claire jumped back with a little shriek.

Jessica's own screech echoed Claire's. She pushed herself into a sitting position, her face washing scarlet.

The window was open two inches, and now she rolled it down the rest of the way. "Oh, God, where am I?" Her voice was a brittle rasp.

"In a truck in the parking lot," Claire answered. Jessica still looked blank. Had someone drugged her and left her here to die? Claire elaborated. "You're at the Minor High twentieth reunion. Specifically, you're in the parking lot for Ye Olde Pioneer Village." Still shivering, Claire crossed her arms. "I thought you were dead. You were lying all crooked with your eyes half-open."

Jessica scrubbed her face with her hands. "Just dead to the world. And the eye thing is the price I have to pay for having such big ones. It used to drive my college roommate crazy." She batted her lashes at Claire.

"Did you spend the night out here?" Jessica's silence was answer enough. Claire took a step back and looked at the pickup. "Whose truck is this, anyway?"

"I'd rather not say." Jessica's tone was less controlled than her words. She sounded pleased with herself. Unlocking the door, she opened it and hopped out, pulling her denim miniskirt down into place as she did so.

"You were making out in a car all night? What's the matter with going into the hotel? At least it's got nice soft beds and privacy."

"And no gear shift," Jessica added. Her lips curved up into a private smile. "You've got to understand that what happened last night —finding Cindy's body—was a shock to the system. I mean, seeing someone dead! Touching them with your own hands." She spread her hands, with their French-manicured nails, in front of her and regarded them as if they didn't belong to her. "It's—it's primal. Something you feel deep in your gut—and you react from your gut. At first we came out here just to talk about Cindy, about how we felt. And then one thing led to another. We both forgot about who we were in high school, and just remembered who we are now. A man and a woman. Alone together."

Jessica looked past Claire, at the horizon, as if she beheld a vision. "After seeing death, well, I think anyone is entitled to go a little crazy. Cindy was young and beautiful, but that didn't stop her from dying. It makes you realize how fleeting life is. And then you find yourself clutching at life." Her gaze dropped back to Claire. "Plus he talked the bartender into selling him a bottle of Wild Turkey to go. Seeing how this was an emergency and all." Jessica seemed to be perking up. Her face was animated, her eyes alight with the thought of how naughty she had been. How many times had Claire seen the same expression on her face in high school? Jessica's self-esteem had always been found in a man's arms. She had slept with the rich-boy sons of doctors and lawyers, the ones who owned brand-new convertibles, the ones who skied competitively or who had, at seventeen, already traveled extensively through Europe. Claire guessed that this latest conquest had also been a member of Minor's ruling class. Twenty years ago, Claire had gotten a vicarious thrill hearing about Jessica's conquests. Now she just wondered when Jessica would grow up.

"So you end up making out in a car in a parking lot? Right next to a hotel that's full of soft beds with clean sheets?" Jessica was silent, so Claire filled in the explanation herself. Her latest conquest must have had a wife waiting for him in one of those beds. "And your Romeo leaves you sound asleep in a car when there's a murderer on the loose?"

Jessica looked away. She spoke to the shimmering asphalt. "I must have fallen asleep and he didn't want to wake me. We watched the sun come up, so it's not like he left me alone in the dark. And he locked the doors before he left. Besides, he was sure that the person who killed Cindy did it because it was Cindy, not because they were a homicidal maniac. "

"But it's hot in there. Hasn't he read those stories about kids dying in locked cars in the summer?"

Jessica shot Claire a sullen look, the same one she was prone to giving Claire twenty-plus years ago, whenever Claire pointed out that sleeping with someone didn't necessarily mean he would talk to you in the daytime. "He cracked the windows, didn't he?" She tugged her fingers through her hair, the side of her mouth pulled upward by a personal smile. "There's one good thing about being thirty-eight. I don't have to worry about being grounded." She tilted her head as she looked at something past Claire's shoulder. "Hey—what's going on?"

Claire turned. A small crowd had gathered in front of the hotel, next to a black-and-white police car. The lights were flashing, but the siren was off.

"Let's go see what's up," Jessica said. They walked across the parking lot and joined the crowd.

"What's going on?" Claire asked the man standing next to her.

He didn't take his eyes off the main door. "I hear they got him."

"Got who?" she said, but just then Kyle shouldered open the door. Ahead of him he pushed a handcuffed Hispanic man. The other man was short and young and slender, with dusky skin and black straight hair that looked as if he trimmed it himself. He was dressed like a dishwasher or a busboy, in black polyester pants and a white shirt topped with a grimy white apron. His eyes were wide and confused, and he seemed to be talking to himself. "No. *Madre de Dios! No maté a nadie!*"

Claire understood a few of the words, courtesy of her *Let's Learn Spanish!* tape that she had listened to a few times and then had shoved in her glove compartment and never taken out again, another self-improvement scheme abandoned. *No! Mother of God! I didn't kill anybody!*

He tried his English out now, appealing to the crowd, which watched him silently, avidly. "I didn't kill no womens!"

Everyone turned at the sound of screeching tires. A black Mercedes SUV raced through the parking lot straight toward where they were gathered. The door was flung open even before it came to a halt. Kevin jumped out and ran toward Kyle and his prisoner, so single-minded that he didn't even bother to close his door or take his keys from the ignition. Behind him, the car beeped impotently. Kevin's hands were balled into fists, his face a mask of anger, his lips pulled back in a snarl. Before Kyle or the police officer following him could re-act, Kevin launched himself at the man being arrested for the murder of his wife.

His fist caught the smaller man on the side of the head. The dishwasher would have fallen if Kyle hadn't kept him upright by yanking on his handcuffs. The other cop started forward, hand resting on the butt of his gun, but he was too slow. Kevin was already raining a flurry of blows down on the prisoner's face. Bright red blood splattered the man's stained apron and Kevin's white polo shirt, first spurting from the smaller man's nose and then from a seam that Kevin opened up on his cheek.

The crowd was stunned into silence, so that Claire

could hear the sound of every punch landing, the grunts each of the two men made as the blows were given and received, even the drops of blood falling like rain on the sidewalk. Only a few seconds had elapsed, but the Hispanic man seemed on the verge of unconsciousness. His head lolled, whipped back and forth with every punch.

A shriek cut through the awful sounds, and Belinda ran out the front door of the hotel. She wore only a white terrycloth bathrobe, and her feet were bare. Her eyes were like two holes burned in a blanket, and her hair was an uncombed mess. She stopped a few feet away and reached her arms out, imploring.

"No, Kevvie! No! This won't bring her back."

With his left hand, Kevin made a shooing motion, as if Belinda were a pesky fly. With the other hand, he landed another blow, this one to the dishwasher's ribs. Claire thought she heard a muffled snapping sound.

Finally realizing he was hurting more than he was helping, Kyle let go of his prisoner, who fell to his knees and then sideways onto the sidewalk. His head made a sickening, hollow thunk. Kevin paused for a moment, his hands fisted, one foot raised, torn between punching or kicking. In that moment, Kyle took two quick steps around the fallen man and grabbed Kevin in a bear hug. Off-balance, the two men staggered together. Meanwhile, Kyle's sidekick had drawn his gun. Now he held it out before him in a two-handed grip. First he pointed it at the prisoner, but he was still, except for a thin stream of crimson blood beginning to wind down the sidewalk. Then he focused it on the two struggling men.

"Halt!" he yelled out. "Halt or I'll shoot!"

At first, his words had no effect, but when he repeated his threat, Kevin sagged, his arms still draped around Kyle's shoulders so that they resembled a pair of drunken dancers.

"Belinda's right, man. This won't solve anything," Kyle said. His words were soft, pitched for Kevin's ears, but the crowd was still hushed, so everyone heard them.

"But he killed her! He killed her!" Kevin's voice was more of a moan than a shout. His eyes were so wide the whites showed all the way around, and his mouth was pulled down at the corners, a rictus of sorrow and anger. "He killed my wife."

"But you killing him won't solve anything. Think of your daughter. She needs her father with her, not in jail for the next thirty years."

Kevin stepped back from Kyle and put his face in his hands. Just before he hid it from view, Claire thought she saw a strange, uncertain expression cross Kevin's face.

Kyle seemed at a loss as to what to do. His gaze went back and forth from his prisoner to his prisoner's attacker. "I'm afraid I'm going to have to arrest you," he finally said, but his words were weak and unconvincing. There was a murmur from the crowd. "I'll ask the judge to go easy on the bail, though. What man wouldn't go temporarily insane in a case like this?" He turned to the younger policeman. "Mike, take him on back to the police station. I'll stay here and wait for the ambulance." Mike opened the back door of the squad car, and an un-handcuffed Kevin got in without even a backward glance for the man who lay, barely breathing, on the sidewalk.

Kyle turned to wave his arm at the two dozen stunned spectators who had watched the savage attack in silence. "And the rest of you—show's over, folks!

Break it up and get out of here!" Now that it was too late, Claire found herself wishing that she had intervened, found a way to stop the lightning-quick blows before they had done so much damage. When no one moved, Kyle's face began to redden and he yelled even louder, "Go on, get out! Now!" Everyone finally started to walk quietly toward the hotel's brass doors as the police car left the parking lot.

Her gaze on the fallen man, Claire remained behind. Two years before, she had taken a one-day first-aid class at the Red Cross. Her half-remembered encounter with a rubber Resusci-Annie doll hadn't prepared her for a much messier reality. On the other hand, she was afraid this guy was going to bleed to death on the sidewalk. Kyle was calling for an ambulance on his cell phone, but would it come in time? Fleetingly thankful that her sports bra was black and sturdy enough to pass for a top, Claire pulled her T-shirt over her head and knelt down. Beneath her knees, the concrete was slick with warm blood.

Looking at the man's swollen, bloody face, she tried to remember her first-aid training. She had a vague memory of the instructor writing down the letters A, B, C, and saying that they were the first priority. Only what did the letters stand for? Airway, bleeding, cardiac? Alimentary, brachial, cuticle? Even if the first three didn't sound quite right, she decided they were close enough.

Airway. Even though the man's breaths sounded labored and somehow gravelly, at least he was breathing. And if he was breathing, she figured his heart must still be beating, so that meant she didn't have to worry about the C word. That left bleeding. Turning her attention to the numerous cuts Kevin had opened on the man's face,

Claire dabbed at them tentatively with her T-shirt, trying to decide which needed the most attention.

Only a few seconds had passed, but it felt like hours. Time fell into place again when Rachel Munroe burst out of the hotel's doors. She was dressed in a damp T-shirt and shorts, and her hair was still in wet curls from the shower. As she shouldered open the door, she was reaching into a satchel, and now she tossed Claire a pair of pale vinyl gloves while slipping on another pair.

"Take off his handcuffs!" Rachel commanded Kyle, while her fingers felt the fallen man's pulse. Her tone was such that Kyle sprang into action without question. While he fumbled with a set of keys, Rachel ran her hands lightly over the man's body, stopping every now and then to probe. "Have you called an ambulance?" When Kyle nodded, she barked, "Then get me a blanket. He's going into shock." Finally, she turned to Claire while she straightened the man out so that he now lay face up on the sidewalk. "I need you to hold his feet on your lap. I want whatever blood he has left to go flowing back to his brain and heart." Claire quickly complied.

"Would you mind telling me how you let this happen?" Rachel demanded of Kyle, who had returned with a gray blanket. "How could you let someone attack a defenseless man?" Her voice was surprisingly low and powerful, given her fine-boned, diminutive frame. "Right now I can tell you that at a minimum he's got a broken nose, a fractured cheekbone, possibly a skull fracture, three or four cracked ribs, and I wouldn't be surprised if his hearing's been damaged. And you just stood back and let it happen."

"Hey, this jerk killed Cindy," Kyle answered, stung. "Why don't you spare some worry for how she died?"

"What makes you so sure he did it?" Rachel asked. "This is America, you know. Ever hear of innocent until proven guilty?"

"Someone tried to use Cindy's ATM card about two last night." With his index finger and thumb, Kyle rubbed his red-rimmed eyes. "I guess I mean this morning. On the surveillance camera, you can see a man spread all her ID out on the little metal ledge and start systematically going through the numbers he found on different things. According to the computer, he tried punching in her birthday, the first four digits of her Social Security number, her street address, etc. All the usual things people use for their PINs. Until finally the ATM swallowed the card. And this guy, this Juan de Jesus, matches the pictures we got from the bank's camera. The night manager says Juan"— Kyle exaggerated the "whaw" sound in Juan—"was out in the parking lot taking a smoke break about the time the medical examiner thinks Cindy died. He must have seen Cindy weaving out to her car, fishing around in her purse for her keys. Maybe she even took her wallet out. And the sight of this nice-looking lady, drunk, holding a wallet full of money, well, that's just too much for this mope. He's a wetback who's only been in this country for a month or so. Maybe once he found that the streets aren't really paved with gold out here, he decided to take matters into his own hands."

Rachel shook her head and didn't answer. Instead, she began to lay gauze over the worst of the cuts, only an inch long but deep and still pulsing blood. "Whatever he did, he didn't deserve this. And no matter how good they sew him up, he's going to be left with a nasty scar right here over his eyebrow. It's kind of ironic in a way," she added, putting down another layer of gauze that was immediately soaked through. "I'd say this cut was probably made by Kevin's wedding ring."

Twenty-one

Clutching her once-white T-shirt, now heavy with blood, Claire made her way to their room, glad that the hotel corridor was empty. She tensed when a door opened farther down the hall. At first she thought it was Belinda, but then she realized it was Belinda's daughter. The girl went the other way. Claire took her room card key from her back pocket and slipped it in the slot. Dante was gone. On the bed, the sheets were pulled up, and when she went in the bathroom, a damp towel hung neatly on the rod. That was one of the little things Claire liked about Dante, that he always tried to minimize the work of the waitress or hotel maid.

A note propped on her pillow told Claire to meet Dante in the dining room. Filling the sink with cold water, she put her T-shirt in to soak. Scarlet billowed in the water, so much that the whole sink soon seemed as if it were filled with undiluted blood. Claire's empty stomach convulsed at the sight. She swallowed hard. Her whole body was trembling, shaking with the need for food, sleep, and at least a few hours without the sight of bodies, real or imagined.

She took a quick shower, averting her eyes from the sink when she pulled back the curtain. After dressing in tan cargo shorts, Birkenstocks, and a scoop-necked white T-shirt, Claire went back to the Feed Trough.

At first she looked for Dante by scanning the now nearly full room for a dark-haired man eating alone. She finally spotted him at a table with three other people. Claire blinked. Twenty years ago, no one would have imagined Tomisue Borders and Alex Fogel sharing a table together. Tomisue had been the daughter of a mill rat, and even at fourteen she had possessed a reputation, breasts of startling proportions, and tiny blue eyes raccooned with mascara. Alex had been a star athlete, equally good at football, basketball, and baseball— enough to guarantee his popularity at Minor.

It was more than likely that the two of them had never spoken in high school, but now they seemed to be having a good time. Looking well-fed and somehow sleek, Alex was dressed in an expensive golf shirt and slacks. A huge diamond ring glittered on his pinkie. Tomisue sat next to a man who was clearly with her, since they looked like a matching set, both blond and denim clad. While Claire watched, a smiling Tomisue said something to Alex, shaking her exaggerated mane of blond hair, teased tawny curls streaked with platinum. She lightly punched Alex's shoulder, which just made everyone laugh harder.

Tomisue pushed her chair back and went to the buffet line, passing by Claire without noticing her. Her petite frame was balanced on high-heeled cowboy boots, and from the aroma that accompanied her it was easy to guess that the only reason she fit in her tiny jeans was that she chain-smoked three packs a day.

"Good morning," Claire said as she pulled out the empty chair beside Dante. Everyone said hello back, including Tomisue's companion. His collar-length hair was blond, too, and also dyed, although not as aggressively. His denim shirt was open to the nipple line, and he wore a gold pendant.

"I'll give you the rundown," Dante said, "and spare you the trouble of asking. Alex here," Alex inclined his head with exaggerated graciousness, "is currently managing a golf club in Phoenix. And Tomisue"—she smiled as she sat down, her plate stacked high with pancakes—"is a checker at that Safeway store we passed on the way here. And next to Tomisue is her husband, who's a welder. His name used to be Tommy, which caused some confusion, but now it's the New K103 FM. The New K103 FM, I'd like you to meet Claire Montrose."

"What?" Claire thought she had been following the conversation, but clearly she had been wrong.

The New K103 FM spoke around a mouthful of quiche. "It was a contest. I changed my name for Super Bowl tickets."

"Ticket," Tomisue corrected him. "You won one ticket. We still had to pay for my ticket and the airfare."

"And you had to keep the name?" Claire asked. "Even after the contest was over?"

He shrugged. "It was part of the contract I had to sign to get the tickets." Tomisue tossed him a look. "Ticket. But everyone always remembers me now. That didn't used to happen before."

"What do people call you for short?" Claire asked.

"Mostly 'K.' Or the K-man. Or if they forget my

name, they call me 'Super Bowl guy' or 'radio station guy.'"

Claire sneaked an embarrassed glance at Dante, but he didn't look as if he thought these people were weird. And, she guessed, they weren't any weirder than the people he knew in New York. After all, was it any stranger to christen yourself after a radio station than it was after an insect? Dante's friend Ant had done just that, and, ever since, the CD from Ant's band Muck had been on the Billboard Top 100.

"You just missed the meeting," Dante said. "They took a vote to see if people wanted to cancel the reunion."

"And what was the result?" Claire asked.

"It's still on," Alex said. "A lot of us didn't fly back here just to turn around and fly home again. Besides, if Cindy were here, she would want us to do it. She always liked a party." Tomisue and her husband nodded solemnly.

"I told Dante that I saw you out there with Rachel Munroe," Tomisue said. "Helping that guy that killed Cindy. Is he gonna live?"

Dante touched her hand under the table. He quirked an eyebrow at her, and she could tell he was concerned with how she was feeling, seeing so much violence in less than twelve hours.

"I don't know. He's unconscious. Rachel was mostly worried that he might have some kind of head injury."

"Cindy's husband clocked him pretty hard," the New K103 FM said.

"I think I'm glad I wasn't there to see it," Dante said. He turned to Claire. "When Tomisue told me what happened, I went back and tried to find you, but everyone was already gone. You doing okay?"

Claire gave a shrug. She didn't know how she was feeling.

After an exaggerated scan of the room, Alex leaned forward. In a low voice, he said, "I was kind of surprised to see who they arrested."

"Then who did you think did it?" Tomisue asked.

Claire could tell that Alex was the kind of guy who liked to gossip, all winks and suggestive nods. Had she known that about him in high school? Had she ever talked to him in high school?

"Well, Wade was pretty mad at Cindy back when she broke up with him."

Claire stated the obvious. "But that was twenty years ago."

"Yeah, but a couple of people told me that they saw him and her fighting last night, not that long before she was killed," Alex said, ticking his index finger. "Then a little while later I happened to be looking for Wade, and I couldn't find him. Wherever he was, he wasn't in the Hoe-Down Room." Now his middle finger joined his index. "And about ten minutes later I went into the bathroom and someone was in the handicap stall, choking and moaning. And you know what I saw when I looked under the door?" Around the table, heads shook or shoulders shrugged. "Cole-Haan tasseled loafers."

"So?" The New K103 FM asked.

"So! Those are the same kind Wade was wearing last night. I noticed them because I've got a pair just like them at home in my closet."

"But what was he doing?" Tomisue wrinkled her nose.

"Before this guy got arrested, I was thinking maybe Wade argued with Cindy, accidentally killed her, and then got sick. See, if we won a game, he used to swagger around afterwards. But if we lost, he would hide in the bathroom, puking his guts out—and making noises just like that."

Tomisue shook her head. "I had my money on that guy, Logan." She must have caught the look on Claire's face. "Of course now I know that isn't what happened."

Claire's stomach growled loud enough that everyone could hear it. "Excuse me. I'd better go feed the beast."

Tomisue cocked her head. "You mean you're pregnant?"

Claire felt herself flush to her hairline. The curse of the fair-skinned. "No, no. I just meant my stomach was empty." The smells of eggs, potatoes, and Sterno mingled as she waited her turn for the breakfast buffet. Tomisue's question made her pay more attention to the children in the room than she normally would have. Her classmates all seemed to have offspring of one kind or another—from kids who were on the verge of graduating high school themselves to babes in arms. A woman sitting in a corner of the room, the wife of a guy Claire vaguely remembered from her history class, was lumpily pregnant. In Minor, though, the pregnant woman was in a definite minority. People tended to have their kids young.

If it weren't for Susan Sarandon and the fact that Claire's new Ob/Gyn had confided that she had had both her kids after she turned thirty-five, Claire would have felt depressed as she looked at the evidence of her classmates' fecundity. It was one thing to be a late bloomer and it was another to wither on the vine.

As Claire was walking back to her table, someone called her name. It was Rachel, damp again from another shower, her hair a mass of black-and-silver springy tendrils.

"I'd like you to meet my husband, Chad. He's a pediatrician, too. We're in practice together." Chad, a man with short, dark receding hair, half-stood to take her hand in a firm grip. "And these are my kids, Jeremy and Melanie." The kids, Claire guessed, were about five and seven, with bright blond hair that matched neither of their parents'. Rachel smiled at her children, then turned her attention to Claire. Her face wore what Claire imagined was the assessing gaze of a physician. "I wanted to see how you were feeling after what happened this morning—and what happened last night."

"All right, I guess. The whole thing just doesn't seem real. None of it. Not finding Cindy, and not seeing her husband beat that guy up."

"I appreciated that you were there to help this morning. Everyone else was ready to let that guy die."

Claire shrugged, feeling she had been little more than a pair of gloved hands to hold various bandages as Rachel taped them into place while they waited for the ambulance. After it had screamed off with the still unconscious Juan de Jesus, Rachel had made sure that Claire washed her hands and even her knees with soap and hot water. Then she had examined them closely, looking for the tiniest cut or scrape that might have exposed Claire to HIV if the dishwasher carried it. Claire didn't know who had been more relieved to find that her skin was unbroken—she or Rachel.

Claire realized that Rachel might know the answer to a question she had been considering since the night before. "Since you work with kids, I was wondering if you see many with schizophrenia. Isn't that when you get it—when you're a teenager?"

Rachel nodded. "Probably all pediatricians follow a certain number of patients with schizophrenia. You're thinking of Logan, aren't you? I heard everyone was talking about him last night. The high-risk years are fifteen to twenty-five. They used to blame it on parenting—especially the mother. They called them 'refrigerator mothers.' Now we know it's genetic. To be schizophrenic is to be terribly isolated. I wish I had had more understanding back when we were in school. Instead, like everyone else, I avoided Logan."

Again, Claire found herself wishing that she had done more for Logan, not let him slip from the grasp of friendship. "People last night were ready to blame Logan for Cindy's death. Do you think he could be violent?"

Rachel shook her head. "Very few schizophrenics are violent—only about 4 percent. Those are the ones you hear about, but that's one reason you hear about those incidents—because they are so unusual." Looking thoughtful, she added, "However, if drugs or alcohol are involved, then the probability of violence skyrockets." Claire wondered if Rachel had remembered the squat glass in Logan's hand the night before, complete with a slice of lime. "For the most part, though, it's not that schizophrenics are a danger to others, it's that they are a danger to themselves. For some reason, most of their hallucinations ridicule them, put them down, frighten them."

Claire nodded. "I remember once when I was with him and he was yelling out that he wasn't ugly, wasn't stupid. It didn't matter how much you argued with him—he still heard that. It must have been so hard to have those voices always battering at him."

Chad had been listening intently. Now he leaned forward. "At the same time, to be schizophrenic is to have a strange sort of power. Some of my patients tell me that schizophrenia makes you feel special. Everywhere you go, people are talking about you. You turn on David Letterman, he's talking about you. You go to the shopping mall and someone's on the loudspeaker, talking about you. Sure, they are hallucinations. But they feel real. Some people find they can't give that specialness up. In some ways, it's kind of hard to settle for ordinary life where no one is talking about you, where you're not powerful, not special."

Claire thought of Logan's new life—friendless, working at Arby's surrounded by coworkers who could have been his children. Was there enough in this life to keep him from returning to his old one? "Logan did say something about missing the voices. He said it was hard to get used to them being gone."

Rachel nodded. "That's one reason people stop taking their meds. Another is the side effects. We just got this new class of drugs, but before that people were really zoned. I noticed Logan still has trouble with lip smacking. The scientific name is tardive dyskinesia. That's probably left over from the old meds."

"But he's on the new ones," Claire objected.

"We've found that some people still have the old side effects even after they change meds." She looked at her children, then dropped her voice so that they couldn't hear. "Sometimes when I look at them, I find myself praying that nothing will go wrong inside them."

As Claire took her leave, she thought that must be

one of the unwanted gifts of becoming a doctor—a familiarity with all the ways your body could betray you. When she got back to her table, Claire found that her scrambled eggs and pancakes, never that hot to begin with, were now cool. She ate them anyway, while Dante watched with an amused smile. Sometimes he teased her, telling her she had an appetite like a trucker's. Maybe if Claire had learned how to do the "girl" things, learned how to push away a half-eaten salad, learned how to pick at the main course and refuse the dessert, she wouldn't need to run to keep her figure. But she would rather eat what she wanted and exercise, if the alternative were going through life without tasting, without savoring, without sweating. In fact, Claire decided, she deserved a cinnamon roll. She asked Dante if he wanted one, but he waved her off with a laugh.

Jessica joined her at the buffet line. She raised one eyebrow. "So, what did you make of all that 'Kevvie' stuff?"

"You mean what Belinda said? But they've known each other for probably twenty years."

"We've both known lots of people twenty years. But would you call any guy named Kevin "Kevvie" unless your relationship involved something more along the lines of 'knowing' in the Biblical sense? Besides, I happened to see them out in the hall last night, and they looked like they had been kissing."

"You're kidding!" This did put a whole new light on things.

"And there's something else to consider. What happened was pretty convenient, don't you think?"

"What are you talking about?" Claire asked. "Convenient for who?"

"They arrest a guy who swears he's innocent, and the

first thing that happens is that someone beats him unconscious. He's certainly not doing any talking now. Do you think that could be because Cindy's husband didn't want anyone to hear what the guy had to say?"

MR E

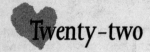

Twenty-two

"What's next on the agenda?" Dante asked with a lazy grin. He bunched the pillow under his head. After breakfast, they had returned to their room, where Dante had given Claire a long, comforting hug. One thing had led to another—and after that to a much-needed hour-long nap.

"Hmm?" Claire answered absently. Wearing only a pair of panties, she sat on a chair and paged through the annual, trying to put old names and faces together with the people she had seen the night before or at breakfast earlier. More and more names were coming back to her, even if they were now connected with people who bore very little resemblance to the teenagers she remembered.

"I asked what we were supposed to do next."

Claire looked up from the rows of painfully young faces. "We're supposed to hang out at the amusement park—and there's also a picnic and picnic-type games. It should be pretty low-key, at least until this evening."

"After what's happened already, anything would be low-key," Dante said. "Why are you looking at your annual?"

"I'm still trying to figure out why some of us got those boxes. We didn't run in the same circles, we didn't have the same friends, and we certainly weren't all friends."

"Same hobbies or after-school activities?"

"No. I worked after school, and the rest did everything from ride horses to grow pot in the basement."

"Did you all have one class in common?"

"No. I probably was in one class with each one of those women, but we weren't all together in any class that I can remember." Claire thought of something else. "Although maybe that doesn't matter. Maybe it's not that we all took the same class—maybe it's that somebody took classes with each of us."

"You certainly don't look much alike."

"Not now. But maybe we did then." Claire had marked the relevant pages with the free postcards the hotel provided, and now she got back on the bed and showed him her picture, as well as those for Cindy, Jessica, Nina, Becca, Jill, and Maria.

Dante slid the annual closer to him on the bed and turned it around. Again, Claire looked at the relevant photos as, one by one, he considered them. Maybe superficially there had been a certain look to them. Or maybe they had looked the way all young people look—slightly unfinished, open to the world.

"The hair," Dante finally said. "You all had hair in the lighter half of the spectrum. Even that Maria's hair is a light brown. And it's all longish, with these curled-up bangs.

"I guess we did have pretty much the same haircut. There were only about three places to get your hair cut in Minor, so we might even have had the same hairdresser. I think that haircut was supposed to look like Farah Fawcett's in *Charlie's Angels*. It always took a while for fads to catch on in Minor. They are probably just now discovering those women's suits with big padded shoulders." Claire kept her voice light, but inside she felt a roll of nausea as she suddenly remembered Ted Bundy's victims, close enough in looks to pass for sisters. What if Juan de Jesus wasn't the real killer? What if Cindy had been murdered by a serial killer who telegraphed his intentions beforehand? Didn't serial killers go after a certain type and then keep killing and killing and killing? She shook her head, but she couldn't shake the thought away.

Dante continued to page through the annual, stopping when he came to the photos of the prom. "So who did you go with to the prom?" He must have seen her face tighten. "Or did you go?"

"No. I went. With Logan. Neither of us had any real prospects of a date. We were both kind of on the edges of Minor. I was too tall, too skinny, and too smart. And he was just too weird. He brought me this huge orchid wrist corsage. I still remember how strong it smelled every time we danced a slow dance. And when we slow-danced, we were careful not to let our bodies touch very much. We'd always just been buddies, and that was the reason we went together. It was like a pact. If you can't find anyone else to go with, we can go together. I think we were both taken aback a little bit to see the other person all dressed up, looking like a grown-up. We were pretty self-conscious."

"And was he, you know—normal that night?"

"For the dance he was. Then later, we went to this party at someone's house whose parents were out of town. Everyone was drunk off their butts on this stuff they called bug juice. You take a new plastic garbage can and fill it with Kool-Aid and whatever alcohol people can steal from their parents' liquor cabinets. The result pretty much takes off the back of your head. It's a miracle none of us ended up in the emergency room for alcohol poisoning. But it did change Logan. He got angry, crazy angry, and started fighting with some other boy. I tried to stop it, but he wouldn't listen to me. He was shouting out, I guess at the voices."

Claire still remembered that night clearly. The two young men had fought in the unlit backyard, scuffling in the darkness, the stars flung too far overhead to give off any light. When someone told her what was happening, she ran outside to try to stop it, her feet slipping in the grass where someone had vomited. Growling at Claire like a rabid dog, Logan had shaken off her arm and then returned to his fight. The ring of onlookers had watched silently, made sullen and immobile by drink. She could still hear the sounds of that night — grunts, the smacking sound of flesh on flesh, and all the while Logan shouting out that he wasn't stupid, wasn't bad, while the other boy mocked him, echoing everything he said—"I'm not stupid!" "You *are* stupid!" Not caring that Logan wasn't reacting to anything that existed in the temporal world.

"Is this the photo that was in Cindy's box?" Dante asked.

"Yes," Claire agreed, glad of the interruption of her thoughts.

"Who was she dancing with?"

"Wade. They didn't break up until just before we graduated."

"But this can't be Wade," Dante said. "That Wade guy's blond. And whoever Cindy is dancing with in this picture is brunette."

2N2R4

Twenty-three

Once they were in the amusement park, Claire didn't have time to wonder who Cindy had been photographed with at the prom. She couldn't walk more than a few feet without people she barely remembered running up to her with a squeal, then throwing their arms around her and hugging her tight. Around her, the same scene was repeated dozens of times, as a kind of giddiness infected the reunited graduates of Minor High. Glad cries of reunion mingled with the cries of the barkers touting three throws for only a dollar. People smiled for no reason and laughed at the slightest excuse. They had survived a brush with death and lived to tell the tale.

Overhead, the delighted screams of riders being whipped through the air only highlighted how lucky they all were to be alive and able to scream for the pleasure of it. Their kids were out in full force, which added to the energy. A few had even managed to coax their parents into trying out the roller coaster, with its double loop.

As she looked at the amusement park rides, Claire guessed it had been impossible to find many that fit the pioneer theme. Oh, sure, there was a little kids' ride where toddlers sat in plastic hollowed-out logs that floated slowly through a trough filled with six inches of scummy water. But most of the rest was the same kind of set-up you could see at any traveling carnival passing through a small town—bumper cars, a Ferris wheel, a ride called the Egg Beater that whirled madly through the air trailing screams. The rides were either meant for toddlers who were happy to go slowly in circles, or for teenagers whose bodies had not yet learned the meaning of the term "motion sickness."

As she took in the ride operators, Claire wondered why Kyle hadn't begun his questioning here. The scrawny, weathered carnies all had the furtive look of ex-cons. Smoking pinched-down hand-rolled cigarettes, they wore faded jeans and blue polyester short-sleeved shirts that exposed the tattoos on their wrinkled arms. And that was just the women.

Claire had planned on avoiding the rides, but when she turned around to say so to Dante, he was already coming back from the ticket booth with two green-colored wrist bands in his hand.

"Whole place is free to Minor graduates and their guests," he told her, grinning as he slipped the band over her hand. "So what do you want to go on first?"

Claire didn't like heights and she didn't like speed and she didn't like knowing someone else was at the controls. Although this pretty much ruled out her enjoying any amusement park ride, she also didn't want to admit her fears to Dante. Finally, she picked what looked like the safest of the rides—the haunted coal mine. They climbed into a seat designed to resemble a coal car and with a lurch they were in darkness. Dante took advantage of the absence of light to sneak in a kiss or two, so Claire missed seeing most of the leaping plastic skeletons and the wailing white-sheeted ghosts. When the car jerked back into the sunlight again, they broke apart. Next they rode the Ferris wheel. Claire endeavored to hide how the sway of the gondola holding them made her stomach lurch. She tried to keep her eyes closed, but Dante wanted her to point out as many Minor landmarks as she recognized. But the old Minor that Claire remembered seemed to be gone, swallowed up by subdivision after subdivision of pale-colored, two-story houses.

Dante's next choice was the Round-Up, a contraption shaped like a giant metal wheel that held people in place by centrifugal force. Claire passed on his invitation, telling him to meet her in the picnic area. Over the picnic tables a big banner reading WELCOME MINOR HIGH CLASS OF '79! drooped in the heat. A buffet offered potato and macaroni salads (both the same unnatural shade of bright yellow), as well as corn on the cob, plasticky-looking dinner rolls, and pale slices of watermelon. Circling a grill the size of a garage door, a teenager wearing a paper chef's hat flipped burgers and hot dogs.

The enervating heat pressed down on Claire. The effect was like going up into the attic and having someone drop a heavy quilt over your head. She sat down at a picnic table. Drooping a little, she realized just how tired she was. Instead of attending the afternoon pool party, she decided she would take another nap, even longer than the one she had taken in the morning.

"Hey, there, Claire. I hear you're like some kind of superhero. I saw you go running this morning, and then I heard you helped that guy Kevin beat up. I'm proud of you for stepping forward. We don't want to go back to the days where people dragged prisoners out of jail and hung them on the nearest tree—despite how guilty they look."

Claire opened eyes she hadn't realized had been closed. Sawyer was standing in front of her, smiling his easy grin. Standing beside Sawyer was his wife, who gave Claire an approving smile. Claire realized that she had yet to hear the woman speak. Looking at her hair-sprayed perfection, Claire straightened up, hoping she hadn't been drooling on her T-shirt. Wiping her hand across her lips, she was relieved to find them dry. "I think I'm getting too old for this much excitement."

"Have you noticed lately that there are a lot less ancient people around, and a lot more people like us?"

"Tell me about it. Jessica and Elaine and I were talking about that yesterday." The three of them looked over at Jessica, who was regaling a dozen people with some story that had them all looking interested. Having survived his bout on the Round-Up, even Dante was circling around. Jessica seemed to have rushed in to fill the popularity vacuum caused by Cindy's death.

"I heard that she's on Broadway now that her soap has been canceled," Sawyer said.

"It wasn't canceled. Her character died. But, yeah, she's acting on Broadway." Claire couldn't help feeling colorless in comparison.

"And what about you? What are you doing these days?"

She wished she had a more glamorous answer. "I volunteer with SMART. It's a program to teach at-risk kids to read."

"That's a wonderful organization. I've made funding it the centerpiece of my agenda for children. That kind of early intervention saves so much trouble down the road." The look in his hazel eyes warmed her. "Say, have you heard anything from Logan?"

Claire shook her head. "I was thinking of trying to call his mother later, see if I can get his phone number. He must have freaked out about seeing Cindy's body and taken off. Maybe he was even afraid of being blamed."

"He didn't seem to be around much last night." Sawyer shaded his eyes from the sun.

"He chain-smokes, so he was out by the ashtrays most of the time," Claire explained. "Logan wouldn't hurt anyone."

Sawyer nodded noncommittally. "I hope you're right. He's not the same Logan you knew when you were growing up. Who knows what years of schizophrenia plus basketsful of drugs have done to him? Logan seemed—" Sawyer hesitated, shaking his head "—I don't know. Not quite right."

Claire straightened up, feeling like a lioness defending her cubs. "You of all people should know not to stigmatize the mentally ill. Inside, Logan's the same person."

Sawyer turned to his wife. "Could you excuse us for a moment, Elaine?" She nodded, and while she was walking away, Sawyer touched Claire's shoulder. "I've never told anyone this, but Logan was violent at least once back in high school. Do you remember that exchange student from Ecuador? That girl with the thick black braid that went down her back? Once after school was over I caught him shaking her by the shoulders and banging her head against the locker. She was so afraid she couldn't even scream. Too afraid to file charges. And

Logan ended up being committed the next day, so I didn't have to decide how best to follow up. But I'll never forget the look on his face. He didn't even hear me when I yelled at him to stop. I had to pry his hands off her."

Claire sagged. Her friend had always been so gentle with her. But was there another side to him? And could he be like that even now, now that he was on medication and taking it?"

She excused herself to go get something to eat, leaving Sawyer to the mercy of an old classmate who launched into a plea for farm subsidies before Sawyer even had a chance to say goodbye. She passed Richard, who was trying to explain something to Maria and Jill by laying out watermelon seeds on the top of a picnic table. "Now imagine," he was saying as she passed, "that you could ramp up the bandwidth of the circuitry and . . ." Claire noticed that neither of the two women looked very interested.

Picking up a paper plate, she took a place in line. Even though she was standing a few feet away, the coals from the giant barbecue felt hot enough to smelt steel.

The person in front of her turned around, and she realized it was Jim. "Enjoy your run?" he asked.

"I should have gone earlier." She took a hamburger bun from an open plastic bag. "Say, do you know if anyone has seen Belinda since what happened this morning? I'm worried about her."

"I went by her room," Jim said. "I only talked to her a little bit. She'll hold it together for a minute or two, then she starts weeping. That daughter of hers, Vanessa, is no help. She's interested in some boy she just met here. What my mom used to call twitterpated."

"It's Wade's kid, if you can believe it. Seems kind of

incestuous." She squirted ketchup and mustard on her bun, then added pickle slices. "Maybe I'll go down and talk to Belinda this afternoon."

The sweating teenager manning the grill plopped a hamburger that was charred black on the outside onto Claire's open bun. She started walking toward the circle of people—including Dante—that still surrounded Jessica. Claire took a bite of her hamburger as she walked, then gagged when it dripped blood. Resolving to become a vegetarian (if she didn't die from E. coli first), she tossed the entire plate of food in a garbage can already overflowing with half-eaten and hastily discarded burgers.

"So what plays have you been in recently?" Dante was asking Jessica when Claire joined them.

"Have you heard of *Dirty Habits*?" It was something of a silly question, because *Dirty Habits* had exploded in popularity after someone had taken a potshot at Nicole Kidman (and missed by a mile), disturbed by her portrayal of a lesbian nun involved with an older nun played by Glenn Close. That and boycotts by every Catholic agency, as well as a stinging denunciation by Rudolph Giuliani, had been enough to make tickets impossible to get. "I play Nikki's other love interest."

"The novitiate?"

Jessica blinked. "Um, yes. Of course, with those darned habits they make us wear, even my own mother wouldn't recognize me." She sighed. "I had to fight tooth and nail to be able to come back here for the reunion. Luckily, I thought to have it included in my contract."

"Dante lives in Manhattan," Claire said. She was trying not to envy Jessica her tanned legs and her ability to look glamorous even at a picnic. The actress wore pressed khaki shorts and a black sleeveless turtleneck. Claire tried to hide the ketchup stain on her shirt by tucking it even more deeply into her shorts. "He works at the Met."

Jessica pushed her sunglasses up her nose, so all Claire could see was her own mirrored reflection as Jessica looked from Claire to Dante. "So have you seen *Dirty Habits?*"

"It's a wonderful show." Dante put out his hand. "You're to be congratulated."

They shook hands, setting the dozen silver bracelets on Jessica's right arm to jingling. "Do you think I'm dressed appropriately?" Jessica appealed to both of them. "Me in my Kenneth Cole leather slides and my Ray-Bans and my Coach bag and my Donna Karan silk turtleneck. Maybe I'm not dressed right for Minor anymore."

Dante's tone signaled that he was about to make a joke. "You're worried you're not dressed for the part?"

Jessica gave Dante a playful shove in the center of his chest. "Oh, you! There's nothing worse than a punster."

Claire hoped neither of them could see her eyes behind her sunglasses. While she was still fuming, Dante turned to her and asked her if she wanted to go get a sno-cone. As soon as they were out of earshot, he said, "So what proof do you have that she was ever on *Until Tomorrow?*"

"Who—Jessica? What do you mean?" Claire was having trouble switching gears. "My mom used to tape the show and I'd watch it when I got home from work. She was on almost every episode. Why are you asking me this?"

"Because the woman who played the novitiate was black."

In the enervating heat, her brain seemed to be working in slow motion. "You mean the part Jessica said she had."

He nodded.

"Are you sure?"

"I just saw it last week."

She started to ask again if he was certain, but one look at his face let her know he was. "Is that why you were over there listening to her stories?"

"Let's just say it was an interesting blend of fact and fiction. According to Jessica, she's kind of like Forrest Gump—she's been on hand for anything important in the theater world."

"You think she lied about everything?"

"Oh, she probably does some acting. But I'll bet she waits a lot more tables."

"Maybe she started making it up on the plane," Claire said, remembering her old friend's impulsivity, always coupled with a burning desire to be loved. "She probably started worrying about how she was going to answer everyone's questions about how she was doing."

"Just like you were before we came."

"Yeah, but it's worse for her." Claire felt a spurt of pity. "She was really important in school. And she was such a good actress. Nobody was surprised when she was on that soap opera—but they would have been shocked if she came back from New York City and said she was waiting tables or doing something menial. I guess she just couldn't live with that idea."

While they were fixing their sno-cones, Becca appeared beside Claire. She pumped the last drops of something labeled BLUE RASPBERRY onto her crushed ice. It was the same color as Windex.

"Are you having a good time, Becca?" Claire asked.

"It's been interesting, that's for sure." She leaned forward and dropped her voice. "Kyle thinks I was maybe the last person to see Cindy alive." Her eyes were wide with excitement. "I went into the bathroom and there she was."

"What time was this?" Claire asked.

"A little after eleven-thirty."

"Did you talk to her?"

"I didn't talk about anything. I just listened to Cindy. She was bragging about her job as a cheerleader consultant, about her trip to Kauai, about her new SUV and how fast it can go."

"Doesn't sound like much fun," Claire said sympathetically. She was already losing any fear of speaking ill of the dead.

So, it seemed, was Becca. "The worst thing was the *way* she bragged about everything."

"What do you mean?"

"It was all by pretending to complain about it. Her job required so much travel to so many exotic places. And their nanny had gotten sick and hadn't been able to go to Kauai with them, so Cindy had to watch after her daughter herself. The kid's eleven, and Cindy made out like she was having to run after a toddler!"

This sounded like the Cindy Claire remembered. "So what are you doing with yourself these days, Becca?" And then was immediately sorry she asked.

"I'm a bronze-tier PermaFood distributor. It's a line of premium dehydrated food. Everything from vegetables to main courses to desserts. All of it guaranteed to last at least twenty-five years. Remind me and I can get you a brochure from my room later."

Claire shook her head. "That's okay."

" I tried to get Cindy interested in it last night in the

bathroom, too. She didn't even answer, just kept using all those little jars and bottles lined up in front of her. And then she sprayed her hair with a whole cloud of hairspray. I just about gagged. Served her right that she had to use one of those puffer things afterwards."

"Puffer?"

"You know, a whatchamacallit." Becca brought the back of her thumb to her lips, fingers curled, and made a puffing sound with her lips. "One of those asthma inhalers."

And just a few hours before Becca had seen her using an inhaler, Claire had also heard her using one. Were you supposed to use them that close together? "Did you tell Kyle about her putting on new makeup?"

Becca shrugged. "Yeah. He was mostly interested in what time I saw her."

Had Kyle, by the nature of his sex, missed an important clue? Why would a woman go to the bother of putting on a fresh coat of makeup near the end of an event? Was it just because she didn't want her public to see anything less than a perfect mask? That made more sense if she had only been checking for smears and smudges. But to completely repaint the canvas seemed to imply something more. Had Cindy been preparing herself for a special encounter? Had she gone out in the parking lot to meet someone?

RUCNNE1

Twenty-four

He rapped softly on her door, twice. The hotel corridor was empty, but still he felt a shiver of fear as he waited for her to answer. People were out in the sun, having fun, relaxing now that "the killer" had been caught. A strange sort of gaiety possessed them. Death had passed by so close that they had smelled his dank breath, and that made the warm summer air all the sweeter.

When Belinda opened the door, her face was swollen and damp, blotched with red. "Oh, hi." Her plump hands pulled the top edges of her white terrycloth bathrobe closer together.

"I just came by to see how you were doing," he said, slipping inside and closing the door behind him. A quick glance around the room showed him they were alone. His breathing loosened now that he was hidden from prying eyes. "I've been worried about you." Leaning forward, he gave her a quick, one-armed hug. When her arms went around his back, he felt a brief spurt of surprise. She clung to him for a moment, and over her shoulder he made a face that she could not see.

Then Belinda let go. Without speaking she turned away and sat on the bottom edge of one of the two unmade double beds. He sat across from her in a chair fashioned from plastic to look as if it had been hand-hewn from a log. The TV murmured in the background. Even in her grief Belinda could not bear to switch off the set. Clothes were scattered everywhere around the room—heaped on the other bed, strewn across a bureau, half-hanging from the hangers in the closet. The door to the bathroom was open, and more clothes lay puddled on the floor.

"Sorry about the mess." Belinda waved one hand vaguely. He noticed that her nose and upper lip were chapped. "My daughter Vanessa came with me. You know sixteen-year-old girls. It takes them forever to decide what to wear."

"This whole thing must be very upsetting for her."

Belinda gave him a bitter smile, her lips quirking down at the corners. "Not really. She didn't see what I saw. The whole thing isn't real to her. She can't imagine what it's like to be with someone you've known your whole life, only she's dead. I mean, Cindy's body was there, but it was empty." Tears spilled from her eyes and ran down her cheeks, but she made no attempt to stop them. "I think Vanessa thinks the whole thing is exciting. Like a TV cop show or one of those *Scream* movies or something. And yesterday she met some guy in the video game room, and she's all stirred up about him. Sixteen and she thinks if you spend two hours talking to someone it must be true love. Maybe it's genetic, since her father seems to have the same idea about his new assistant." At the thought of how life had betrayed her, her weeping intensified. She ran the back of her hand underneath her nose and then wiped it on the lap of her bathrobe. He hid his disgust.

"Maybe now is a bad time," he ventured, leaning forward. "Honestly, I don't know what to do. I only know I want to help you in whatever way I can. Is there anyone you would like me to call to be with you? Or do you want me to go away and leave you alone?"

"No." Her answer crowded his query. "No, I don't want to be alone. There've only been a couple of people who have stopped by, and they don't stay for long. Maybe people don't know what to say. So don't go. 'Cause when I'm by myself, then I just keep thinking about it and thinking about it. If only I had gone out to my car a few minutes before. Maybe that would have been enough. Kyle told me they think that the dishwasher guy must have done it right before I came out there. If I had gone out twenty minutes earlier, maybe Cindy would still have been alive. Twenty minutes earlier and maybe I could have frightened that guy off. That's all. Twenty minutes. And now Cindy's dead."

"You can't think about that," he said, more harshly than he had intended. "You'll just go crazy." He himself had been awake most of the night, playing out different scenarios. Imagining himself reasoning with Cindy instead of panicking. Imagining that he had never agreed to go out in the parking lot at all. Imagining that twenty years ago, he hadn't made the mistake of allowing himself to be seduced by her. "And look at what you did this morning. You were there for Cindy's husband. If you hadn't stopped him, he might have killed that guy. Then where would he be? His wife would still be dead and he would be doing ten to forty. He didn't need that."

"I couldn't let Kev—Kevin keep hitting him. Even though it makes me sick to think about that Mexican guy putting his hands around Cindy's neck, I couldn't just let him get killed in front of me. At least the judge let Kevin out on bail so Alexa didn't have to be alone. She's only eleven, you know."

He steepled his fingers. "Maybe you should think about going home. It must be very stressful, being in the same place where—it all happened."

"What am I going to do if I go home? At least here, there are a few people who understand. Like you." She gave him a wet-eyed, trusting look.

He leaned forward and gave her knee a pat, careful to avoid the place where she had wiped her hand. "That's why I came by to see you. I couldn't stop thinking about you, about what you've lost. You and Cindy were so close. Best friends for more than twenty years."

"Yes," she agreed. "Yes." She was starting to sob again in earnest, high-pitched little yips.

"I can understand how upset you are. Especially when you think that you must have been out there right after it happened. Too bad you didn't see anything."

She shook her head. "That's what Kyle kept saying. He kept bugging me, saying I must have seen something. But I told him I didn't see anything."

"Nothing?" he asked, keeping his face carefully composed. "Maybe you saw something little. Something so small it didn't mean anything. Maybe there was, I don't know, a piece of paper by her body that blew away before the cops got there. Or you heard something, heard the guy's voice, heard him talking to Cindy. Or maybe you saw this guy's car, you know, saw his car when he drove away."

"A car." Belinda sat up straighter on the bed. "I had

forgotten about it until you said that, but I do remember a car going by right before I saw Cindy. I remember looking up, thinking it was going too fast, but then I saw the, you know, the body—and I stopped thinking about anything but that." She looked at the phone. "I'll have to call Kyle. He was talking about hypnotizing me."

He remembered how, in a panic, he had started to drive away, before he realized that his absence would betray him, before he realized that the only possible solution was to go back and act as if nothing had happened. Now he put his hand out and touched Belinda's wrist. "Hypnotize you?"

"Yeah. He said a hypnotist can take you back in time and freeze everything in your mind. You know, like pressing the pause button on the VCR when you want to see the movie credits. He said they could make it be so that I could see the details around me for every step of that walk, turn my head to the left and see everything that in real life was just a blur. And like a video camera, he said you could zoom in and out. He said that you can read the license plates of cars, or see tiny scars on people's faces." She pulled her hand back and looked at him, some bit of intelligence flickering briefly in her eyes. "Why are you asking me all this?"

"Cindy and I were, were close." He folded his hands and dropped his gaze.

Her next words froze his blood. "I know how close you were," Belinda said softly. "She told me about it. Maybe Cindy is looking down and smiling right now. You helped me remember about seeing that car. Maybe there was a reason you were supposed to come and talk to me today."

"I think you're right. There is a reason." He opened his arms to her and leaned forward. She paused, eyeing him uncertainly. He could tell Belinda thought he was going to hug her. Instead, he yanked on her bathrobe tie, pulling it from around her waist. "What?" she began, reflexively clutching the edges of her robe together. In one quick motion, he wrapped the tie around her neck.

He was on her so fast, his knees pinning her shoulders to the bed, there wasn't even time for her to scream. He did what he had to do, but he turned his face away. He didn't want to watch Belinda's bulging eyes accuse him as her mouth twisted and silently spat his name.

He spent the next five minutes wiping everything down with a wet washcloth he found in the sink. And while he worked, he had an idea. It entailed a bit of risk, but if it worked out the way he thought it would, then no one would suspect him. It was, he decided as he polished the doorknob, a perfectly wonderful idea. He giggled a little at the thought of it, until he caught himself. And then, in silence, he leaned down and gathered up Belinda into his arms.

♥ Twenty-five

Claire woke up from her second nap of the day feeling about as tired as she had when she lay down. With the curtains drawn the room was dim and undefined, just like her thoughts. She had dreamed about Logan, that much she was sure of. The old Logan, skinny and funny and smart. Where was he? Why had he disappeared? Was he all right, or had Cindy's death pushed him back into the place where the voices whispered in his ear?

The bedside table held a directory of hotel services, a *TV Guide*, postcards of glamorous-looking people playing slot machines (although from what Claire had seen, the instant the photos were finished the models had been replaced by matrons in polyester), and the Minor phone book. Claire had forgotten that an entire phone book—both yellow and white pages—could be less than an inch thick.

There were three entries under West—but none of

them were Logan or started with an L. There was an E. West, though, who lived on Ash Creek Road. Claire couldn't remember Logan's mom's name, but she did remember the name of her old street. When she was little, the older kids had called it "Ass Creek" and when Claire had repeated it, Jean had threatened to wash her mouth out with soap.

She reached for the phone, but didn't pick it up. Would Mrs. West even talk to her? The older woman had been fiercely religious, convinced that everyone was going to hell, except for the twenty or so people who attended her particular church. Once, Mrs. West had smugly explained it all to her, about how Claire was preordained to spend eternity drowning in a lake of fire. The eerie thing had been how Mrs. West had smiled at the thought.

When she looked up from the phone book, she saw that Dante was awake.

"Before we get ready for dinner, I think I need to go for another trip down memory lane," she told him. "Would you mind driving?"

"Sure. Why don't you want to drive?"

"I'm starting to live in the past so much I'm having trouble seeing what's really here. If you drive, you won't get confused by how much everything has changed in this town, the way I would."

Claire didn't even attempt to give Dante directions, letting him pick up a map from the hotel's front desk instead. As a result, while it might have taken her an hour of driving in confused circles, it took him less than ten minutes to arrive at her old neighborhood.

Back in the days when Minor had been a small town surrounded by farm fields, Claire and her mother and sister had lived on the wrong side of the tracks. Now that Minor was home to expensive three-thousand-square-foot homes, their old neighborhood was more like the wrong side of the moon. The yards were filled with old appliances, cars up on blocks, and the remnants of children's plastic toys.

Claire hadn't thought of their old rental home in years, but now here it was, looking as if it belonged in a ghost town. It had needed painting even when she lived there, but it seemed as if no one had taken a brush to it in the intervening twenty years. The boards were now a weathered gray decorated with long, curling strips of deep green paint. More flakes of paint littered the ground along the edges of the house. The other houses around it were only in marginally better condition.

One house stood out from all the rest. A freshly painted doll-sized two-story not much bigger than the separate garage that sat next to it, it had an eerily perfect bright green lawn. Claire had a sudden memory of Mrs. West picking up fallen leaves by hand, one by one. She had harbored some belief that a rake would injure the grass.

As they went up the walk, Claire thought she saw a curtain twitch in Logan's old room on the second floor. Lifting the shiny brass knocker, she let it fall with a hollow thud. It was a long moment before she was sure she heard movement inside the house, and then Claire couldn't tell if the sounds she heard were from someone coming down the stairs or down the hall. Finally the door opened soundlessly to reveal a woman wearing a blue housedress, white apron, and yellow rubber gloves. Her swollen legs ended in white slippers.

"Hello, Mrs. West. Do you remember me? I'm Claire Montrose. I used to live next door. And this is—" she hesitated, uncertain what title to give him, and finally settled for none at all "—Dante Bonner."

As she spoke, Claire held out her hand, but it was ignored. She had forgotten that it would be.

"Oh, I remember you all right," Mrs. West said. Her tone was not at all welcoming. Underneath a black hairnet, she had the same tight, blue-white home permanent that she had had when Claire was growing up. Maybe there was a thirty-year stockpile of Toni down in the basement. Now she wiped her gloved hands on her apron and walked back into the house.

She left the door open, though, so, after hesitating a moment, Claire and Dante followed. Out of habit, Claire kicked her shoes off at the door. Watching her, Dante did the same. They left them on the mat, next to two identical pairs of run-over brown loafers, and followed the clear vinyl runner to the living room. Mrs. West was slowly settling herself into a dark blue armchair covered in a heavy plastic slipcover.

Claire and Dante perched on the very edge of the couch. It crinkled under their weight. The floral pattern looked as fresh and unfaded as the day it had come into the room, twenty-two years before. Like the recliner, the couch had been swathed in specially fitted heavy-duty plastic with an odd, pebbled texture. Everything in the house that could be protected was. Clear plastic runners criss-crossed the blue shag rug. The cream-colored shades of the two floor lamps were still wrapped in the plastic that had swathed them in the furniture store. Underneath a black cloth slipcover squatted the long rectangle of a console television.

In high school, Claire had seen Mrs. West as just frugal. Now she supposed the older woman would be diagnosed with obsessive-compulsive disorder. With Mrs. West's conviction that everything should be wrapped up tight against the real world, that flesh should never touch flesh, it was a wonder that Logan had managed to come into the world at all. Logan's father had died of cancer when his son was twelve, and with him had gone the last brakes on Mrs. West's beliefs.

"I came because I was worried about Logan," Claire began.

"He hasn't lived here since he first went into that hospital." With a sigh, Mrs. West leaned her head against a white antimacassar draped on the back of the chair, over the plastic covering. She pushed a lever on the side and the footrest swung out to elevate her grossly distended legs.

Maybe he hadn't lived here, but Claire was sure Logan still kept in touch with his mother. "I need to talk to him." She pitched her voice a little loud. Could Logan be somewhere in the house, listening? "It's about what happened at the reunion."

"Bad business." Mrs. West nodded her head, looking not at all perturbed. "Heard about that on the radio."

"Well, that Kyle Kraushaar who was in our class— maybe you remember him?" Claire interrupted herself, but got no reply from Mrs. West. "He's chief of police here now. This morning he arrested someone for Cindy Sanchez's murder. It looks like a dishwasher at the casino killed her and stole her purse." Even as Claire made sure her words were crisp and carrying, she thought about what Sawyer had seen twenty years before, Logan with his hands around some other girl's neck. She hadn't told Dante, not wanting to taint Logan in his eyes. "So Logan doesn't need to worry about anyone blaming him for anything."

"Maybe they should," Mrs. West said. "Satan talks to that boy—don't you know that? I tried to get him to sit down and read the Bible with me, but it didn't do any good whatsoever."

Claire shook her head, knowing even as she spoke that she was wasting her breath. "It's not Satan, Mrs. West. There's something physically wrong with Logan's brain. It's just as real as any other physical illness. Besides, he doesn't hear the voices anymore. He told me that."

"He did, did he?" The older woman raised one eyebrow. "What God has joined together, let no man put asunder."

As she recognized the old words of the marriage sacrament, Claire felt a chill. Dante leaned forward. "Do you think God put the voices in Logan's head?"

Mrs. West addressed her answer to Claire. "Everything is foreordained. You know that. It's why our church doesn't bother with proselytizing. Were you meant to spend eternity in heaven, you would already have believed."

"But if you believe everything is predetermined, why did you sit down and read the Bible with Logan?" Claire asked. "Why did you do that if you thought it wouldn't do any good?"

Her eyes were small and anguished. "He's my boy, isn't he? It took me a long time to submit myself to God's yoke."

"Can you give me his phone number? It wasn't in the book."

"He doesn't have a phone," the older woman said, giving Claire an idea of how bleak Logan's life must be, when every house had more than one telephone and even twelve-year-olds carried their own cell phones.

"Did Logan come here last night, Mrs. West? Or have you heard from him?"

"I told you, I don't know where he is." Her yellow-gloved hands twisted on her lap.

"Even so, I want to leave this with you." Claire got up and put a slip of paper on top of her suddenly still hands. "It's got my room number and phone number at the hotel. The hotel even has voice mail, so he could leave me a message. And I also wrote down my home phone number in Portland."

In the car, she put her head in her hands. They drove back to the casino without speaking while Dante rested one palm lightly on her back. After he had turned off the ignition, they both sat in the still and stuffy confines of the car. Finally, Claire said, "I think he was there, Dante. I think even if Mrs. West thinks Logan is lost in the next life, she still cares what happens to him in this one. I think Logan was there and he heard every word we said."

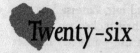# Twenty-six

A blast of hot air met Vanessa when she opened the door to the hotel room she was sharing with her mother. It felt like it did when you stuck your head too far inside the oven to see if your Papa Murphy's pizza was done. Making a face, Vanessa walked over to the heating unit underneath the window. The little dial had been cranked all the way to the left. What had her mom been thinking? There wasn't a thermostat, but Vanessa bet the room was at least one-hundred degrees. She turned off the heat, and then turned up the air-conditioning to the maximum setting.

Where *was* her mother? Vanessa decided that Belinda must have changed her mind and gone to the reunion. In a way, it was a relief that she was someplace else, instead of here, sitting in a chair staring in the direction of a TV game show while tears rolled down her red and swollen face.

Her mom was beginning to act as if Aunt Cindy really

had been her best friend. Belinda thought Vanessa didn't notice things, but she did. Like Vanessa noticed how Aunt Cindy always treated her mom, paying her no attention unless she wanted something. Then she could be as sweet as pie. And since her dad left, Vanessa had noticed something else. Twice she had picked up the upstairs phone to find it already in use—and her mother talking to Uncle Kevin in a low voice.

Vanessa walked into the bathroom and leaned over the counter cluttered with two dozen cosmetics. Looking at her face, she was torn between self-criticism and exultation. Despite her slinky name, which conjured up images of a smoldering-eyed dark beauty, Vanessa had inherited her mother's pale and pudgy looks. For once in her life, though, Vanessa thought she looked like a woman, not a girl. Her eyes were shadowed, her lips swollen from kissing. She thought she looked like a woman who had spent all day and all night doing exactly what Junior had so badly wanted to do.

Vanessa didn't know what she wanted or didn't want. After meeting in the video arcade the night before, she and Junior had spent the rest of the evening talking in the Snak Shak. In just half an hour, he was holding her hand, and by the end of the night she was sitting in his lap, exchanging lingering kisses until the fat old woman who ran the place told them to knock it off.

When Vanessa had finally come back to the hotel room, she had found her mother hysterical. Not because of how late it was, but because Belinda had been the one to find Aunt Cindy's body. Vanessa shivered at the thought. She hadn't really liked Aunt Cindy, but it was scary and strange to think of her lying dead. Vanessa hadn't known how to comfort her mother, who had wept and cried out all night long, even after she finally slept. It had been a relief to leave soon after she woke up to meet Junior.

Most of the day she and Junior had spent on the amusement park rides, kissing in anything that offered a moment of darkness. They had only split up a few minutes before to get ready for what promised to be a big evening out. Junior planned to borrow his father's credit card and take Vanessa out to dinner in the casino's fanciest restaurant—the End of the Trail.

But what would she wear? First she looked at her own clothes, but none of them were right. They were all too babyish. Then she turned to her mother's clothes, which were not only nicer but less wrinkled, since she had hung them in the closet. Their figures were similar enough that she could freely borrow from her mother's wardrobe. And since Vanessa's father had taken off, there was more to borrow. Belinda now favored low-cut tops that showed off her ample freckled cleavage.

Vanessa finally chose a cream-colored knit top with cap sleeves and a narrow slit that would end just above the little bow in the center of her bra. After a moment's consideration, she took Belinda's black leather jacket from the back of a chair, even though her mother had expressly said she was never to wear it.

Shimmying out of her clothes, she kicked them in the direction of her open suitcase. Her T-shirt ended up half-under the bed. Had she bent down to pick it up, Vanessa would have seen her mother's body stuffed under the bed frame, seen Belinda's purpling face, her eyes wide and unblinking, the whites pink from broken blood vessels. Had she spent another few minutes primping, she might have answered the door when the killer knocked on it ten minutes later. Instead, Vanessa left her T-shirt where it lay and left the room, going back to the arms of Wade's oldest child, Wade Junior, at eighteen two entire exotic years older than Vanessa.

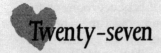

Twenty-seven

Several months prior to the reunion, Claire had gone shopping for a new dress to wear to Saturday night's big dinner and dance. But after a few perilous moments in a Saks dressing room where she had actually considered wearing a backless dress cut so low it would have ruled out wearing any undergarments at all, she had come to her senses. The first time she had gone to New York City she had both met Dante and bought a beautiful dress. She had worn it only once, to dinner with another man, a man who turned out to be a charming fraud and swindler.

The dress, though, was a keeper. Cut from apricot-colored satin, its sleeves and bodice were made of sheer netting. The color set off her hair, and the dozen darts that nipped in her waist made her look curvy rather than lanky. Dante had asked whether he should pack a tux for the reunion (he owned several because he often attended fundraising events for the Met), but Claire had told him just to bring a dark suit. This was Minor, after all, a place where the women might dress up, but the men never would.

In fact, she had worried that she might be over-dressed, but the Westward Ho! banquet room glittered with sequins, bugle beads, and gold lamé. The outfits looked a little out of place among the room's decorations—hay bales, bleached cow skulls, and fake cactuses wearing bandannas. A few of the men were dressed in Levi's and T-shirts, but most were wearing suits (although some of them looked as though the last time they had been out of the closet was for high school graduation). One side of the room was a dance floor, the other was filled with large round tables, covered with white tablecloths. As a centerpiece, each was topped with an old cowboy boot filled with strawflowers. Along one wall was the buffet, ending with planked salmon. While it was probably more likely the pioneers had been subsisting on wormy hardtack by the time they reached Oregon, Claire figured that idea wasn't nearly as marketable.

Flash! Claire jumped as a roving cameraman ducked in to take her and Dante's picture. She was reminded of how Richard Crane had always hidden behind his camera, taking so many pictures that he faded into the scenery.

Claire and Dante found a place at a table with Maria and Jill, who by coincidence were both wearing cream-colored pantsuits. Jessica, a vision in a midnight blue off-the-shoulder silk dress, snagged the chair on the other side of Claire. Dressed in a black sleeveless dress with a mandarin collar, Becca took a seat directly across from them. Claire was beginning to feel that the man-to-woman ratio was distinctly unbalanced, until Becca cajoled a passing Wade to sit next to her, and Richard stopped by and asked if he could sit with "all you lovely ladies." He looked embarrassed when they all chorused agreement. Jessica patted the chair next to her and immediately launched into full-flirt mode.

By the time Dante and Claire joined the buffet line, it snaked all the way to the entrance doors. Behind them, people began applauding and whistling. Claire turned to find Kyle, red in the face, being hailed as a hero. Finally, flushed and nodding, he put his hands up to still the noise, then walked over to the bar in the corner.

"Hold my place, would you?" Claire asked Dante, then followed Kyle. His face soured when he saw her, but he turned toward her and away from the others, who still crowded around him, slapping him on the back and offering to buy him drinks.

"What's the matter, Claire—you want to stick your nose in things again?" His words were loud enough that several people turned to look at her. She saw that he was already a little drunk, even though he had just walked in the door. "You should be happy that the bad guy is locked up and the rest of us are safe."

At that a couple of the men raised their glasses in tribute. "Here, here."

She put her hand on his arm. "I didn't come here to criticize you."

At Claire's touch, Kyle softened immediately. "I'm sorry I snapped at you. I'm dead on my feet. I was up all night."

"Maybe you should go home."

"What—and wait another ten years before I see everybody?"

Claire thought to herself that Kyle was also enjoying

the limelight. Out loud, she said, "I did have a couple of things I was wondering about."

He groaned theatrically, but didn't walk away.

"Like how did Kevin know to come back just when you were taking that guy to jail?"

Kyle looked away. There were lines of fatigue etched on his face. "Kevin called me early this morning. He was angry, saying why hadn't I arrested anyone yet for Cindy's murder. Screaming that the statistics show that if someone isn't arrested for murder in the first twenty-four hours, then chances are good no one's ever gonna be." He scrubbed his face with his hands. "I got defensive, told him that this morning we would take someone into custody. I didn't tell him where, though, but I guess it was probably easy enough to figure out that whoever did it was probably still here at Ye Olde Pioneer Village."

"I've been thinking—are you sure it was this dishwasher guy? He just seems so—little. Cindy's probably two inches taller and at least his weight. Wouldn't it have been hard to strangle her? It seems as though she could easily have fought him off."

Unconsciously, Kyle began to twist his hands together, reminding Claire of the marks on Cindy's neck. "Maybe. Except for two things. We've got the blood-alcohol level back on her. It was point-one-three, making her well over the legal limit. Kind of explains the cheerleading routine thing." They both looked at each other, remembering Cindy shaking her pompoms—and her breasts—in Richard Crane's face. "And the other is that the pathologist says her airway was already compromised before she went out in that parking lot. She's got asthma, and it wasn't very well controlled—at least not last night." Claire flashed back to the blue inhaler she and Nina had seen in Cindy's hand. "This Juan guy might not even have meant to kill her."

"What does he say about what happened?"

Looking down at his shoes, Kyle ran the back of his thumbnail over his lower lip. "We probably won't be asking him any more questions for a while."

"Is he still unconscious?"

Reluctantly, Kyle nodded. "He seems to respond to his name. And he's squeezed his wife's hand a few times. There's some bleeding in the brain. The doctors say they don't know when he'll wake up—or what kind of shape he's gonna be in when he does."

"And is Kevin already out on bail?" Claire couldn't hide the anger in her voice.

"Hey—the judge made the decision about bail, not me, Claire. He's one of Minor's most prominent citizens. Or at least one of the richest. He's not considered a flight risk. And there's a lot of sympathy for a man who finds himself going temporarily off on the man who murdered his wife."

"Have you thought about whether Kevin might have had another reason for beating that guy up?"

"What do you mean?" The expression in Kyle's small brown eyes was unreadable.

"Maybe he did it so he wouldn't talk—so he couldn't tell you he wasn't guilty. I think"—Claire ventured Jessica's hypothesis—"I think maybe Cindy's husband was having an affair with Belinda."

"What makes you think that?" For once, Kyle looked as though he was really listening.

"When she tried to stop him from beating up that guy, she called him Kevvie. No woman would call a man that unless she was intimate with him." It didn't sound as convincing as it had when she and Jessica had both heard the way Belinda addressed Kevin.

"So? They've known each other for nearly twenty years. And you've gotta remember—I've got proof. I've got that guy on tape with Cindy's ATM card."

"But what about what he said when you arrested him? I heard him saying something about being innocent."

Kyle shrugged. "My Spanish isn't too good, and he doesn't have any English. Something about how he didn't do it—how original! Just once I'd like to have some SOB tell me he was guilty."

"Did he say anything else?" Finding it an effort, Claire kept her voice nonjudgmental, patient.

"Maybe something about finding Cindy's wallet in the garbage bin." Kyle didn't meet her eyes. "It's an easy out. That way he can claim he's not the guilty one. That he just took advantage of an unexpected opportunity."

"He could be telling the truth, couldn't he? Couldn't the person who killed Cindy have taken her wallet and then dumped it later? Maybe whoever did it even put it in a place where they know someone might find it and keep it? Like in the garbage outside a hotel kitchen?"

"Anyone can make up a story to fit the facts," Kyle said. "Maybe aliens did it. Maybe it was a contract Mafia killing. Maybe it was a flukey suicide. But I think what happened is that this guy tried to take advantage of Cindy and things got out of control."

Claire thought of what Martha had said. Occam's razor. The simplest explanation that fit the facts. Was Kyle's the simplest? Did it fit the facts? "Did you find semen on her body?"

Kyle flushed, as though they were both back in seventh grade health class, squirming bundles of hormones. "No. We didn't. You ever stop to think that maybe this mope couldn't get it up—and maybe that made him so mad that he killed Cindy?" He shook his head in frustration. "And that's all I'm gonna say about this, Claire. I shouldn't even have said as much as I have to you." He turned back to the bar before she could ask any more pesky questions.

When Claire turned back around, she saw that Dante was next in line for the buffet. She hurried to join him. As she tried to fit everything she wanted on one plate— slices of melon, steamed asparagus spears with hollandaise sauce, boiled new potatoes, a roll, tortellini, and finally salmon—she began to question what Kyle had told her. But if Juan de Jesus hadn't killed Cindy— who had?

As she and Dante walked back to the table, he asked her what she and Kyle had been talking about. She summarized it briefly for him.

"I don't think the dishwasher did it, Dante. That's what Kyle wants to think, but maybe it's too easy." She stopped talking as they took their places at the table.

The expansive mood of the afternoon seemed to be carried over to the dinner. People laughed, teased, boasted, and ordered drinks from the two harried barmaids that circled the room. Letting the conversations eddy around her, Claire wondered if she was wrong to think that it hadn't been a stranger who killed Cindy. But wasn't that what Kyle was leaving out of the equation? That Cindy was the type of person who was more likely to be killed by someone she knew than by someone she didn't? And what about what Nina had told her? Who had Cindy been primping for? Remembering the aloof way he had watched his wife, Claire was willing to bet it hadn't been Kevin. And if Kevin had been having an affair, that might give him reason enough to kill his wife. Had she discovered his affair—or had Kevin discovered one of Cindy's own?

There were other people to consider, too, Claire thought. Wade, for one. Cindy had lost herself in someone else's arms at the prom. She had broken up with Wade a few days later, and everyone remembered how haggard he had appeared back then. Even watching Cindy from behind his dark glasses, his face had been naked with longing.

And now that she had Sawyer's information, could Claire even rule out Logan, who might have heard one voice he couldn't ignore, urging evil?

And knowing that Cindy's airway was already compromised, could even Belinda be ruled out as a suspect? It would be easy to become hysterical if you had just killed someone. And Cindy's death would be a neat way of freeing up Cindy's husband. The problem with figuring out who might have killed Cindy, Claire realized, was that there were too many people who had good reasons to have done it.

The baked salmon had been consumed long ago, the ears of corn reduced to gnawed cobs. Claire pushed back her chair and excused herself. She was pleased to see that she had managed to make it through the entire meal without spilling a single drop on her dress, which surely qualified as a miracle. But after she had taken only a few steps toward the hall—and the bathrooms—Jessica caught her arm in a rustle of silk.

"Let me walk you out," Jessica's breath was warm against her ear.

"What? What are you talking about?"

"Let me hold your arm and walk you out."

"Why?" Claire asked. Even though she felt a brush of annoyance, she continued to move forward as Jessica requested, her old friend's arm looped through hers, their heads close together and hips bumping.

"There's a big brown glob stuck on the back of your dress."

"What?" Claire started to look behind her, but Jessica tugged her arm.

"Don't look! I don't think anyone else has noticed. And you don't want them to. It looks kind of, um, like . . . "

"Like what?" Claire could feel the redness creeping up her neck and ears.

"Like something biological." Jessica raised her free hand to her mouth to stifle a giggle.

"Oh, crap, Jessica. Or I guess I should say not crap. I know what it is. It's a Raisinette. There's this vending machine right outside our room, and I got some Raisinettes because I was hungry. I was eating them on the bed before I got dressed. Then I sat down right before we left to fix my shoe—and I must have sat on one." Suddenly the absurdity of the situation overcame both of them. They barely made it to the safety of the hall before sagging with laughter.

"Here I am swanning about and I've got what looks like a piece of shit stuck to the back of my dress."

"I've done worse," Jessica leaned her head back against the red flocked wallpaper, which looked more suited to a turn-of-the-century bordello than a pioneer's rough-hewn cabin. "Once I was having dinner with a producer, and after I went to the bathroom I tucked my skirt into my nylons. I walked the whole length of the restaurant's dining room with people staring at my butt. And not just at an ordinary butt—but at my butt looking big and bulgy." She wiped under her eyes, then inspected her knuckle. "Damn—my mascara's running. Come on—let's both get cleaned up."

Claire followed Jessica into the bathroom. Twisting and turning, she couldn't see the Raisinette, even in the mirrors above the sinks. She could feel it, though, on the underside of the curve of her bottom. She tried scratching at it with her fingernail, but it wouldn't budge. When three more women came into the bathroom, Claire put her back against the wall.

"I only could ask this of a friend," Claire whispered in Jessica's ear, and suddenly it felt as if that's what they were, friends, "but do you think you could help me get this thing off?"

"Sure," Jessica said, and grabbed Claire's hand. Obediently, and ignoring any odd looks, she followed the other woman into the handicapped stall. Jessica put down a paper cover, then perched on the very edge of the toilet seat and gestured for Claire to turn around. "Can you lean forward or something? I'm going to try to peel it off in one piece." Claire bent down and put her hands on her knees.

The whole absurdity of the situation—her punctured vanity, her preposterous position, and the fact that they were now hiding out in the handicapped stall—caused giggles to continue to bubble forth from Claire. She was glad that the sound of the other women's chatter and the constant flush of toilets drowned most of it out.

"There," Jessica said finally. "I managed to get it off in one piece. Thank goodness for acrylic nails. That sucker was really stuck." She stood up and handed Claire the flattened Raisinette, which was now about an inch and a half in diameter, with a raised center from the raisin.

Claire made a face and dropped it in the toilet. Tomorrow, she resolved, she would give up eating junk food for good.

"Is there a stain?"

"Not much of one. Your dry cleaner should be able to get it out. Luckily, it's sort of in a shadow."

"A shadow?" Claire began, then stopped. "Oh, I get it." She bet size-four Jessica's butt had never been accused of casting a shadow. Mentally, she shook herself. It was silly to feel jealous, especially now that she knew how insecure Jessica was. She tried again. "I really appreciate your covering for me. Scraping something off my butt in the handicapped stall is going above and beyond."

"I'm known for doing my best work in the handicapped stall," Jessica said. She smiled a private smile, but didn't explain further. "Besides, don't you remember how you saved me in Mr. Grotting's history class in seventh grade?"

Actually, Claire had forgotten until now. "Oh, yeah. That was the day you wore white jeans and your period started."

"I started to get up, and then you pulled me down. At first I got mad at you, because I didn't know what you were doing. Then I figured it out, and I thought I would just die. When everyone had gone you took off your sweatshirt and tied it around my waist and walked with me to the office to call my mom. If it weren't for you, I would have been the pariah of seventh grade. The Girl Who Bled on Herself."

"When you're thirteen, nobody wants to know that kind of thing happens."

"No one likes to know that kind of thing happens now. Women are all supposed to be perfect. We're not supposed to have periods or get wrinkles or age spots or crow's feet or stretch marks. We're supposed to look eighteen forever." Jessica sighed, ignoring someone who rattled the door. "In New York, I'm starting to feel so old. In fact," she looked up coyly through her lashes, "on the back of my head shot it says I'm thirty. If I put down I was thirty-eight, I'd be washed up. The only parts you get if you're thirty-eight are moms. Frumpy moms. And at the same time, every bus that stops in the Port Authority terminal is filled with eighteen-year-olds with perfect skin, pert little breasts, and legs that go all the way to the ground. And of course they not only act, but they can sing, they can dance. And kids are the only thing producers want these days. Somewhere in New York or L.A. right now, some twenty-four-year-old is lying to some producer, saying she's eighteen. When she's just beautiful and perfect the way she is."

Jessica's blue eyes were shining like sapphires, her dark hair springing up in tendrils from where she had pulled it back. She was completely beautiful, but Claire knew she would be as deaf to that message as any of the twenty-four-year-olds she was lamenting. Instead, Claire opened the door to the handicapped stall.

"Let's go back to the party before we miss Sawyer's speech."

2Q2STOM

Twenty-eight

When they slipped through the door to the Westward Ho! room, Sawyer was already speaking. He was a natural orator, blunt and folksy. When he made eye contact with you, for a second it was as if he were speaking directly to you, not thinking about the others at all. Even the waitresses paused, surprised as flies trapped in amber, to hear him evoke years-old memories. He began with a brief reference to the Fourth of July and his time in Vietnam. For a minute, his expression shifted, became shuttered. Claire thought to herself that he must never have come to terms with the chunks of time gone missing from his life in the POW camp and then the rehab hospital.

"I didn't know then what I was fighting for," Sawyer said. "But when I became a teacher, it began to make sense to me. I saw all these young people who were hungry. Not hungry in a physical sense, the way I had seen peasants in Vietnam, but hungry for their lives to have meaning. Still, there were those in Minor whose lives had meaning even then. Like Richard Crane, here." Richard glanced up. Even with his hair falling over his eyes, Claire could see that he was coloring deeply. "He had a life of service, even then. Although he admired them, he didn't want to be the football player making the winning touchdown," Sawyer nodded in Wade's direction, causing him to straighten up, "or the actress taking a bow after a standing ovation," and Jessica gave a little gasp and put her hand on her chest. "No, Richard was content to take their pictures so that others could connect with that moment. And today millions of people worldwide are making connections with the help of his modems." There was a smattering of applause from the audience.

"Or take Martha Masterson. She's doing gene therapy research now, did you guys know that? Someday, children born with cystic fibrosis won't have to die, thanks to her. Do you know how much pride I feel when I think about her being in my biology class? Even then, though, I could sense that she would soon move past anything I could teach her."

Sawyer went on to flatter most of the people who were there, effortlessly weaving in everyone from the garbage hauler ("his company has tirelessly promoted recycling") to the travel agent ("spreading some of our wealth—and along the way, our ideals—to third world countries"). He mixed the serious with the not-too, telling funny stories, like the time Alex built a working replica of a guillotine for history class and nearly severed his index finger, or the time Jim ate a cigarette butt to avoid being suspended for smoking—but then got so sick that he voluntarily gave up cigarettes for nearly a month.

Jessica was sitting between Claire and Dante, and at one point Claire's vision focused on the other woman. She was watching Sawyer with her lips parted, her eyes soft and dreamy. Even twenty years ago, Sawyer had had that effect on women, and his rugged handsomeness probably didn't hurt him at the polls now. Claire told herself that she would still vote for Sawyer if he were wall-eyed, fat, and balding, but she had to admit that his looks and beliefs made for a pretty nice package. While she was thinking this, Sawyer went on to hit the high points of his platform (children are our future, public schools need to be fully funded, the plight of the environment can't be ignored), without ever specifically mentioning that he was running for governor.

The finer points of the last part of his speech were lost, though, when the Minor Miner mascot appeared behind Sawyer and began waving to the crowd. People broke into laughter, and he stiffened, perplexed and nearly angry, unaware that a giant miner had loomed up behind him, wearing a headlamp and coveralls and waving its enormous four-fingered hands. When he finally turned around, he abandoned his speech with good grace and led the crowd in their old cheer.

We don't need picks,
We don't need tools,
To beat you guys,
'Cause Minor rules!

Although the Minor Miner traditionally never spoke, he accompanied the chant by swinging his giant foam-rubber pick up and down in a chopping motion, which the crowd accompanied with rhythmic clapping. For a moment, Claire thought of Cindy, of how she would have run to the front of the room to join Sawyer and the mascot, how she would have kicked and yelled and shaken her hips. Looking around the table, at the faltering expressions on the faces of Wade, Richard, and even Jessica, she knew they were thinking the same thing, too. It was, Claire realized, easier to like Cindy now that she was dead.

After the chant was over, preparations began for the dancing. A DJ started spinning records (actual records, too, not just CDs) while the hotel staff pushed in a karaoke machine. On the low portable stage that Sawyer had just vacated, Jim began setting up amplifiers and guitars. When Dante went to the bathroom, Claire walked over to talk to Jim. They had to raise their voices to be heard over a medley of Donna Summer hits.

"So are you going to play 'Louie, Louie' tonight?"

He shrugged, but couldn't hide his smile. Jim was always at his happiest when he was making music or making love—or just about to do either. "Wait and see. We're not scheduled to start playing for an hour. You won't hear none of this disco stuff, that's for sure." Donna Summer's voice finished swooping through the last notes of "Bad Girls." Jim winced when Olivia Newton-John began popping the notes on the bubble-gum sweetness of "A Little More Love."

The Minor Miner waddled by them, high-fiving (or high-fouring) anyone who put up a hand, occasionally swinging his pick. For the most part, he was ignored, although the occasional guy would come up, knock on his head, and wittily shout "Anybody home?"

"I started thinking about Cindy when I saw the Miner," Jim said. "She would have loved to have gotten up there, reliving her glory days. She would have had us all on our feet, cheering."

There was something about his tone. "You liked her, didn't you?"

He looked away. "Remember when we broke up?"

"Yeah?" She drew the word out. Jim hadn't wanted to formalize their relationship at the time by even using the term "breakup."

He plucked at a string. "It was because I was starting to see Cindy." Jim didn't have to explain what "see" meant.

Her heart constricting with an old, half-remembered pain, Claire made herself think back. "But she was dating Wade then."

He shrugged. "It was like a secret thing for both of us. I'd park by Safeway at the end of the shopping center and she would get in my car. We would drive out to the river and go skinny-dipping. I knew she was slumming, but I didn't care. She didn't want anyone to know about us. Maybe her parents didn't, and maybe the teachers didn't, and maybe even the other girls didn't, but I'll guarantee some of the guys at least guessed. Cindy collected guys. She used to sing that Blondie song, you know, the one that talks about a girl putting another notch on her lipstick case."

What a cliché, Claire thought. *Cheerleader slash whore.*

She must have murmured the last word underneath her breath, because Jim reacted with a protest, the expression in his green eyes hardening. "She wasn't a whore. She was just Cindy. Her dad was a doctor who was never around, even when she was really little. And when he was, he criticized her. So you could never tell her enough that she was pretty or funny or had something to say that you wanted to listen to. She needed to hear it all the time."

It was strange to think of Cindy as vulnerable or insecure. When they were teenagers, Claire had hated Cindy for the way she picked on others, for the way she always had to be the center of attention. Now the perspective shifted. Had all Cindy's actions been fueled by a deep insecurity?

And there was another facet to Jim's story. Claire tilted her head to one side, thinking. "Okay—so who else?" she demanded suddenly.

"What?" She could tell Jim knew what she was asking, but he didn't want to answer her question. He pretended to tune his guitar.

"Who else did she sleep with?"

Grimacing, he raised his shoulders to his ears. "What does that matter?"

"It matters because I'm beginning to doubt that the dishwasher killed Cindy. And if he didn't—well, someone who used to sleep with her would probably have more reason to kill Cindy than someone who didn't."

His gaze was as inscrutable as a cat's. "Does that mean you would put me on the list of suspects?"

Her answer came on the heels of his question. "Of course not, Jim. I know you pretty well, remember? And you would never do that. So who else?

He gave in. "I don't know everyone besides me and Wade. There was Alex Fogel, and Brian Jones, and a couple of other guys from the football and basketball teams, I think. Oh—and once I saw her with that old buddy of yours, Logan."

"Logan!" Claire couldn't believe it. In an odd way, it felt more of a betrayal than learning that Jim had slept with Cindy.

"Cindy always liked a walk on the wild side. The best way to get her to do something was to tell her that she shouldn't or she couldn't."

Claire hardened herself. "Do you know of anyone else?"

"I'm sure there were, but I don't know anyone else for certain. From the way she talked, I think she was even sleeping with one of her parents' friends. Some older guy that would really get in trouble if anyone found out about them. A little taste of forbidden fruit." He looked at her with flat eyes and she could tell that he was angry with her. "Does it make you feel better, knowing all that?"

She answered him honestly. "No. But don't you care if the wrong person is in jail for killing Cindy?"

"If it's the wrong person, then, yeah, sure I care. But you asked me the wrong question." His finger slid down a string until it made a low squeal. "You should have asked if I want to see the right person in jail." Before she could answer him, he turned around, set the guitar down and walked away, pushing through the wine-red curtain that hid the service entrance.

Claire stared after him, unsure of his meaning. In the back of her mind, though, she counted the reasons to link Jim with the crime. He had once been Cindy's lover. And he had disappeared for a while after they found the body. Had he been disposing of Cindy's wallet in the casino's dumpster? And, she realized, there was yet another reason to wonder if Jim was involved. Cindy's body had been found less than thirty feet from his car. Was that more than just a coincidence?

An arm slipped around her waist. She turned. Dante.

"That Jim of yours didn't look too happy."

"You know he's not 'my Jim.' But yeah, you're right. He thinks I'm asking too many questions about who might have killed Cindy."

"What did he tell you?"

"That Cindy slept around, which wasn't really a surprise. She slept with him, though, and I didn't know that."

"Does that really matter now?"

"Sure it does. Someone who once had an intimate relationship with her would probably be more likely to kill her than a stranger, don't you think? And it sounds as if she went through boys like scratch paper, so one of them might still be mad about being treated that way."

"Who were some of the other guys?"

"Besides Jim and Wade, Jim said Alex Fogel—that guy from breakfast, remember?—and some other guys from the football and basketball teams." Claire looked down at her feet. "And maybe Logan, once." When she looked up, Dante was watching her intently.

"Sounds like she had her fingers in every pie of yours. Does that make you dislike her more?"

"What—are you looking at me as a suspect?" Then she turned serious. "No," Claire heard her own answer with surprise, "I guess I'm starting to understand Cindy a little better. I think she was one of those people who lived all on the surface, but underneath she was lonely."

BWHO UR

♥ Twenty-nine

During a break in Jim's set—which had had the crowd on its feet, cheering—the DJ put on "Chuck E's in Love." Even though it wasn't really a slow song, Dante pulled her into his arms and out onto the dance floor anyway. "Has anyone told you anything interesting about what really might have happened to Cindy? Or have you overheard anything?" she asked him.

"No, but I didn't know you needed me to be snooping."

"You're an outsider here. People might talk more freely in front of you. Kind of like they do in front of a waiter or behind the bus driver. I've already noticed that when I join a group, people tend to switch subjects."

"You're not exactly subtle, though, are you? You've already told a bunch of people that you don't think the dishwasher did it. Well—who else does that leave? Only the people in this room. They might resent the fact that you suspect them."

"But I don't suspect all of them." Dante pulled back to look at her better and Claire laughed. "All right, I don't suspect three or four. You, for instance. I'm pretty sure you didn't do it. But it seems as if a lot of other people could have. I wish I were a pillar or one of these stuffed cactuses or even that guy over there with the camera—something or somebody no one pays any attention to." She pulled Dante back so that they avoided running into the lumbering mascot. He was moving blindly and slowly around the room, pausing every now and then to wave enthusiastically and totally cluelessly. "He reminds me of a presidential candidate," Claire whispered to Dante.

"I don't think the mascot can hear you," Dante said in a normal voice. "He's got all that padding around his head." The Minor Miner stopped waving for a moment and turned his big pasted-on felt eyes in their direction.

"You just gave me an idea. Do you have some money—ideally four or five twenty-dollar bills—that I can have?" That was the nice thing about going to an event like this. Claire didn't need to worry about carrying a purse, since everything was already paid for and Dante was keeping the hotel card key in his wallet.

"Yeah. I'm afraid to even ask why." He pulled five twenties from his wallet and handed them to her anyway.

She tore each bill down the middle.

"What did you do that for?"

"I plan on appealing to the oldest human emotion—greed."

The high school kid wearing the Minor Miner costume hadn't been able to resist the lure of $100—even if he only got half of it right away, stuffed into his four-fingered fist. She told him he would get the other half if he let her wear the costume for the rest of the night, and after a moment of silence, he had nodded his giant head.

He had retrieved his things and a big, lightweight black box from the janitor's closet, then met Claire and Dante in their hotel room as they had arranged. The Minor Miner went into their bathroom, and a skinny high school kid with a buzz cut and a pierced nose, wearing jeans and a T-shirt came out, carrying the costume in his arms. He wouldn't hand it over until Claire had promised not to talk while wearing the costume, never to act out of character, not to lose or damage any part of the outfit, and at the end of the night to leave the costume, in its box, with the front desk. Only then did he set the costume on the bed (all of it neatly folded, with the exception of the head and foam-rubber pick), and hold out his hand for the other halves of the bills.

"Thanks," he said, stuffing them into the front pocket of his jeans. "Oh, and I forgot to warn you not to let anyone take off your head. For some reason, guys like to try it. Once I almost got deheaded by two drunk guys at a football game, but I managed to get away."

Thinking that she had more motivation not to be revealed than he would ever guess, Claire agreed not to let anyone take off her head.

"And high-five people, because if you shake their hands, they try to take off your fingers. Oh—and watch out if there are any kids around. You can't really see anything below about waist level, so the first thing you'll know about there being any kids is when one of them runs into you full speed."

"Okay, okay. I don't have to worry about that tonight.

The event is adults only." Claire was impatient to go back to the party and see if her ruse would work. When he started to launch into a recital of the finer points of belly bumping, she opened the door and shooed him out.

Dante helped Claire out of her dress. She let him sneak a few kisses, but she was too eager to get back to the dance to let him do more. First she slipped on the dark blue Lycra pants. They were thick with padding, and the outside was slick as satin, except where it had been snagged by the various Velcro fasteners that held the costume together. Then came the heavily padded shirt, again dark blue, which zipped up the front. These two pieces formed the backdrop for the miner's costume. Next came a huge flannel shirt and then oversized denim overalls sized to fit about a 400-pound man. She was finding it harder and harder to move, so Dante snugged the straps so they wouldn't fall down.

The Miner's big black boots had been fashioned over men's hightop tennis shoes. Claire slipped her feet in them, for once grateful that she wore a woman's size ten. She waddled into the bathroom to look in the mirror. A laugh spurted out of her. Her head looked puny, perched on top of her now outsize body.

She maneuvered her way back to the bedroom (remembering to lift her feet high off the ground so she wouldn't catch the big boots on the carpet). The dark blue hood came next. It reminded her of a medieval knight's garb, a single piece that flowed over her head and shoulders, with an oval opening cut out for her face. Finally she lifted the miner's head and looked inside it. It had been built around a bike helmet. She lowered it in place and fastened the strap under her chin. Inside the head, it wasn't as stuffy as she had thought— the huge eyes were made of some kind of black mesh, with glued-on felt dots for the irises. Dante helped her pull on the two four-fingered hands, much larger than her own, handed her the foam-rubber pick, and then they were ready to go.

Claire quickly discovered that she could only see by looking at something at a slight angle, so the pupils of the fake eyes didn't get in the way. She had no peripheral vision to speak of, and what vision she had was dimmed about 30 percent by the mesh of the eyeholes. The costume probably weighed thirty pounds, and she was beginning to baste in sweat. And as the costume heated up, it began to release the faint but lingering smell of vomit.

When they reached the door of the Westward Ho! banquet room, Dante went on ahead of her, to deflect suspicion. Claire tried to open the door herself and found that first, she couldn't see the knob, and second, that after she finally found it she couldn't open it with her outsized hand.

"Let me help you with that, good buddy," a voice said. She turned. Wade. He opened the door, then propelled her forward by slapping her on the back.

At first, Claire found herself smiling at people whose gaze met hers. A social smile, lips pressed together, accompanied by a little nod. All of it invisible under the costume. The costume required broad gestures, she began to find. The big wave. Chopping her pick wildly. Arms held out wide for a hug. A certain walk seemed right, too, exaggerated, pumping the arms, raising the knees a little higher than necessary. The head was already growing unbearably heavy. The weight certainly encouraged her to stand up straight—her back hurt too much if she did otherwise. You could break hardened criminals down by simply making them wear the costume for a few hours, she thought, as yet another man punched her playfully on the shoulder, almost knocking her over. Didn't people realize that there was someone underneath the foam rubber?

Claire remembered seeing rainbow-haired clowns forced to wave at intersections to draw attention to store openings, or avoiding the Fred Bear who occasionally roamed the Fred Meyer store, dressed in an oversized blue shirt. Next time the Fred Bear guy wanted a hug, she would give it to him. It was too embarrassing to find yourself acting for someone you thought was standing right next to you, only to turn your head and figure out they had left.

But all the downsides of the costume were balanced by one giant upside. While she walked around the perimeter of the room, occasionally accidentally running the edge of her miner helmet into the wall, her fellow graduates treated her—or her alter ego, the Minor Miner—as if she were invisible.

Claire saw Alex Fogel lay down a twenty-dollar tip for one of the barmaids, as a woman looked on admiringly, and five minutes later she saw him come back and pocket the tip before the barmaid got to it.

She overheard Cherie and Todd Walter, the pet psychics, arguing about whether Cherie had had too much to drink. Todd left the room, and a few minutes later Claire saw Cherie sweet-talking another man who didn't seem to mind her half-mast eyes and the way she slurred her words.

From the other side of the room, Claire saw Kyle answer his cell phone. He didn't say more than a few words, but his expression froze and his face turned purple. Before she could make her clumsy way in his direction, he hurried out of the room.

Hidden inside her costume, Claire was free to wince as Tomisue tried her hand at karaoke, warbling off-key through "Stand By Your Man."

Claire watched Maria and Jill, who sat in one corner of the room, turn down every request for a dance, preferring to reminisce with each other. She saw Wade leaning in close to whisper to Becca. And Claire witnessed Jessica flirting with Richard, laughing up at him, touching his shoulder and then the nape of his neck, leaving him with a slightly stunned look that mingled dizziness and delight. Layers within layers, Claire thought, as she caught sight of Martha watching Richard fawn over Jessica. Martha's open face was unable to hide a faint frown of envy. And all the while, she saw Dante circling from group to group, person to person, trying to get someone to confide secrets in a stranger.

People treated Claire as if her costume were reality, as if there were nothing inside it, no human being with ears. Now as the evening wore on and the drinks flowed, they wanted to include the Minor Miner in their festivities. They made chopping motions with imaginary picks whenever they saw her. One guy she didn't recognize pulled her on to the dance floor, and she danced for a few minutes while Jim growled out "Satisfaction" in a passable imitation of Mick Jagger. Some of the men, the drunker ones, began to shout and grab at her and bang on her head. Claire realized she had no way to indicate distress, that her mascot face would keep right on smiling happily no matter what they were doing to her.

When it got particularly bad and she began to worry about breaking her promise and losing her head, Dante rescued her by inviting the ring of men around her to accompany him back to the bar for a free drink. Afterward, her bladder sent up a distress signal, the same one it had been making for at least an hour, increasingly urgently. She would have to take a break and go to the restroom. With luck, she could manage to pee without taking off too much of her costume.

Out in the hall, she headed for the women's room.

"Hey, where you going, big guy?" Someone grabbed her arm. Brian Jones, another of Minor's old football heroes, was grinning at her, his face as relaxed as she had ever seen it.

Wade stood next to him, weaving slightly. "Don't want to give the ladies a scare!" Together, they took her by the arms and walked her toward the men's restroom. At first, Claire wanted to resist, but then she realized she wasn't a person anymore, she was something more, something that didn't automatically fit into a category. She just hoped that the men's restroom had stalls just like the women's.

Trying to fit it into the stall, she banged her head a few times, but finally managed by inching in sideways. Behind her the two men were laughing and joking. Leaving her head on, Claire took off only the costume's hands and carefully laid them over the toilet paper dispenser.

"Where'd you get this, anyway?" Brian's voice. Claire narrowly missed dropping one of the overall straps in the toilet.

"Same guy we went to twenty years ago. Only now he's got three kids to support."

Claire managed to tug the pants down to her knees. The costume was so bulky she couldn't really sit, but even squatting the relief was worth it.

Afraid that one of the two men might decide to pop his head over the stall, Claire finished peeing and tried to get herself back in working order as fast as possible.

"So where were you last night, man?" Brian's voice again. "I looked all over for you and I couldn't find you for at least twenty minutes."

Wade snorted. "You're not going to believe it, man!"

Brian was already laughing. "What?"

"That little minx Jessica was giving me a blowjob in the bathroom!"

"No way!" Brian's voice mixed incredulity with admiration. "Someone would have seen you!"

"Nah—we went in the handicapped stall and Jessica sat on the edge of the seat. But get this—she insisted on putting one of those paper covers on it first!"

While both men exploded into laughter, Claire realized that this explained everything—Wade's absence the night before, and even the sounds Alex Fogel had heard coming from the bathroom stall.

When she came out, Wade and Brian were still laughing, heads close together over a small silver hand mirror that lay on the counter. Three lines of white powder remained.

"Hey, not in front of the mascot," Brian said, elbowing Wade in the ribs.

"Maybe he'd like a little taste." Wade knocked on her head. "How about coming out of there and joining us? On the house."

Claire shook her mascot head and waved her four-fingered hands to show she wasn't interested. To her horror, she noticed that she hadn't quite managed to pull the right one down in place (it was hard to do the second, once the first was on) and that a strip of pale,

nearly hairless—and definitely not masculine—skin
was showing.

PB4UGO

Thirty

Before she slipped the card key into the slit, Vanessa fingered the side of her throat with a private smile. It felt tender, and even a little raised. She'd bet there was a suck mark there. Wait until all the girls at school saw that—and heard that she now not only had a boyfriend, but that he was two whole years older! The one thing she wouldn't tell them was that they hadn't really gone all the way. She would just smile and look mysterious.

Junior had wanted to, of course. They had rolled around on one of the two wide beds. Vanessa had even let him pull up her top and touch her breasts—but nothing more. He had thought she was afraid, but it wasn't fear of getting AIDS or a reputation that stopped her. What if she didn't do it right? What if she not only didn't do it right but did it all embarrassingly wrong? So in the end, they hadn't done it, although low in her belly it felt full and hot and achy.

When they had heard Junior's father laugh right outside the door, Vanessa had had about a second to scramble into the bathroom, clutching her bra and top. Hurriedly, she had pulled her clothes on and then looked in the mirror. Her face was scarlet, her eyes small and guilty. It took all her courage to turn the handle and walk out of the bathroom.

But the adults hadn't seemed to mind. Not only was Junior's father there (a nice-looking guy, but paunchy) but there was a woman with Wade, a woman named Becca who smiled up at him from the shelter of his arm. Vanessa was shaking by this point, but they never asked what the two of them had been up to, and they didn't lift an eyebrow when Junior said he would escort Vanessa back to her room.

He had kissed her in every alcove and deserted hallway on the way back, but when they got to her hallway, she told him he had to go. It was two in the morning, and her mother was going to be furious. It wasn't exactly the right time to make introductions. They would see each other in the morning, she said, and between kisses they agreed to meet at 7:00 A.M. at the Feed Trough. All the hung-over adults wouldn't be up yet, and they would have the place to themselves in peace. And maybe, she had finally agreed, just maybe, if Wade came down for breakfast, then the two of them could sneak back up to his room. Actually, she thought she might be even more frightened of things in the daytime (what if he took that hard lump out of his pants?), but when she had said it Junior had grinned from ear to ear and called her beautiful. For that moment, she had decided it was worth it.

The light above the handle glowed a steady green. Vanessa pushed open the door to the room she shared with her mother.

At first, she thought Belinda was sleeping. But as Vanessa's eyes adjusted to the dark, she could see that while her mother was lying down, she wasn't under the bedcovers. In fact, her bathrobe was open.

"Mom," Vanessa whispered, but it came out so soft even she didn't hear it. "Mom?" she tried again, a little louder. Her mother didn't move, and there was something about her stillness, the chest and the belly not rising and falling, that Vanessa could not deny, no matter how much she wanted to.

She was shaking so hard she thought she might fall down. Too afraid to turn around, she took one step back, then another, until the doorknob poked her in the back. She put one hand on it, and reached with the other for the light switch. For one second only, she looked.

Then she turned and opened the door, her free hand clawing at it, and ran into the hall. Vanessa began to scream and scream and scream, and at the sight of the first face that poked out of another door, she fell like a rag doll onto the carpet.

After Claire's narrow escape from the bathroom (Wade and Brian had been too interested in what was laid out in neat lines before them to notice any discrepancies in her costume), Claire had returned to the reunion. She spent the rest of the evening trying to eavesdrop, but all she overheard were boozy expressions of good fellowship or boring recitals of what people did all day at their jobs. Finally she motioned to Dante, he nodded, and they had met back at their hotel room.

Claire was down to the Lycra pants and shirt of the costume when a woman began screaming in the hall. Dante opened the door, and they ran out together.

At first, it all seemed terribly familiar. A goggle-eyed Belinda, frightened past coherency, collapsed on the carpet. In a split second, Claire realized she was making the same error she had that morning, mixing up Belinda with her daughter.

"My mom . . ." was all the young woman could stammer out, as she pointed at the door that still stood open. Claire and Dante went in together.

Belinda made a terrible messy contrast to the neatly made bed on which she lay. The bright light of the room offered no shadows, no vagueness, the way the darkness had softly enfolded Cindy. Belinda was a nearly clinical study in death. It was almost, Claire thought, as if she were on display.

The signs of Belinda's terrible struggle were everywhere. Her open white terry cloth bathrobe was speckled with dark spots of dried blood. Bloody furrows gouged her neck. Tracks, Claire guessed, made by Belinda's own desperate fingers. Her swollen, bloody tongue protruded between her teeth. The whites of her open eyes were red, and her eyelids and the bridge of her nose were purple. On her naked chest was a round wine-red circle—probably the bruise, Claire realized, left there by the killer's knee as he held her down.

And in curled fingers of her right hand was a familiar wooden shape—a box carved into a rough heart. Without touching it, Claire leaned down to look. The box was open, and inside was a picture of Belinda. Claire recognized the picture she had looked at with Charlie as they paged through the annual together. Belinda, her face upturned in a sycophant's smile in the direction of what would have been Cindy, if she hadn't been mostly scissored away—reduced now to a sweater-clad shoulder and breast. The picture curled at one edge, where the glue had loosened, and Claire could see a bit of the photograph on the other side.

Kyle couldn't blame this on the poor dishwasher, Claire thought as a fine tremble sluiced over her. When Dante put his arm around her, she jumped. Was he thinking the same thing? Was he wondering which woman who had received a box would be the next to die?

TXNS00H

Thirty-one

Outside the room Vanessa had been sharing with her mother, a small crowd began to gather. Jim was there, and Tomisue, and the New K103 FM. So was Wade, with Becca. Claire noticed that the back of Becca's dress was only half zipped. Belinda's daughter was still on her hands and knees, rocking back and forth and moaning. Claire lifted the girl to her feet and held her close for a few minutes, keeping quiet while the girl muttered furiously, mindlessly, into her ear. Then Wade's son arrived and put out his arms. Belinda's daughter turned away from Claire and fell into them. More and more people were beginning to gather, so Claire rejoined Dante in the room. With the toe of his shoe, Dante nudged the door nearly closed, to try to keep the sight of her mother's violated body from further burning itself into the girl's memory.

"Look," Claire whispered to Dante as they waited for Kyle to arrive. They were the only two people in the room, but it seemed right to whisper in front of Belinda's body. It was as if they were granting Belinda the respect the killer had stripped from her. "Look at her throat. Didn't Cindy's look different?" It was easier, Claire found, to look at Belinda's body one part at a time, and, at all costs, to avoid looking at her eyes.

Dante cocked his head. "When I checked Cindy's pulse, I remember I could see the marks of fingers on her throat." Around Belinda's neck was a thick, unbroken purple line that grew even wider just under her chin. "He must have put something around her neck and pulled on it."

Claire noticed something else that didn't look right, but before she could say something, Kyle shouldered open the door to the room, followed by Marc, the cop who had taken their names and addresses—was it only the night before? Claire watched as Marc visibly paled. Even Kyle, presumably hardened by years of police work, couldn't stifle a groan at the sight of their old classmate's violated body.

Claire realized another hard truth. Belinda's death meant that a man had been beaten insensible for nothing. A fury born of mingled fear and frustration rose up in her. "So tell me, Kyle, do you still think Juan de Jesus is guilty?"

Kyle seemed faded with exhaustion, all color leached from him except for his bruised-looking eyes. He shook his head, but he didn't meet her eyes. "No. Because he died this evening." Seeming to move in slow motion, he turned his wrist and looked at his watch. "I guess I should say yesterday evening."

"Oh, no," Claire breathed. She remembered kneeling in his warm blood, tentatively touching his face with her hands.

"The doctors say a clot must have broken off and traveled up to his brain. He had a massive stroke. They tried to save him, but . . ." Kyle shook his head again. "Go on, get out of here. I've got a murder investigation to conduct. And don't touch anything on your way out."

The hotel was well soundproofed, so as the night wore on Claire heard very little of the comings and goings that must have marked the investigation. Even so, she could not sleep. She started when Dante brushed her hair back from her face.

"What are you thinking?" His voice was a whisper.

"I'm wondering if Kevin Sanchez decided to rid himself of all the troublesome women in his life."

"Pretty drastic way to go about doing it, don't you think? Aren't lawyers supposed to be calm and rational types?"

"I've already seen what he's like when he's angry. We know he's capable of violence."

"If Kevin did it, then he'd have to be crazy," Dante said. "Kyle may not be a genius, but if Kevin was really sleeping with Belinda, I'm sure he'll find out about it. And if you decide to kill both your wife and your lover, you have to realize that the first person the cops are going to come looking for is you."

"Maybe he wasn't thinking when he did it," Claire said. But something bothered her. "Except I'm beginning to wonder about Belinda. About the way she looked."

"Yes?" Dante propped himself up on one elbow.

"Did you notice how her right side looked different?"

"You mean, how it was a different color?" It had

been a purplish red, while the other side had portions that were blanched white.

"If she had been lying on her back the whole time, shouldn't both sides be the same color? What if her body was in one position when she died, but later someone put her in a different position? That could account for the two halves of her body looking different. And there was something about the way she was laid out. It was as if she was—posed."

"Maybe there are two killers," Dante said. "Maybe the second killer wanted everyone to think that the same person who killed Cindy was the one who killed Belinda. So he arranged Belinda's body to make her look like Cindy."

"Two killers?" Claire shuddered. "Do you really think there is more than one person from my high school class who's a murderer? And to strangle someone—that seems so, well, personal, for want of a better word. I mean, with a gun, you might shoot someone in the heat of the moment. You could do it before you even have a chance to think it through. You could even be a block away. But strangling someone—you have to touch them with your own hands, and you have to mean it, and go on meaning it, even if it takes five minutes for the person to die." The room was warm, but Claire pulled the covers more tightly over her shoulders.

Dante draped his leg over hers. He was so furry, it was like adding another layer of blanket. "Well, strangling's quiet and less messy than shooting someone. And you don't have to worry about buying anything special to do it. You've got all the tools at hand, so to speak."

The pun broke some of the tension that was filling Claire. She groaned and pretended to push him way.

"And once you started strangling someone," Dante continued, "you would be afraid to stop. Afraid of being arrested as soon as the person drew breath to scream. And didn't Kyle tell you that Cindy was having problems with her asthma? Maybe whoever killed Cindy didn't mean to. Maybe they got into a fight and it got out of hand."

"Why kill Belinda then? And what about the boxes? What do they mean?"

"Maybe the boxes," Dante said, "are just a cover-up. Maybe whoever gave them wanted to throw people off the trail by giving them to a bunch of different women, but only planned to kill two. Maybe the killer was someone who was tormented and teased by both Cindy and Belinda."

"Only someone who didn't go to Minor would come up with that theory," Claire said. "Belinda could actually be pretty nice, especially if you got her on her own, without Cindy."

"Okay, say someone did give each of you a heart-shaped box and now plans to kill you. But why? You guys don't really have anything in common now. Except each of you is single—or at least unmarried —right? Except for Cindy."

"But that wasn't true earlier in the year," Claire said slowly, remembering her conversation with the pet psychics. "I heard she and Kevin filed for divorce, but then got back together."

"That's not going to look good for Kevin," Dante said. "Does Kyle know that? And how do you know it?"

"Someone who lives here saw it in the paper. It's so small they even print all the court proceedings."

"Back in high school, was there one relationship you all had in common—one friend, one—" Dante hesitated "—one lover? Did Jim sleep with Belinda as well as with you and Cindy?"

"No. I'm sure he didn't." Claire shook her head. "You make Minor High sound like Peyton Place. I think relationships overlapped more than I knew. But I can't think of one person who was an enemy—or a lover or even a friend—to all of us."

"Could all of you know a secret that this guy wants to cover up?"

Claire shook her head. "If that's true, I don't know what it is. And if there is a secret, so far, he's been pretty darned successful at keeping it hidden."

But as Claire lay staring into the darkness, she found her thoughts returning to Jim. Cindy's body had been found near his car. And despite what she had told Dante, even at seventeen, Jim had had something of a reputation as a stud. Was it possible that he had slept with Belinda, too? And of all the people she had talked to, he was the only one who had said he talked to Belinda after Cindy's murder. Had he been trying to provide himself with an alibi in case any of his fingerprints were found in the room?

TIH5 HO

♥ Thirty-two

In the middle of the night, Claire hadn't thought she would ever be able to sleep, but here it was, morning, shafts of sunlight slid past the thick curtains patterned like flour sacks. Looking at her watch, she was surprised to find it was nearly nine o'clock.

When she and Dante pushed open the door to the Feed Trough, they found it packed with reuniongoers, all surrounding a young cop she didn't recognize and an unshaven, exhausted-looking Kyle. The people crowded around him didn't look much better.

"It's a serial killer," declared Becca. "Any one of us who got those boxes could be next!"

"I don't know about the rest of you, but Jill and I are leaving," Maria said. She put her arm around Jill, who only came to her shoulder, and left it there. "It's not safe here anymore." Like the shift of a kaleidoscope, Claire finally figured out that the two women were something more than old friends.

"But how do we know the killer won't follow us wherever we go?" Nina's hair bristled on one side, looking as if she had just gotten out of bed—or no longer had the energy to devote to her hair. "Most of us live here, or in Portland. In less than an hour, he could be at our door—especially since that damn reunion booklet we all got has our home addresses in it."

"What about the boxes, Kyle? Did they give you any clues?" Martha asked. Of all the women who had asked questions, she seemed the calmest—but then again, she hadn't gotten a box. "Did you get fingerprints off them? Have you gone back and figured out who took wood shop?"

Kyle shook his head. "No fingerprints. And the boxes themselves are a dead end. They were imported by the truckload last Valentine's Day. Every Pier 101 and Cost-Plus and knickknack store in the country sold them. They were hand-carved, sure, but by people in Malaysia."

"What about Kevin?" Claire asked. "Have you talked to him?"

Kyle's jaw tightened. "Kevin's been sitting in jail since eight o'clock last night, charged with manslaughter in Juan de Jesus's death." The people who hadn't heard about this additional death began to murmur to each other, but Kyle raised his voice and soldiered on. "He's lawyered up and refuses to say anything, but the coroner says Belinda died sometime between nine and midnight. Belinda's daughter says her mom wasn't in the room a little before eight. And we have a casino surveillance tape that shows Belinda outside the casino entrance at 9:08 P.M. So there's no way Kevin coulda done it."

"What about Logan West?" Jessica's voice had the power to cut through the babble. "Has anyone talked to him?" Richard patted her arm.

Claire's heart sank as people began to mutter in agreement. Could Logan really have killed Cindy and Belinda?

"We're looking for him right now. In fact, we have received some information that indicates he may have a pattern of violent behavior." Kyle looked in Sawyer's direction and gave an almost imperceptible nod. "We wanna bring him in for questioning. If you see him, don't approach him yourselves. Just back off and call 911." His tired gaze roamed around the room. "I can understand if some of you want to leave, especially you ladies who received boxes. But Nina's right—going home is no guarantee of safety. If you do leave, make sure we have your name, address, and phone number, in case we need to contact you later. If you decide to stay, the casino has offered to eat the cost of the rooms tonight, as well as to give everyone here for the reunion a voucher for fifty dollars of casino gambling. Remember, you could be safer here, in numbers, than you would be at home alone."

When people started to break up into little groups— some leaving, others picking up trays for the breakfast buffet—Claire pulled Kyle aside. She didn't want to start a lynch mob if she were wrong. "I should have told you this before, Kyle."

"What is it now?" His voice was flat, his eyes red-rimmed with exhaustion.

"After that group of us found Cindy's body, Jim disappeared for a while. Later, he asked me to say we were together. He said he went home to check on his girls, but I'm not sure I believe him."

Kyle's expression didn't change. "He's a dealer, Claire."

"What?" Claire felt off balance.

"He figured he'd make a quick buck selling pot—and maybe a few other things, although he hasn't told me that—to some of his old buddies from high school." Claire thought of Wade and Brian and their white lines on a mirror. "He told me about it last night, after Belinda's body turned up. He took off after Cindy died so he could get rid of his stash. Says he threw it out." Kyle's voice underlined the word says. "I guess he figured being charged with selling pot was better than being charged with murder. I told him I've got my hands too full with solving these murders to charge anyone else with anything else—at least right now."

GN2POT

Thirty-three

"So what should we do?" Dante asked Claire. They were back in their hotel room. "Go or stay?" His hands hovered over his open suitcase.

"Hmm?" Claire answered absently. She sat on the bed, looking at the picture of the honor society in the annual again, the same photo where she stood in the middle of a dozen people, the same photo someone had cut apart to get to her, and then tucked her image alone in a heart-shaped box.

"Should I pack up or change for the pool party?"

Claire didn't answer. The annual in her lap showed her with her hair in her eyes, with her face slightly angled to the ground. But hadn't the photo in the box been different? Hadn't it showed her with her bangs shaken back from her eyes, her face lifted up? Or was she simply imagining things? A minute ago, when she had looked again at her old self, Claire had been sure something was different. Now, the more she looked, the more she didn't know what to think.

Still without answering Dante, she picked up the phone. "Jessica McFarland's room, please," she told the hotel operator.

While the operator transferred her, Claire said to Dante, "I think maybe there's something different about the picture I got in that box. Like maybe—" she stopped as Jessica said hello. "Jess?" How long had it been since Claire called her that? Since she had started believing what Jessica kept trying without success to tell herself, that she was better than other people? "Remember the photo you got in your box? This is a weird question, but do you think it was exactly the same as the one in the annual?"

"Give me a second and I'll see."

"What do you mean you'll see? You don't still have your box, do you?" Even as she said the words, Claire realized that this particular move of Jessica's shouldn't surprise her.

"It kind of slipped my mind to turn it in. Besides, if Kyle had wanted to check for fingerprints, he had a half dozen other boxes to look at. And by the time I figured out that it might be important, I had touched it so many times that it would only have had my own fingerprints on it. And I guess the fingerprints of all the people I've shown it to."

Claire was amazed by Jessica's nonchalant attitude. "Maybe one of the people you showed it to was the murderer. Did you ever think of that, Jessica?"

"I didn't show it to Logan, if that's what you mean. Besides, one box more or less wasn't going to make a difference. Kyle already had six samples—why did he need a seventh? But do you know what this box could mean for my career? This morning, I was on the phone to someone who's a stringer for *People*, and he's already running it by them back in New York. I can see the headline: DID THIS ACTRESS ESCAPE A SERIAL KILLER? With a big head shot of me looking beautiful and mysterious. Black-and-white and my face half in shadow—it's more dramatic. And holding the box, of course. This could really get me noticed."

Claire sighed. The one good thing about Jessica having kept the box was at least Claire could put her curiosity to rest right away. "Well, could you go compare the photo in your box to the one in the annual?"

Jessica was gone for so long that Claire began to think maybe she had been disconnected. Then she thought she heard two people talking in the background, so Claire stayed on the line a few minutes longer. Finally, just as she was about to hang up, Jessica came back on the line.

"It's gone, Claire. My box is gone!"

"What do you mean, it's gone?"

"I had it in my purse, but now I can't find it. And I've turned my room upside down. Someone must have taken it."

"Who knew you had it?"

"Probably most of the people from our class. I didn't tell you because I knew you would just make me give it back to Kyle."

"But why would someone else take it?" Claire asked.

The other woman made a little "puh" sound of amazement. "A souvenir from a serial killer? Do you know how much you could get for that on eBay? Or maybe someone else has a private stringer for *People*." Jessica's voice should have sounded dejected, but it didn't. "Anyway, I can't talk any longer. Richard Crane was just here. He wants to spend the day with me. He told me he wants to keep me safe. You know, Claire"— her voice was that of an adolescent, on the edge of a giggle—"I think he really likes me. Maybe I won't need to be worrying so much about *People* magazine after all. Anyway—I've got to go."

"Jessica—wait. You never told me whether you thought your picture in the box was—" Claire stopped when she realized she was already talking to a dial tone.

Dante said, "I take it we're staying?"

The next phone call Claire made was to Kyle. She arranged to meet him downtown at Minor's police station, a stucco building that felt blessedly cool inside after being in the un-air-conditioned Mazda. Kyle looked dead on his feet, swaying slightly when he came out to talk to them. The circles under his eyes made him look like an old basset hound.

"You said you needed to see me?"

"I need to see the picture that was in my box. I think there's something that's different about it from the picture that ran in the annual."

For once, Kyle didn't argue. They waited a few minutes while Kyle got the boxes from the evidence room. Each was bagged in brown paper. With latex-gloved fingers, he opened Claire's box. She opened up her annual.

Claire bent over the pictures and looked back and forth. Even though she had been expecting it, it was like a shock of icy water. The photos were clearly a little bit different.

Kyle leaned closer. "Nearly the same," he said slowly, "but not quite."

"Could you see what's on the back?"

"Sure. They had to separate each one when they were looking for fingerprints." With the edge of a paperclip, he turned over the photo.

The back was plain white photographic paper, not another page from the annual.

"What about Cindy's?" Dante asked, but Kyle was opening up the bag before Dante finished the sentence. The back of Cindy's photo was also white.

"I just assumed they were cut out of the annual," Kyle said. "I didn't even think of looking on the back."

"These are matte prints, not glossy," Dante said. "Makes them look a lot like the kind of paper that was in the annual."

"Maybe," Claire said slowly, "maybe sometimes a photograph reveals more by what it doesn't show."

Kyle tilted his head. "You mean who got cropped out?"

Claire shook her head. "No. I'm thinking—who took these pictures?"

She knew who it was now. Had he liked them all in high school, unable to distinguish between them, happy enough that they were all girls? When had his attraction slowly twisted into hate? Claire remembered the way he used to smile at her in calculus. A quick little nervous smile followed by his head ducking, the shock of dark hair falling over his eyes, hiding his expression. When he had looked at her like that, had he been dreaming of kissing her—or killing her?

Dante said, "These photos are so similar to the ones in the annual, they must have been taken at the same time—by the same photographer. So who took the photos for your yearbook?"

Claire didn't answer him. Keys in hand, she was already running to the main door. "Come on!" she yelled over her shoulder at Kyle and Dante. "He's got Jessica!"

HIHO AG

Thirty-four

"I have something important to ask you, Jessica," Richard said. He took her hand. They were sitting hip to hip on the Ferris wheel.

Jessica returned the clasp of Richard's damp fingers. Something rose up in her, as if they were meeting as spirits as well as bodies. She had worked so hard last night to get him to notice her, had embraced the spotlight now that Cindy was gone. She had come to her senses and realized that she had to live in the here and now, live in the world where the past of high school didn't matter, where even Wade Merz was nothing but washed up. Only the present mattered, a present where Richard Crane rattled around in his mansion and had no idea how to meet women. If only she had realized when they were both sixteen how important he would be!

"Just ask," she said, wishing that she were sitting on his right, so that he could see her best side.

"I used to watch you, you know. You were so beautiful. And popular. You had so many boyfriends. I felt as if I couldn't talk to you. The only way I could get near you was with my camera. You would walk out on the stage and command it. Just as you commanded my heart."

"What did you want to ask me?" She could feel the smile deep inside her, but she wouldn't let it out, not yet.

"Do you trust me?"

"What?" She was off-balance now, uncertain what he was really asking her. Part of her had been hoping that he might pull a black velvet jeweler's box from his pocket. With a ten-carat diamond as big as a dime.

"Do you trust me? Do you think I would ever hurt anyone?" Richard's hand felt icy now, icy and cold. She wanted to pull her own hand away, but did not.

Another part of her took over, playing the part he needed, buying her time to think. "Of course you couldn't hurt anyone, Richard," Jessica said in a gentle, soothing voice, in the tone you would use with a child or a madman. Inside her, she heard her own voice, her real voice, shrieking that she had to get out of here. Their gondola rocked gently as they rolled to the top of the wheel. Up here, she could see forever, see past Minor, tiny as the toy town it really was, past the fields that surrounded it, golden with summer wheat, and all the way to the mountains in the distance, still scarved in white. "I know you couldn't." She hesitated. "Why do you think I would think that?"

He hung his head, while his hand still gripped hers fiercely. "Because of the boxes. I gave them to you ladies, but I swear, I never meant any harm to come of it. It was like—like a tribute. But then something went terribly wrong. Things have gotten all mixed up."

Jessica remembered Cindy's dulling eyes, imagined the bloody furrows marring Belinda's throat. And then she had a more terrible vision. She had seen Until Tomorrow on TV often enough that she could think of herself in the third person, easily imagine what her body would look like, spread-eagled, head lolling back, tongue nearly bitten in half.

Down on the ground, she saw four people pushing their way through the crowd, running whenever there was a bit of open ground. She squinted. Claire and Dante, accompanied by Kyle and another cop in uniform. As Jessica watched, Claire pointed up in their direction. The two police officers drew their guns, and the crowds began to part before them.

"No." The word was torn from Jessica. Had he told Cindy how much he admired her, sweet-talked Belinda until she let him into her room? Shaking her hand until he finally freed it, Jessica scooted back as far from him as she could. The gondola swayed under them. Her stomach lurched as the car began to fall forward, toward the ground.

"No, Jessica!" Richard cried, his face twisting. He only had eyes for her, not for the policemen who were too far away to offer her any help. "You don't understand!"

The car was now at the lowest point in its revolution. Making a split-second decision, Jessica stood up and stepped over the silver restraining bar. She looked to the operator, but his attention was caught by the people running toward him. The platform was only a few feet beneath her, but the car was beginning to ascend. She had to jump now, before it was too late. She put her right hand on the edge of the car. With a sob, Jessica vaulted her legs over.

And was stopped short as Richard leaned forward and grabbed her left arm, shouting, "What are you doing?" Jessica had braced herself for the ten-foot fall, but now she was halted with a jerk that felt as though it would rip off her arm. The car continued its inexorable rise as she hung, dangling. Red-hot pain sliced through her arm and shoulder. The two people in the car below theirs were screaming for the ride operator to stop while they stared at her dangling feet. But the Ferris wheel continued to turn. The momentum of her leap had turned her body into a pendulum that swayed from side to side. The car rocked violently back and forth in response. With a pop, she felt something give in her shoulder.

Jessica's focus narrowed to her arm, to the ring of pain around her shoulder and the second ring where Richard's hand dug desperately into her arm. Originally he had grabbed her forearm, but now his hand had slid until it was just above her wrist. And, she realized, she was still slipping within his grasp.

"Hold still!" she heard him shout. There was no one whose eyes she could look into, no one she could plead with or gain reassurance from. All she could see were the giant spidery red arms of the Ferris wheel, and the backs of the baskets directly opposite. As their gondola rose higher and higher, she saw that the ride operator was finally, frantically pulling at a lever.

With a tremendous lurch, the ride came to an abrupt stop.

"Jessica! No!" she heard Richard scream, just as she was torn from his grasp. And then the ground was rushing up to meet her.

She had a split second to think that they would find her just as broken as Belinda and Cindy. And then Jessica didn't have any time to think about anything else.

Thirty-five

After the crowd watched Jessica struggle with Richard and then fall to her death, it was all Kyle and the other cop could do to prevent a lynching. While the two men trained their guns on Richard, the ride operator followed their shouted instructions and let off the passengers, car by car. Sobbing and staggering, the riders disembarked, averting their gaze from the horrific sight of Jessica's broken body. As his gondola slowly made its way around the circle, Richard sat slumped, his hands over his eyes.

As they realized what had happened, the other carnies stopped their rides and let off their passengers, too, so that by the time the gate to Richard's car was finally opened, a couple of hundred people had gathered around the Ferris wheel. When he dropped his hands to push himself off the seat, it was clear Richard had been weeping. The eerie silence was broken by someone hissing as Kyle stepped forward with a pair of handcuffs.

That hiss heralded an explosion of nearly unmanageable anger. People began to scream at Richard, shouting "Murderer!" and "Killer!" Richard had never been close to anyone in high school, so there was nothing to balance the bloody reality of Jessica's death. Next to Claire, Tomisue suddenly bent over, her hands on her knees. Claire thought the other woman was overcome by emotion, until she straightened up with a small stone in her hand and threw it straight-armed like the softball star she used to be. It opened a cut just above Richard's eyebrow.

Kyle whirled around, his hand on the butt of his gun. "Calm down, people!" he shouted, but his voice was drowned out by a chorus of catcalls, boos, and threats.

Martha pushed her way through the crowd and put her own body in front of Richard's. She screamed back at his tormentors, begging them to leave him alone. But her pleas were unanswered. The crowd was rapidly becoming a mob.

Another stone whistled past Kyle's ear. He cupped his free hand around his mouth. "If you people don't disperse now, I will charge you with inciting a riot!" While no one threw any more rocks, his threat did not result in anyone leaving.

Then Sawyer, hampered by his limp, cut through the crowd. His strong orator's voice rose above the shouts and catcalls of the crowd. "Stop! This must stop! People, we are not a lynch mob! Would you dishonor Jessica's memory with more blood?"

Sawyer was perhaps the only person the mob would have paid attention to. At his words, it quieted and became a crowd again. Into the silence, Richard said, "I gave those boxes out of love. Not hate. Out of love. Don't you understand?" His gaze went to Nina and then to Becca as he spoke, and finally to Claire, his dark eyes pleading. While he spoke, blood continued to run down his cheek and plop into the dust. "I didn't kill anyone. Why would I want to kill the ladies I loved?" Before he could say anything more, Kyle pushed on his shoulder and marched him away. Richard's head was bowed so low that the dark sweep of his hair covered both his eyes.

With no place to focus its anger, the crowd began to disperse. Martha was left standing alone, tears streaking down her face, her hands hanging empty by her sides. Her expression wasn't sad or shocked, though—it was angry. And she was staring at Claire so fiercely that Claire finally felt she had to say something.

"I'm sorry."

"Sorry!" Dante started as Martha spat out the word. "You know Richard. Do you really think he is capable of killing anyone?"

"How well did any of us really know him?"

Claire's question had been rhetorical, but Martha treated it as if it were real. "I knew him. We were on yearbook staff together. We spent hours in the school darkroom, just talking. He has the most brilliant mind of anyone I've ever known, but he never figured out women." Shaking her head, she summoned up a smile, tears sparkling on her eyelashes. "He never saw that I was interested in him, for example. I don't think he ever even noticed that I was a girl. I was just his pal, that's all. I used to watch him, you know, while he developed photos of all of you. Cindy, Jill, Maria, Nina—all of you." Martha added, almost to herself, "Except Belinda. I don't ever remember him talking about her. But there must have been something that attracted him. Cindy and Maria were cheerleaders, Jessica was an actress—

but sometimes it was something little." Her mouth quirked down at the corners. She reached out her hand in the direction of Claire's curls. "With you, it was your hair."

Dante spoke up. "Why did he give those women the boxes?"

"I think he gave those boxes to single women he had had crushes on in high school—or women he thought were single—and hoped that one of them might love him back. I don't think he really knows any women now. Most of the people in his line of work are men, and he has so much money that I think that it insulates him from meeting anyone new. Maybe high school was the last place Richard actually met girls. Maybe he's living in the past. But that doesn't mean he would kill anyone."

"How can you say that?" Dante's voice was gentle. "You saw him push Jessica out of the Ferris wheel."

Claire answered before Martha did. "Are you sure that's what happened?"

Dante turned to her. "You saw it happen, Claire. So did a hundred other people."

But while Martha had been talking, Claire had been replaying the scene in her own mind. What *had* she seen? When the four of them—Claire and Dante, Kyle and Marc—had first entered the amusement park, they had fanned out, searching for Jessica and Richard. Then Dante had shouted and pointed at the Ferris wheel and the two dark heads close together in one of the cars. They had begun to run toward the Ferris wheel, Kyle and Marc drawing their guns, but it had felt as ineffectual as running in a dream.

As Claire had watched Richard and Jessica, something changed between them. She had been able to see it even from several hundred feet away, how they drew apart, how they both stiffened and their mouths opened wide as they seemed to shout at each other. And then there had been a sudden blur of bodies. And the next thing Claire knew, Jessica had been dangling from Richard's hand, her free hand clawing at the side of the swaying basket.

Now Claire said, "What if Richard didn't push Jessica? What if she jumped instead, and he tried to catch her?"

A few people had been watching them curiously, but Martha paid them no attention. "That's what I've been trying to tell you guys."

"Why would she jump?" Dante asked, his expression skeptical.

"Say Richard gave several women—including me—boxes," Claire began, thinking out loud. "As Martha said, it was his way of showing some kind of old affection toward us. But then two of those women turn up dead. So now he's frightened. But Jessica has been acting as if she's his new best friend. He thinks he can go to her and she'll listen to him. So Richard decides to tell her about this horrible coincidence, perhaps ask for her help or advice—."

"—but Jessica jumps to conclusions and thinks he's confessing to being the murderer," Dante finished for her. "So she makes a split-second decision and tries to get away from him by jumping out of the Ferris wheel, but instead it all goes wrong. It could be." He slowly nodded his head. "It might have happened that way. She is—was—an excitable person. But isn't it a huge coincidence that someone is killing the same women Richard gave his boxes to?"

Suddenly, more pieces of the puzzle fell into place for

Claire. Martha didn't remember Richard developing pictures of Belinda. Jessica had said her box had gone missing. And in her mind's eye, Claire saw Belinda's body again, how it had been laid out on the bed almost as if it were on display, the heart-shaped box in her dead hand. And Claire remembered something else about the photo inside that open box. She was sure she had seen the dark edge of another photo on the back where the picture had curled up, away from the box. But the backs of the other photos—the ones in the boxes that had all been turned over to Kyle—had been white. Could someone have stolen Jessica's box, cut Belinda's picture from the annual, and used it to try to cast suspicion on whoever had given the boxes?

Claire sketched out her idea to Martha and Dante. Then she said to Martha, "If they'll let you talk to Richard, ask him if he gave Belinda a box. And if he didn't, ask Kyle to look at the back of the photograph in that box. I think someone is trying to frame Richard for these murders." Claire realized that if she were right, the irony would be that the murderer had probably gotten his idea from Jessica, with her hysterics over her own heart-shaped box after they had discovered the one in Cindy's dead hand.

"You could be right," Dante said. "But aren't you forgetting something? If Richard didn't kill Cindy and Belinda, who did?"

Martha didn't answer with words. Instead, she just cut her gaze to Claire.

"You think it's Logan, don't you?" It was hard for Claire to say the words.

Martha had pulled her keys from her pocket, and now she looked up at Claire, her gray eyes serious and sad. "Jim told me that Belinda said Logan was watching Cindy Friday night, just staring at her. She said he scared her."

Claire protested. "But everyone was watching Cindy. That's what Cindy wanted."

"So then why has Logan disappeared?"

"I don't think he could handle seeing Cindy's body. He's—fragile." Claire hesitated, realizing she might be damning her old friend with her own words. Was Logan so fragile that something could have snapped inside him, leading him to murder? She thought again about what Sawyer had told her, Logan with his hands around another woman's neck twenty years before. A wave of exhaustion swept over her. There was no other answer. Logan must be guilty.

Martha held her car key at the ready. "I don't know the real answer, Claire. All I know is that Richard didn't do it. And that I'm going to do everything that I can to help him. Thanks for giving me something that might just do that." Her determination lit her from within, turning her plainness into a fierce beauty. She walked off without saying goodbye.

Dante said, "I hope Richard finally sees her for who she is."

Claire watched the other woman walk around knots of people with long strides. "He would have to be blind if he didn't."

The entire amusement park had to be shut down for several hours while it was evaluated as a crime scene. Hastily, the hotel management moved the survivors of Minor High class of '79 into the Feed Trough, where they delivered a quickly prepared speech about the wonders of spending more time at Ye Olde Pioneer Village. Clearly, management was afraid of the impact on business when word got out that there had been three murders at their resort in as many days.

Those who opted to stay would not only get free lodging that night, but the bill for their entire stay would be torn up. Each guest who chose to remain would also receive a coupon good for a three-day stay at a later date. As an added enticement, they were reminded of the glories of that evening's fireworks show—the biggest, they were assured, in Oregon. Possibly even west of the Mississippi, according to one of the more eager assistant managers. There were more inducements offered—casino scrip, a midnight buffet—but looking around, Claire thought that they probably weren't needed. Most of her old classmates wanted nothing more than to be with each other, to tell each other the stories of where they had been when each event had taken place, to rehearse again their terror and relief.

Claire and Dante, on the other hand, decided to leave. Claire felt she would only be able to finally sleep in her own house, in her own bed. But as they packed, she moved more and more slowly as she began to see the holes in Martha's theory that Logan must be the killer. For one thing, if Belinda had really been so afraid of Logan, would she have even let him into her room?

And why had Belinda left her room? Vanessa had said when she came back to their shared hotel room to change for dinner, her mother had been gone. As she sobbed in Claire's arms, the girl had said she thought her mother had decided to attend the reunion, even though Belinda had been a weepy mess just a few hours before. And Kyle had said that a surveillance tape had showed Belinda walking past the casino in the early evening. But could there be another explanation?

Claire finished packing and sat down on the edge of the bed. "How much would you say Belinda and her daughter looked alike?"

"Quite a—" Dante stopped as he saw where she was going. "You're thinking about the tape, aren't you?"

"What if Kyle just assumed Belinda was on that tape because Vanessa had already told him her mother wasn't in the room? But you've seen how much they look alike. And what about what Vanessa was wearing last night?"

"That black leather jacket." Dante stopped folding the pair of slacks he held in his hands.

"Belinda's jacket. And then there's something else. Vanessa told me that when she went in their hotel room to get ready for dinner, the heat had been turned up until it was incredibly hot. She had to turn off the heat and crank up the air-conditioning to make it bearable."

"But why would Belinda do that?" Dante asked. He put his pants in the suitcase and then zipped it closed.

"Maybe Belinda didn't." Claire's brain was racing so far ahead that she didn't bother to explain what she was thinking. "How does Kyle know when she was killed?" she demanded. "How do they fix the time of death?"

Dante sat down in the chair opposite Claire. She had his full attention now. "Partly by when she was last seen, I would think."

"But we know that might be wrong."

"Don't they look at the stomach contents during the autopsy?" He answered his own question. "Except that she was so upset she might not have eaten anything. So—what other way is there?"

Claire was so excited that her answer crowded Dante's question. "I think they take the temperature of the body to see how long it's been cooling. And if the body was someplace hot for a while——."

"——then that might screw things up." Dante tilted his head. "But Vanessa was in that room and said her mother wasn't there. So where was Belinda?" He hefted his suitcase and opened the door of the room.

Claire picked up one of her own and followed him out the door. After making sure there was no one in the hallway, she answered Dante's question. "Maybe her body was in the closet or under the bed."

"Maybe. I'm not sure how much Kyle would welcome another theory from you. Are you going to call him and tell him that Logan must have hid Belinda's body for a while?" Dante held the elevator door for her as Claire went inside the empty car.

"Logan?" Claire echoed. "But Logan couldn't think like that. I mean, if the theory is that he went crazy and ran around killing people, why would he go to all the trouble of planting a box on Belinda or messing with the estimated time of death?"

"Why couldn't it be Logan? You said he was one of the smartest kids in school."

"But he doesn't need to supply himself with an alibi by screwing up the time of death. He already doesn't have an alibi, since no one has seen him." As they stepped outside, Claire thought of something else. "But someone who was at the reunion banquet would have a reason. Maybe they wanted people to think there was no way they could have done it because at the time of death, they were surrounded by three hundred people." Outside, even though the sun had already gone behind the hills, the heat was still oppressive. Claire's mind was ticking away. She was missing something, something important, but what was it?

"You need to get this lock fixed," Dante said as he opened the trunk without benefit of a key and put his suitcase inside. "So you still think it was someone you went to school—."

Claire interrupted him. "An older man!" She threw her bag in, not even minding when a zipper opened and some clothes spilled out.

"What?"

"Jim said Cindy was also sleeping with an older man. Someone she really had to keep a big secret." The last piece of the puzzle fell into place as she realized Belinda would probably have known all about Cindy's secret lover. No wonder she had had to die. Claire slammed the hatchback closed. "He thought it was one of her parents' friends, but—."

Someone called her name in a hoarse whisper. "Claire!"

They both turned toward the sound, Dante stepping ahead of her. When a man's head popped up over the edge of the adjacent car, Claire let out a muffled shriek.

It was Logan. He shuffled toward them, still wearing the clothes he had the night of Cindy's murder, although the suit jacket and red tie were gone. Even in the rapidly fading light, it was clear he was a mess. His once-white dress shirt was now stained and splotched, his pants dirty at the knees. His hair stood up in tufts. Logan looked as if he hadn't bathed or slept indoors since Friday night.

"I need to talk to you. I've been watching your car. I need to tell you something." His voice was only a shade above a whisper, and his eyes kept darting around, although there was no one in sight.

"I think I know what it is. You saw something Friday night, didn't you?"

Logan was silent, but Claire thought she could read the answer in his eyes.

"What did you need to tell us, Logan?" Dante prompted. Claire could hear the tension in his voice. He still thought Logan was guilty of the killings. Overhead, there was a sudden rolling boom, and they all jumped before they realized it was just the first fireworks. Gold flickers spread across the sky. Behind the wooden stockade fence, the crowd shouted approval.

When Logan didn't reply, Claire said, "You know what happened to Cindy and Belinda, don't you?"

He didn't answer her directly. "I've tried to kill myself so many times. I've walked out into traffic. I've put a knife against my own throat while I watched in the mirror. Jumped into the river wearing my winter coat and a pair of work boots. But I've never tried to hurt someone. Never. You have to believe me, Claire." Lit up by a burst of silver fireworks, his blue eyes blazed at her. "Tell me you believe me."

She had to raise her voice to be heard over the thunder of the fireworks. "I believe you, Logan. So what do you want to tell me?"

"I was out here that night. Friday night. In this parking lot." He smacked his lips, reared his head back, then continued on. "I was walking through the parking lot with a cigarette. The whole reunion thing was overwhelming. I just had to get away for a while. Sometimes I feel like I don't belong in the world anymore. I've never used an ATM card, a CD player, the Internet. There are people from our high school with grandchildren, and I've never been on a date."

Claire nodded her head as she looked into his burning eyes. Above them, a firework exploded red, then another one, higher up, dripped white sparks, followed by a third one, higher still, that turned into blue pinwheels.

"And then I heard someone running. I crouched down, I don't know why. Well, I do know why. I was embarrassed. I had been talking to myself out there, trying to talk myself into going back. And then I see him go running by me, and he's got this black rectangular thing in his hand." His hands sketched a shape in the air. "It was a woman's wallet."

"Who was it that you saw?" Dante asked.

Claire answered for him. "It was Sawyer, wasn't it?" Sawyer, the one who had told her that Logan had been violent toward women in the past. Sawyer, Cindy's walk on the wild side.

Nodding, Logan made a sound that was a cross between a bray and a moan. "I didn't know what it meant then. But when I saw Cindy's body, I knew who had killed her. And I knew I had to leave. Because who would believe me? The word of a crazy man against our next governor?" For a minute, there was only the sound of his labored breathing. "Do you know how much I looked up to him?"

Dante asked, "Did he see you?" His shoulders had relaxed, and Claire could tell that he finally believed Logan.

"No. I don't think so. But if he had looked me in the eye, then he would have known. I couldn't hide my thoughts from him."

This sounded too much like the old Logan to Claire. "I have to ask you something, Logan. Have you stopped taking your meds? Are you hallucinating again?"

His answer was firm and his gaze didn't waver. "No."

"Why now? Why are you telling us now?"

"Because my mom told me about Dick being arrested. And I knew I couldn't let that happen. You have to go with me, Claire. You have to tell them I'm not crazy anymore." He opened his mouth to say something more.

At first, before Logan crumpled to the ground, Claire thought the sound she had just heard was another firework. But then her brain put the sound together with the red blossoming across Logan's T-shirt, and she realized that he had been shot. Claire screamed, but the sound was lost in the explosion of fireworks and the gasps of the crowd behind them.

In the next burst of fireworks, she saw Sawyer standing behind Logan's fallen body, coolly taking aim at her and Dante with a handgun. At the same moment Dante jerked her to one side, pulling her down to safety behind a car. She felt more than heard the bullet whistle past her ear.

"Come on and keep low!" Dante hissed in her ear, and they took off running in a half crouch, zigzagging between the rows of parked cars. It was impossible to shout for help, to hear their pursuer, or even to know if Sawyer were firing at them. The boom and hisses of the fireworks offered perfect concealment. The only thing they had going for them was that Sawyer would be hobbled by his old injuries—but his gun meant that he didn't need to get close to them to kill them.

All too soon, they came to the edge of the parking lot and a fence Claire had never noticed in the daytime. Both of them were crouched behind a red Ford Festiva, not the best car for hiding behind. To their left lay the glass doors of the hotel, radiating golden light a hundred yards away. Behind those doors lay help—but could they get to it before they were killed? Somewhere to their right was Sawyer. Dante raised himself a couple of inches and peeked through the car window, then settled back down again. His lips brushed against Claire's ear. "We'll have a better chance if we separate. You keep along the edge of the fence and I'll make for the doors."

She put as much force into her whisper as she could. "No. We stay together." She was afraid that Dante planned to sacrifice himself to save her.

Their decision was made for them when a bullet sang above their heads, close enough that her ears rang. Dante tugged her to the right, and they ran down one row, up another, their heads bowed so low that they almost brushed their knees, left, then right, then left again, until finally Claire had no idea where they were in relation to anything. Where was the hotel, the fence line, or even the amusement park?

Claire turned her head and realized that the only important thing to know was where they were in relation to Sawyer. Because he was only thirty feet away, holding the gun straight out in front of his body with both hands. The round eye of the gun looked back at her. She lunged forward frantically, praying she could move an inch or two out of the path of the bullet. The gun cracked just as the toe of her sneaker caught on something. Claire landed in a heap.

"No!" Dante screamed from behind her. She heard him run past, but whatever happened next was covered by the sound of a firework exploding overhead in a shower of silver sparks.

Frantic as a bug on its back, Claire struggled to her feet. As she pushed herself up, the fingers of her right hand caught the edge of whatever had tripped her, something cool and slender that glinted in the light of the fireworks. A broken car antenna. She turned and ran after Dante.

Dante was on the ground, with Sawyer on top of him. Sawyer's back was to Claire. The gun was in Sawyer's fist, but Dante's hand was wrapped around the barrel, so that it pointed up, midway between the two men. As Claire watched in horror, Sawyer began to force the gun downward, twisting it so it pointed right at Dante's head.

Now thankful for the noise of the fireworks, Claire ran up behind Sawyer, looped the antenna around his neck, and pulled. Sawyer gurgled a scream, reaching up with one hand to try to pull the antenna away from his neck. The thought flashed through Claire's mind that this must be how Sawyer had felt while he strangled Cindy and Belinda. She began to drag him off Dante.

And then the antenna snapped in half.

The sudden shift in tensions changed everything. It left Sawyer with a bloody furrow on either side of his neck. It let Claire go sprawling backward, the two broken halves of the antenna in her hand. It let Dante succeed in bucking the other man off. And it left Sawyer sitting on the ground holding the gun.

He looked at them, shaking his head, and to Claire's amazement a smile played about his lips. Then, still smiling, Sawyer shrugged and leveled the gun at her again, not even bothering to get to his feet. There was no place to go, no hiding place, no bargain to make, no options left. She squeezed her eyes closed, wondering how much it would hurt, or if she would feel any pain at all. She realized she couldn't die like this. There must be something she could do. Maybe if she rushed Sawyer, she could buy time for Dante, if not herself.

All this had taken only a second, but when Claire opened her eyes again, Logan was staggering up behind Sawyer. In his upraised hand was Claire's jack. There were still about fifteen feet separating them. Was there any way she could buy time? Could she claim she was pregnant, tell Sawyer she had always loved him, offer him money? Then Dante shouted, "I thought you were for gun control!" Claire realized he was trying to draw Sawyer's attention.

Sawyer's grin broadened and his gun never wavered. "Things aren't always what they seem."

The jack caught him right above the temple. Then Logan collapsed on top of the ex-teacher he had admired so much.

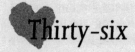

Thirty-six

He was about ready to leave—it was nearly one in the morning and he wasn't a kid anymore, despite what some of the others at the reunion seemed to think—when she caught his arm outside the restrooms.

"I've been looking everywhere for you!"

Cindy was even drunker than she had been earlier, Sawyer realized, as he looked at her red, red mouth and the smear of lipstick across her front teeth. She held his arm for balance as much as to get his attention, although he noted that she didn't miss the opportunity to press her cleavage up against him.

"We need to talk, don't we?" Her wink was as broad as a vaudevillian's.

"We do?" he echoed. An icy shard of fear pierced his heart. There was a good reason he had been with groups of people all day, never alone, never accessible. He didn't want any old memories being trotted out.

"I got what you sent me."

"Sent you?" Her words put him off balance. "But I didn't . . . "

"Come on—let's not talk in here." She pulled him along behind her, through the brassbound glass door, out into the warm night, past the silent sleeping rows of cars. He let himself be towed, fearing any resistance would attract the kind of attention he most definitely didn't want.

In a darkened corner at the far edge of the parking lot, she was in his arms before he knew it, pressing herself against him. For a second he met her with lips open in surprise. But when her tongue slipped into his mouth, he put his hands on her shoulders and pressed her away.

"Cindy, I'm sorry, but this isn't—."

"Isn't what?" Her smile faltered.

"Some things are better left in the past."

"What are you talking about? You send me this box with our picture in it, then you act like you don't even want to know me."

"What are you talking about?" Their picture? They had never been photographed together, he was sure of it. Such a thing could have ended everything.

She pressed a wooden box in his hand. It was shaped like a heart, with a hinged lid. And when he thumbed it open, he saw Cindy's face, and a sliver of the back of the dark-haired man who held her in his arms.

"This is me?" he asked. Shot from the back. Shot in the back is more like it. He never knew that picture was taken.

"Remember?" Smiling at the memory, she took the box back from him. "I was with Wade that night. But I pulled you out on the floor and made you dance with me. Just one dance. When I got the package you sent and saw what was inside, it was like it all happened yesterday. Remember," she said, wobbling on her high heels, grinning at him sloppily, her lust reasserting itself as she pressed herself against him again, "remember that time in the art supply room?" In her heels Cindy was only an inch or two shorter than he was. Now she stepped behind him and kissed the back of his neck. "Remember how you kissed me like this and you wouldn't let me turn around and then you put your hands up under my shirt and . . . "

He spun around to face her. "No, I don't remember, Cindy. I don't want to remember. That was all a long time ago. I'm married now. We both are. We were just kids then."

"Kids?! You weren't any kid. You were a man. That's why I liked you better than those boys in school. You knew what you were doing. Remember when we used to sit underneath that old pine tree or fir tree or whatever in the hell it was? The one where the branches came all the way to the ground like a tent? And we would get high and then you would take off all my clothes piece by piece and just look at me." Her voice softened with the memory.

He had kind of forgotten some of this himself. This did not seem good at all. The press would have a field day if she came to them. DID TOP GOV. CANDIDATE HAVE SEX, USE DRUGS WITH H.S. GIRL? And maybe she picked up on his thoughts, because the next thing she said was, "Think of that Kennedy, the one who was putting it to the babysitter. That was the end of his political career, wasn't it?"

"Cindy," he appealed to her, knowing already that his tone wasn't right. "Come on, sshh, let's not make waves."

She was angry now, eyes blazing, breathing even

more audibly than when she was aroused. "I could make some waves. I could make some goddamn waves. I could tell them all about how you pressured me to get an abortion, how I was never able to have kids after that!"

In the distance, a car door slammed. They both froze for a second.

Then Cindy said, loud enough to be overheard, deliberately provocative, "So I'm not good enough for you to fuck anymore, is that it, Sawyer? But I was in high school, wasn't I? I was good enough for you when I was seventeen!"

With every word, his panic rose. His ears filled with the sound of his own heartbeat—but did he also hear footsteps? He grabbed her to calm her down, then clapped his hand over her mouth. Not hard, no, but more as a reminder that they were in a very public place. "Be quiet," he hissed into her ear. "Someone's coming."

Instead of doing what he asked, Cindy struggled harder and let out a muffled scream. Worse and worse. He couldn't have people finding them like this, not when Cindy was angry and feeling rejected. She'd shout out the old sordid details to the next person who came along. He pulled her back against his chest, his left hand still over her mouth, and wrapped his right arm around her shoulders. She was fighting in earnest now.

"Hush," Sawyer tried to whisper in her ear, to calm her the way he used to calm the children when they were babies. Sometimes a whisper worked better than a shout. "Hush."

But she wouldn't or couldn't hush, instead intent on fighting him. He could feel the screams trying to push their way out of her throat, and all he could think of was making her be quiet, before everything went even more horribly offtrack. If he could just make her be quiet, then he could explain it to her, explain that things were different then, that times were different then, that he had gone to war a boy but come back a man who had seen too much and done too much and who sometimes needed to seek sweet solace in the arms of a girl who knew nothing of the world.

And suddenly Cindy was unmoving in his arms, too still, her body slumping forward. Dead weight.

And finally, he did what he had to, almost mechanically. His memories were not of twenty years before, but of nearly thirty, and the ghosts that accompanied him wore black and came barely to his shoulder. In Vietnam he learned to separate what it was necessary for his body to do from what his heart was feeling. He took his heart and put it away in a box, to keep it safe. He learned that accidents happen. That there was more than one way to consider any given situation.

Before he walked away, he leaned down toward Cindy. "Hush," Sawyer said again, and now she couldn't contradict him. "Hush." Then he walked away.

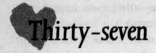

Thirty-seven

In the next few days, the facts of what had happened were teased out, then pieced together with a few guesses to make a complete story. Sawyer's two killings seemed not to have been premeditated, but rather the result of a sudden terror that secrets were about to be revealed. The first murder had covered up his two-decade-old affair with a high school girl. Like many another killer before him, Sawyer had found murdering one person had led him to kill again, for fear that the first crime would be revealed.

Once his killing fear had passed, though, he had proven adept at covering up his tracks. He had ripped at Cindy's clothes the way a rapist would, then put her wallet where it would be sure to be found by the banquet staff. But once Cindy's body had been found, Sawyer realized that his fingerprints might be in places they shouldn't be. Pretending to worry about the dead woman's modesty, he had leaned down to pull her shirt closed—and thus created an explanation for any prints that might be found on her buttons, or even the cloth of the shirt itself. It was the same reason he had been sure to touch—in front of witnesses—the heart-shaped box Cindy had been holding in her hand.

In the case of Belinda, Sawyer had used several ruses to throw off the scent. First, he had read enough crime reports to know that the time of death would be estimated by taking the body's liver temperature, which would cool at a given rate. His hope had been to interrupt that cooling process long enough to provide himself with an alibi. Hiding Belinda's body under the bed, he had turned up the heat as high as it would go. Sawyer had guessed that Belinda's daughter would return, sooner or later, and that she would both turn down the heat and note that her mother was gone.

Later in the evening he had sneaked out of the dance for five minutes, the stolen key card in his back pocket, just long enough to arrange Belinda's body on the bed, heart-shaped box in hand. Sawyer knew, from Jessica's boasting, where he could procure a box. (His own annual had yielded the necessary picture.) He got help from an unexpected corner when Vanessa borrowed Belinda's leather jacket, and was later identified as her own mother on a blurry surveillance tape.

It appeared that Sawyer's wife, Elaine, might be charged as an accessory, for she had been the one who had stolen Jessica's box from her purse after having offered to keep an eye on it while the other woman went to the bathroom. Elaine now claimed to have been told by Sawyer that he wanted the box so he could turn it in to the police. She had bolstered her claim by filing for divorce and refusing to speak to him.

Kevin had hired the best defense lawyer on the West Coast, who planned to plead temporary insanity. He was out on bail now and spent most of his time seeing anger and grief counselors.

As for Logan, the doctor said he would have an ugly scar and lose some of the range of motion in his right arm. Kyle had pulled a few strings and arranged for a job to be waiting at the Minor library for Logan as soon as he was discharged from the hospital. When Claire and Dante had visited him in the hospital, he had confided in them his dream of becoming a social worker. Somehow, Claire had a feeling—or maybe it was only a hope—that he might make it.

"Just one more kiss," Dante requested. The flight attendant standing at the airport gate ten feet away made a show of looking at her watch. She had already made the last call for boarding, but it would be a long six weeks before Claire and Dante saw each other again. Closing her eyes to block out the other woman's face, Claire complied with Dante's request. Finally, she came up for air.

"I never told you, but I thought the reason you spent so much time talking to Jessica was that you had a crush on her."

Dante laughed. "I know a million Jessicas in New York. They all worry too much about what people will think about them to be who they are. And you, well, you talk to waiters and women in supermarket lines and strange dogs. I kind of like that in a girl."

"Woman," Claire corrected Dante. "I'm a woman."

"Sir, we're boarding," the flight attendant called out.

"Don't I know it," Dante said, before dropping a final kiss on Claire's lips and then turning on his heel.

IBCNU

Appendix

Key to License-Plate Terms

-CSHFLW	Negative cash flow (*many states fill in any space on a vanity plate with a dash*)
2N2R4	Two and Two Are Four
2Q2STOM	Too Cute To Stay Home
AMBER	Amber
ANIL8	Annihilate
AWAWEGO	Away We Go
BWHO UR	Be Who You Are
BYTDAPL	Bite the Apple
GN2POT	Gone to Pot
GON4EVR	Gone Forever
HEBGBZ	Heebie Jeebies
HE WON	He Won
HIHO AG	Hi Ho, Silver (*AG is the periodic table designation for silver*)

IBCNU	I'll Be Seeing You
ICUNIYQ	I See You and I Like You (*said in an Elmer Fudd accent*)
ML8ML8	I'm Late, I'm Late (*a perfect plate for a white Rabbit*)
MR E	Mystery
OPNYDE	Open Wide
PB4UGO	Pee Before You Go
RD4MOR	Ready for More
RKNROL	Rock and Roll
RUCNNE1	Are You Seeing Anyone?
TAGURIT	Tag, You're It
TIH5 HO	Oh, Shit (*seen in a rearview mirror*)
TOUCHE	Touché
TXNS00H	Who's Next? (*seen in a rearview mirror*)